THE FRIENDSHIP OF CRIMINALS

THE FRiENDSHIP OF CRiMINALS

ROBERT GLINSKI

MINOTAUR BOOKS
NEW YORK

THE FRIENDSHIP OF CRIMINALS. Copyright © 2015 by Robert Glinski. All rights reserved. Printed in the United States of America. For information, address St. Martin's Press, 175 Fifth Avenue, New York, N.Y. 10010.

www.minotaurbooks.com

Designed by Steven Seighman

Library of Congress Cataloging-in-Publication Data

Glinski, Robert.
    The friendship of criminals / Robert Glinski.
        pages cm
    ISBN 978-1-250-04996-4 (hardcover)
    ISBN 978-1-4668-5102-3 (e-book)
  1. Organized crime—Fiction.   2. United States. Federal Bureau of
Investigation—Fiction.   3. Philadelphia—Fiction.   I. Title.
    PS3607.L63G45 2015
    813'.6—dc23

                                                    2014040119

Minotaur books may be purchased for educational, business, or promotional use. For information on bulk purchases, please contact the Macmillan Corporate and Premium Sales Department at 1-800-221-7945, extension 5442, or write to specialmarkets@macmillan.com.

First Edition: March 2015

10 9 8 7 6 5 4 3 2 1

This book is dedicated to my giggling kids and beautiful wife, Cynthia, as well as my writing instructors—Elmore Leonard, Dennis Lehane, Patricia Highsmith, George V. Higgins, and John D. MacDonald.

ACKNOWLEDGMENTS

Okay, let's do this:

To my professional team—Kirby Kim, Michael Homler, India Cooper, Lauren Jablonski, and Mythology Entertainment, which optioned the movie/television rights. Any writer would be blessed to have your support and confidence.

To my dog Jasper, in case she reads while we're asleep or not home. Good dog, Jasper.

To my sisters, Ann and Jenny—loyal, loving, and badass. Give this book a shaky review and they'll find you. I'm not joking even a little. Best sisters ever.

To my poker group, fly fishing crew, high school friends, college buddies, law school mates, and brothers-in-law Chris, Patrick, and Todd. You did absolutely nothing to help me with this book except unknowingly lend your names, but the anticipated issues for not including you isn't worth the agitation. So, "thanks."

To my nieces and nephews, Anthony, Meagan, Lizzy, Brandon, Caitlyn, Callie, Christian, Cameron, Christian, Meredith, and Allison. Because sometimes it's just nice to see your name in print.

To my parents, Ken and Sue. Nobody is born into this world with a library card and books. You guys always made sure I had both. And in separate ways, you exhibited the daily benefits of hard work and perseverance. A book doesn't get published in today's market without a little of those trickling down.

To Nicholas Clemente, William Brennan, Nicholas Fausto, and Mike Wallace. Four classics who showed me every day what it takes to be a Philadelphia lawyer—bold, fearless, independent, forgiving, and funny as hell. I owe you all a night at the bar.

To Don "Sonny" Wellington. The ultimate hustler, in the best sense.

To Lisa Joy Gubser, the Washington University graduate assistant in my '89 Western Civilization class who wrote *Your writing style leaves something to be desired* on my very first college paper and then worked all year helping me improve. You changed my trajectory and are the perfect example why we need great teachers. Thank you.

To my mother-in-law, Flo, and sisters-in-law, Courtney and Carrie, who all share my love for the written word. Thanks for the support. And the meat loaf. And the cookies. Love those cookies.

To my wife, Cynthia, and little monkeys, Lyla and Campbell. I can't imagine another husband or daddy receiving more love and encouragement. I hope I've made you proud. It's all that matters.

And finally, to my mom, who as I write this is fighting leukemia. I hope you get to see your boy's first book on the shelf. I really, really do. Growing up, how many times did we have this conversation?

Mom: "Robert, turn off your light. Time for bed."

Me: "But I'm reading a good part."

Mom: "Okay, ten more minutes."

Thanks, Mom. I love you.

THE FRIENDSHIP OF CRIMINALS

I.

CORRAL A HUNDRED LITTLE KIDS and announce Santa Claus, Easter Bunny, and the Tooth Fairy do not exist. Not dead, not gone. Just not real.

Of the hundred, fifteen never believed. They're above the fray, like birds watching a car crash from some distant tree. Three dozen go Code Red, their bodies overwhelmed by the desire to fight, run, or both. Twenty obsess over missed clues. Another twenty-five reject the new reality. They cry.

The remaining four are the cynics. Their zombie eyes hold fast as the conspiracy confirms what they've suspected all along—lies trump truth when people want to believe. Bow-tied rabbits hiding chocolate? Fairies trading cash for human teeth? *What a bunch of suckers, ripe for the picking and deserving, too.* A cold-blooded takeaway, sure, but it's how these future grifters and televangelists filter the world.

Now take these same one hundred kids and gift them a gun. Pistol, rifle, or shotgun—doesn't matter as long as it's designed to stop a human heart. Unlike in the Santa/Bunny/Fairy experiment, the shorties cluster. *Is that a real gun? Yeah, I'll hold it.* No crossroads here.

Little Bernie Jaracz of Port Richmond wasn't any different. Since watching a teenager hypnotize a pubescent cabal with a chrome revolver, he'd wanted a gun. Not to hurt a rival or pursue revenge—he wasn't that kind of kid. Holding a piece just seemed *natural*, like jumping puddles or peeing in the grass. Gun. Hand. Gun. Hand. A pairing meant to be. *Look, right there, a special grip for my fingers. Awesome.*

The boy's wish came true in his grandfather's basement a few weeks shy of his seventh birthday. Without introduction or warning, Big Bern Jaracz withdrew a .38 caliber pistol from his workbench and handed it over. Given the similarity in personalities, the old man would have been surprised if the kid flinched. He didn't. Just something in the blood, Big Bern figured. Stiff as a glass rod.

Left eye squinting, Little Bernie aimed at a spiderweb pulled taut between the overhead joists. Half a dozen hammer falls against an empty chamber had him clearing imaginary barrel smoke and asking if they could go outside. "I want to shoot bullets. Like, for real."

His grandfather shook off the query and snatched the gun, restocking it behind a small wall of coffee cans filled with washers, bolts, and nails. The spot hid another six handguns of various specialties. Two were part of his personal collection; the rest circulated based on market demand.

"Stay out of there," warned the old man, his fist shoulder high. "Your future doesn't happen today. We're in for the long play."

"What?"

"Steer wide of my workbench, boy."

Retired with a city pension, Big Bern Jaracz spent the summer of '97 babysitting Little Bernie because the kid's dad violated probation and his mom was back at the wire factory. "Family takes care of family. He's with me." Truth was, there wasn't anyone else.

So each morning since school let out, Little Bernie washed his face, kissed his mom good-bye, ran past a dozen stoops, and burst through his grandfather's front door without ringing the bell. Never occurred to him why the door was unlocked. Security in the boy's home was a different matter. His mom slapped his cheek if he forgot the dead bolt. After suffering his third red face in as many weeks, he argued Big Bern left his door open, so what's the big deal?

"Because," she said, "no one's stupid enough to wander in with that bear."

When Little Bernie pushed the point, she balanced the coloring in his face. Welcome to Port Richmond.

Inside his grandfather's house, the two bachelors had a routine. The kid made buttered toast while the old man read *The Philadelphia Inquirer* and sipped Sanka. After two cups, Big Bern cleared the dishes, glanced at the phone as though he needed a reminder of its location, and told his grandson they should go downstairs. Time to work.

In the basement—surrounded by the heavy-handed tools of a previous generation—Little Bernie watched Big Bern do his magic. On any given morning, his grandfather might fix a wristwatch dropped off by a neighbor, a shorted-out hair dryer, or a fan with a frayed electrical cord. After puttering a few hours, they returned upstairs for bologna and pickles on Wonder Bread. The meat wasn't the pink loaf the rest of America ate. Big Bern sneered at that mess, calling it dyed baby shit. He purchased handmade bologna from the neighborhood sausage maker, one pound a week since before Kennedy was elected.

Little Bernie made the sandwiches while his partner tuned the radio and boiled water for instant coffee. After each plate was topped with chips, they sat at a wooden table pressed against the back wall, listening to local news or a Phillies ball game. An oil painting of God floating atop gravy-brown clouds looked down in approval. Conversation might brush against a starting pitcher or the next day's project, though more often they settled into the easy quiet reserved for old men and small boys.

During Little Bernie's last week of summer vacation, a historic August heat wave dominated news radio. With the East Coast sitting on a hot plate, broadcasts flip-flopped between weather forecasts and strategies for keeping cool. The routine lasted until Friday, when news broke of an explosion in South Philadelphia. A breathless reporter said a bomb had detonated beneath a man's front stoop, covering the street in brick and body parts. Several names were listed in quick order—too fast for Little Bernie to make sense of who did what but *Anticcio* was repeated most often. The boy liked how the name's first part was a bug. Made him wonder if the man was teased as a kid. He'd have teased him, that's for sure. *Anticcio the Ant.*

Event coverage lasted long enough for him to finish his sandwich and eyeball his grandfather's untouched plate. Repeating the highlights a third time, the reporter promised updates as police released additional information. Little Bernie wasn't swallowing the hook. He didn't need to know any more about the blasted-to-bits insect guy on the other side of town.

The old man had a different take. As the newscast signed off, he rotated his chin toward the wall-mounted phone. A stranger might have interpreted the behavior as a prediction, like he was expecting a call. Anyone familiar with Jaracz knew better. It was a show of will.

When the phone rang, Big Bern pounced before the caller could change his mind.

Staring at his grandfather's back, Little Bernie strained to hear a few hushed words in Polish and a closing grunt.

Hanging the phone up, Big Bern crossed the room in three steps, the subfloor flexing beneath his boots. "Listen now," he said, a hand on his grandson's shoulder. "There's work to do. A job that will push us."

The boy raised his eyes. His grandfather's head seemed to threaten the plaster ceiling.

"I've been given a few hours. What you see today—what we do—you must never speak of. Not to me, not to anyone. But never forget. Over your life, much will change. Remember the old ways. That's how we've survived, how you'll survive when I'm gone." He motioned to the radio. "The bombs in their own neighborhood, with children looking on, that's the new way. Don't yield to that."

The boy's stomach churned. He licked his lips.

"You and me are doing good. We're protecting our family, our friends— shielding what we love."

The boy was fine until the last word. Hearing *love* rattled him. He couldn't recall his grandfather saying it before. Not one time. Emotional markers like *hate, love, sad,* and *happy* weren't compatible with the old man's vocabulary.

Big Bern turned for the sink. "We need to wash our hands before leaving. Use extra soap, scrub hard with the brush, and drink up. We must be careful of the heat. Can't let it distract us." He downed two glasses of water, picked up his car keys plus a second ring, and told the boy to hurry.

With the car radio tuned to news, Big Bern navigated the tight Port Richmond one-ways until they were driving north on I-95, away from the city. Despite the August heat, he kept the air off, thinking maybe he could prep the boy. Working a lifetime outdoors had conditioned him for extreme temperatures, but he worried his grandson would struggle with what was waiting. Not because he was soft. Just not enough time to cure. Yet.

Twenty miles up the interstate, a mile off the exit, they stopped at a dated storage facility wrapped in chain link and razor wire. To one side was a boarded-up adult video store, to the other a stucco warehouse with a four-foot bluebird painted near the front entrance. Dead trees backdropped the buildings.

Big Bern parked a few spaces from the office and nodded to the half-stoned attendant seated behind bulletproof glass. The man stiffened before returning the courtesy. Wasn't often the Polack visited, and any less was fine. Among men with poisonous looks, the one-eyed giant would have been a leader.

Bern kicked the storage door before unlocking it to scatter any mice, pulled it up hard, and waved for the boy to join him. Inside—with the door closed and Third World heat pressing down—he pointed out five black footlockers marked with the same slash of white chalk. Another dozen of different colors and markings were stacked against the wall. Big Bern ordered the black ones dragged beneath the overhead light. Using a second set of keys, he unlocked and flipped the lids in quick succession, telling his grandson to keep his mouth shut and pay attention. *No time to baby-step. Be a man.*

For the next hour, kneeling side by side with sweat raining off their heads, they unpacked, prepped, and loaded twenty-five pump-action Remington 12-gauge shotguns.

Setting the last firearm aside, Big Bern sent the boy to reopen the door while he reviewed the order and scanned the room. Did they have everything they needed? *Think, think, think.* He cursed his age and what it'd done to his confidence, even wondering if it was God's way of retiring him.

The building's front side was now shaded from the afternoon sun, and a slight breeze danced the skinnier weeds. Stretching his arms and shoulders, Big Bern said to stay clear so he could back the car in tight. Six minutes later the shotguns were loaded in the trunk and tucked beneath a heavy wool blanket. Big Bern's last to-do was circling the car, looking for any telltale indicators that might catch a trained eye. "The suspension is holding fine. That's why I bought this car. Stiff Detroit steel," he said, proving his point by pushing on the rear quarter-panel. "Low-riders make the highway cops suspicious."

Exiting the fenced lot, every stitch of clothing soaked through, Little Bernie still couldn't connect the dots. He had no clue where the guns came from, why they were fetching twenty-five, or who was receiving so much firepower. Truth was, that kind of question-and-answer didn't much factor in his moment. All Little Bernie cared about—same as most boys— was holding the guns and impressing the man-in-charge. Did he seize the opportunity and step up in weight class? *Be a man.* By his appraisal, he'd succeeded.

Big Bern agreed, giving him his due before noticing smudges of gun oil on his own hands. *How could I forget cleanup towels? Most important day in a decade and I forget towels?* The details, he chided himself, pay attention to the details. *Don't trip up on the easy stuff.* The kid needed an example, not some lesson in seat-of-your-pants planning. With the violence coming, and the number of men they'd face, strength wasn't enough. To win, accountability was demanded from each component. *Be a man.*

"I'm taking you home," he said, minding his speed on 95. "I can handle the rest alone. People are preparing to push us. And now we'll be ready to push back. It's the old way."

2.

"THIS IS JUNIOR DAVIS."

One syllable was enough for Sonny to know. The investigator's voice—choked off with a vocal tourniquet effect he claimed came from training amateur boxers—was a dead giveaway. Thing was, Sonny had met the man's people, and they all sounded the same. "Hold on, let me get organized."

"Call back. I don't mind. Wife's at choir."

"No. Stay on the line." Sonny had been rereading a postcard in his building's lobby when Junior called. The postcard's front side was a typical Florida beach scene—honeys in neon string bikinis strolling the white sands. The back side was handwriting small enough to pack four lies into three inches. *Dad, still making my meetings. Thirty-six days and counting . . . all different this time . . . God bless sobriety! Love, Michael.*

Pushing through the high-rise's front door, Sonny spit gum onto the postcard, folded it in half, and tossed the mess into the trash. *Wish you luck, son, but I'll believe it when I see it.*

Sonny's destination was a shaded bench beneath a palm tree. A pinkie-sized lizard posed strong before scrambling over the back support. "Okay, buddy, I'm alone. What'd you find?"

"Before I get started, they got Anticcio. Didn't know if you'd heard."

Sonny's mileage with the man warranted a grimace. "I was rooting for him. Old age must have shortened his arms."

Junior's two cents was Anticcio got arrogant, an analysis supported by fifty years of watching Philadelphia hoods murder each other. "Rea taking shots at his car on the Schuylkill showed he was serious. I said at the time, *Anticcio can't play this too cute. The kid is going for it.* Ask Cheeky, he heard me. Judge bangs the gavel on Monte's twenty-year turn and boom, put two in Rea's head that afternoon. Just like that. Don't let the wiseass start hearing the cheers. Hindsight, now."

Other than the personal loss, the change in South Philly leadership didn't mean much for Sonny's business interests. Since buying the sailboat and moving to Florida, he'd unwound, sold off, or walked away from most of his Northeast positions. The same couldn't be said of Bielakowski.

"What about our thing?" asked Sonny. "Any progress?"

"I mailed a report. Invoice included."

"Call to soften the blow? Nice of you."

"Long shot all the way. We talked about this."

Sitting alone didn't stop Sonny from raising a dramatic hand. "There's got to be some part of a story."

"You want to wait for the report?"

"Baseline it."

"Records are thin, lost, or locked up. Doesn't help the orphanage burned before microfiche and computers. You think you left around 1940, so access is needed from '25 through '42. For those years, your name has no real file. We know you were there, can't tell why."

"Christ sake."

"Not saying it's not boxed up in City Hall, just couldn't shake it loose. Sure, you popped up on public registries and a census, but those are simple lists. Nothing attached to explain where you came from, parents, ethnic background, any of that. No names, dates, or details."

"A dead end."

Junior wasn't surprised by the lack of a question mark. Sonny's style never entailed getting dragged into the know, even after hearing he was all trunk, no roots. "Yeah, that's what I'm saying. Not uncommon, with the wars and the way they viewed young girls getting knocked up. A family with a little money, they'd stash a sixteen-year-old until the baby arrived, then do a drop-and-dash at a crosstown orphanage. Plenty of babies weren't even born in hospitals."

Sonny stayed silent. There was no percentage in old news. Looking back for a payoff was a fool's errand.

"As I said, the full report will arrive in a couple days." Junior had a protocol for handling these conversations. Give the information. Pause. Give a little more. Pause. Remind them about the report, suggesting it might provide some measure of closure. Never did, though. Old demons weren't spooked like park pigeons. "Some other stuff in there, too, kind of interesting."

Sonny had also asked Junior to follow up on his memory of an older orphanage boy. No pictures or specifics, just a lingering, hopeful sense of brotherhood. Maybe this older boy cared for him. Maybe he didn't. Sonny couldn't quite pin it down, futile as netting cigarette smoke. Either way, Sonny's only basis was his biased recollection and the drunk, passive-aggressive ramblings of the orphanage's custodian. *I ain't supposed to say nothin' but I heard a boy that used to be here—your brother, they say—got himself killed last week. You know anything about that? No? Oh, that's sad all the way around—him dying and leaving you alone.* First night the custodian teased him with the story, Sonny ran away, lasting a week before a beat cop scooped him up. He'd go on to set the orphanage record, freeing himself fourteen times before they gave up looking.

"Nothing certain there either," said Junior Davis, "except I did find another kid with the same last name at the same orphanage. Pretty strong coincidence." He was careful what he allowed to seep into his voice. Before flunking out of the police academy, his instructor had schooled him on being *clinical*. "First name was Benjamin. Ring a bell?"

Sonny repeated the name, first out loud and then to himself. He had to admit, nothing.

"Long time ago," said Junior. "Anyway, for two years he was included on the same lists and registries. Twelve years older—as you thought. And passed away like the custodian said. Found the death certificate. Pulmonary failure was the official cause. Truth, the boy got shot."

Sonny grunted, his mind rotating the possibility of an actual brother at the orphanage.

Junior didn't want his client drifting too far. "Listen, I wasn't going to tell you. Didn't include it on the invoice, but I found his cemetery. This Benjamin fellow, I mean. Went out there thinking you'd like a picture of the headstone."

"There's a marker?"

"No. That's what I'm saying. No grave site. Whole thing resited for a commercial development. They said the original spot was like a pauper's cemetery. The new location—after they moved everybody—didn't have any individual markings. More like general signage."

"Shit."

"I know, man."

"So I might have had a brother but they planted and replanted him like a bush?"

"Sums it up. How much all that matters is your choice."

And that was the point, thought Sonny. He'd hired the investigator to confirm the gaps, not rewrite two-thirds of his biography. "All questions don't have an answer. Want has nothing to do with it."

Even when appropriate, Junior Davis didn't apologize for disappointing results. He'd learned his lesson. In a day or two—as clients replayed their conversation—they'd twist his compassion into incompetence. Blame the messenger. All the more reason to keep it *clinical*. "You reaching out to Bielakowski on this Anticcio deal? Rea's going to be a handful."

Sonny didn't resist the heavy-handed change of subject. He was ready to march. "Anymore he knows better. Would just be ego to suggest a strategy."

Old-timers like Junior couldn't accept that Sonny and Anton Bielakowski were no longer lockstep partners. A half century of anything was hard to shake, but Sonny moving south pared their business dealings to a once-a-year sit-down. No bad blood, just time, distance, and age playing their parts.

Sonny's cell phone buzzed with a second call. "You got anything else?"

"It's all in the report. Ring me with questions. Oh, and I've got a fighter you should check out. Kid's got a chance. Throws a liver punch like you've never seen."

"Anton bankrolling him?"

"No. Wanted to ask you first."

"Next time I'm up, I'll take a look. Always had a soft spot for body punchers. Gotta run. I'll wire the payment. Say hello to the wife."

Clicking over, Sonny heard an unfamiliar voice. "Mr. Bonhardt? This is Debbie Shenkman from Shenkman's Funeral Home in Fort Lauderdale. Do you have a moment?"

Funding three cremations in six months had moved Sonny up the local parlor call sheet. As his South Florida circle aged, he'd become the go-to financier for any pals dying without money and prepaid arrangements. While people wondered about the reasons, Sonny saw it as simple decency—he hated anyone going out on a losing streak. "Ironic timing, Ms. Shenkman."

Like airline pilots during in-flight updates, the funeral director spoke with a slow, syrupy drawl and a touch of hush. "I'm calling on behalf of the estate of Mr. Charles Duebel."

"Who?"

"Perhaps that name is unfamiliar. I believe his friends—and I apologize if this sounds insensitive—called him Duebber."

Sonny loved the move. The fat bastard—already owing him three grand—was getting the last laugh. "Natural causes?"

"Excuse me?"

"I'm asking what killed him. Bullet or cancer?"

"I'm sure you understand, I'm uncomfortable disclosing those types of details."

"You will if you expect me to foot the bill."

"A stroke is what took Mr. Duebel's last breath. I'm very sorry for your loss."

"Smoked unfiltered cigarettes and ate at gas stations for as long as I knew him. He's probably taking up half your back room."

The funeral director paused a moment, unsure what was expected. "It's true that Mr. Duebel is a large man. That's one of the reasons I wanted to speak with you. We have lovely alternatives for the heavyset."

"Listen," said Sonny, "this is Duebber's idea of a joke, so let's not get carried away. Bill me for the cremation, and I'll get his kids' addresses for the urn. Even if they don't want to pony up, maybe they can spread his ashes somewhere nice."

"Yes, a cremation," said Shenkman, with an angel's kiss of condescension. "Certainly it's an option. But many individuals believe a casket and headstone are necessary to memorialize a loved one."

"Tap the brakes."

She steadied herself for the upsell. A slow month had Dad pounding the table for more revenue, to hell with limited supply. "A headstone provides a sense of permanence, eroding just one inch every ten thousand years. Each person—no matter their status—deserves a respectable *physical* testament to their earthly existence."

Sonny's mind flipped back to what Junior Davis had said about his dream brother. Dead, buried, moved, and gone. Family pets deposited in the backyard got more pomp and circumstance. "Ms. Shenkman, let me ask you a question. What do they call those large tombs with steps and columns?"

"The industry term is *private family mausoleum*," she said, her tone betraying a sliver of enthusiasm. "Yes, very distinguished. A noble and lasting way to be remembered. We'd, of course, have to coordinate with the cemetery. Lauderdale Memorial Park has plots with wonderful views."

"Those are granite, like the headstones?"

"Yes. Sometimes we do see marble, though it doesn't wear like granite. And while bronze has its admirers, the green patina can be a turnoff."

Sun splicing through the overhead palm fronds heated Sonny's legs in thin strips. He shifted over a few inches to keep pace with the shade. The lizard poked its head out, anxious to reclaim the prime real estate. "Once the vault's in place, can it be moved somewhere I don't want? Taken somewhere else?"

"Oh, no," she said, straightening her back. Chasing money was Debbie Shenkman's least favorite part of the job. Fancying herself the new generation of parlor management, she preferred collaborating. The keynote speaker at last year's industry conference called it *Partnering with the Bereaved.* "I assume we're talking about you, rather than Mr. Deubel?"

"Yeah," answered Sonny. "Duebber gets the cremation-and-urn special. The mausoleum is for me."

"Then to answer your question, we at Shenkman's Funeral Home believe a mausoleum is a moral and contractual obligation. For purposes of this conversation, a private family mausoleum is permanent."

"What happens if I don't die first?" Sonny was thinking of his son. Personalities like Michael's didn't have the usual life expectancy. The boy would be lucky to see fifty candles on a cake.

"It's for the family, so yes, others can be interred first. The name—your last name—is above the door, and appropriate markers are mounted to recognize others."

"And cost—a premium lot plus the best granite mausoleum to fit six. What's that run?"

"Instead of talking numbers, let's set an appointment and—"

"I don't want a date. Give me the number."

"Four hundred thousand."

Sonny didn't know if the number was high or low. Didn't really care. "Four hundred thousand for a place that can't be bulldozed for a strip mall?"

"Yes, Mr. Bonhardt. I guarantee it."

That was enough for Sonny. "Send the invoice for Duebber. For the four hundred thousand, is a ten percent cash discount a problem?"

"No. Certainly not."

Sonny's mind was already pressing forward on acquiring the proceeds, an addiction of pursuit that defined his life. "Pull together a couple designs, and I'll call you back in six months to sign the paperwork and drop off payment."

Sonny had a gift for earning. Over a lifetime, he'd made millions—maybe a hundred or more. He also had a counterbalancing gift for blowing it, never saving a damn dime. Every year, to keep the wolves at bay, he needed a minimum of six hundred grand. This year, the bar was even higher. He'd sell his ideas for the majority, plus an extra side con. Hell, maybe just swing for the fences. Get motivated and go big. *Time to get working,* he thought. *Permanence isn't for the poor.*

3.

A Few Months Later

ANTON BIELAKOWSKI POSITIONED the pork shoulder along the table's edge and whispered, "*Spojrzeć*," to get his apprentice's attention. Even though the cold of the cutting room had antagonized the sausage maker's arthritis, he wanted to demonstrate a final trimming technique before retreating. The rest of the recipe—boiling the shoulder with a liver and grinding the meats together with barley, vinegar, and pig's blood—could be taught later, outside the refrigerated room.

With a practiced hand, Bielakowski inserted the blade and made quick work of the inch-thick fat cap. At his age, cuts were a reflexive routine, a mechanical procedure that brushed little against conscious thought. He slid the trimmings into a catch barrel, positioned a second shoulder, and lingered through a lull in the pain as though a stay had been granted. A jolt from his right wrist closed the conjecture, forcing him to yield the knife before dropping it to the floor.

In the locker room, Bielakowski washed with diluted bleach and exchanged his sausage-making apron for brown polyester pants and a button-down shirt frayed from his short neck and coarse whiskers. Tucked within the shirt's front pocket were two pens, a small notebook, and a roll of antacids. The notebook was customized with onionskin paper designed to melt inside a closed hand. Each month started with a fresh notebook, the previous one burned in the back alley.

Passing through double doors, the sausage maker wiggled his fingers at a familiar customer before inspecting the display cases of pierogis, kabanosa, kielbasa, and a dozen other varieties of handmade sausage and prepared foods. Pleased at the deli's cleanliness, he dropped a twenty in the tip jar and asked one of the part-time girls to wrap four packages of meat. One was for his wife and son, two were for widows in the neighborhood, and the fourth was a surprise for a man who preferred capicola and prosciutto.

Bielakowski's wife had made her request that morning over the breakfast table and called the shop at lunch to make sure he didn't forget. Since his hip replacement, she'd noticed slips in his mental acuity. The lapses weren't monumental, just enough that the love notes she put in his shirt now came with cues about upcoming errands or appointments. Bielakowski bristled at the implications, though it was a prideful show. He needed the help and appreciated her and Marcek's strategies for keeping him current. Their assistance allowed him to focus on Tom Monte's family.

A year had passed since U.S. Attorney Richard Codd's historic press conference outside the Federal Courthouse at Sixth and Market Street. Assured all major media outlets had arrived, the highest-ranking law enforcement official in the Eastern District of Pennsylvania tapped the microphone, cleared his throat, and announced he'd negotiated a deal with Tom Monte, leader of Philadelphia's largest crime family. In return for a twenty-year sentence, the mobster would plead guilty to multiple charges of conspiracy, racketeering, and extortion. When the buzz subsided, U.S. Attorney Codd thanked his staff, tossed a complimentary bone to the FBI, and issued a warning to what remained of Philadelphia's crime community—*Fiat justitia ruat coelum*. Let justice be done, though the heavens fall. Cue the band, thank you, and God Bless America.

That same afternoon, four miles south of the courthouse, two of Tom Monte's ranking protégés went all in for the family's top spot. Joe

Anticcio—Monte's number two—was the old guard and presumptive heir. He was challenged by an ambitious young cock-of-the-walk named Raymond Rea who cared more about the spotlight than protocol or paying dues.

Given his age and accomplishments, Anticcio had certain advantages for carrying on his predecessor's legacy. His influence included most of the town's bookmakers, some of the unions, and a relationship with New Jersey and New York. At the same time, young Rea's cupboard wasn't bare. His power came from a personal boldness that caught his adversaries off guard, a cadre of aggressive young soldiers who didn't respect the old ways, and a connection with a South Philly motorcycle club that specialized in methamphetamines and storm-trooper waves of violence.

After months of fighting and three attempted murders, Rea killed the veteran Anticcio by going broad with a bomb. Forget an open casket. There was hardly enough to make the identification. Style points and oddsmakers' predictions aside, Rea understood he'd won a crown of thorns—a bomb would be under his stoop if he couldn't rev up the family's production. As his old boss Tom Monte was fond of repeating, *No one revolts with a full belly. Everyone is thinking it when they're hungry.* Pressed to perform, Rea put his strategy into action the Saturday after Anticcio's funeral when he sent his soldiers en masse to Spring Garden Street. The soldiers' assignment was simple—reintroduce Philadelphia's legendary street tax to every business with a cash register.

During the height of Tom Monte's reign, Spring Garden Street was the northern edge of his taxing territory. He owned everything south to the Navy Yards, which meant he collected without worrying about permission or forgiveness. For other earning opportunities, he allowed his men to stray beyond these boundaries with one exception. Tom Monte didn't care if his guys hassled the Jamaicans in West Philly, the Puerto Ricans in the Badlands, the Irish in the Northeast, the Chinatown contingency, or the drug gangs surrounding Fairmount Park. Every one of them was fair game, every one except the Poles of Port Richmond. The Polish mob was not to be antagonized. Any money or advantage taken from the Poles—however small—came soaked in too much blood to make the numbers work.

A month after taking control and reorganizing Spring Garden Street, Rea's soldiers pushed the tax into unclaimed Northern Liberties. A week later and another ten blocks north in Fishtown, they popped into Lou's Grill & Draft, a bar that catered to unemployed roofers and dice hawks. After downing an hour's worth of liquid courage, Rea's soldiers unplugged the jukebox, hopped atop Lou's bar, and announced the new boss was no longer honoring rules negotiated by dead men. Going forward, everyone—including Lou and those high-hat Port Richmond Polacks twenty blocks north—would be paying Rea's tax. No exceptions.

Never one to overreact—especially regarding youthful mistakes—Anton Bielakowski also believed in consequences for ignorant maneuvering. Before pressing north, Rea should have sent an emissary. Not for purposes of negotiation—Bielakowski would never compromise Port Richmond—rather so they could communicate like men instead of the rooster show at Lou's Grill & Draft. Truth was, he didn't care about Spring Garden, Northern Liberties, or Fishtown. They weren't his, and the Italians were free to work those neighborhoods. But Rea's shout-out regarding the Poles was a mistake.

Bielakowski settled on a three-pronged response. Prong one was a handwritten note. Like its author, the message was modest and straightforward. *If you believe Port Richmond owes you a tax, come get it.*

Prong two involved extending his watchful eye to Kensington, Port Richmond's closest neighbor to the south and west. The move had no financial bearing; Bielakowski historically dismissed the neighborhood as a collection of hack pipefitters, burned-out storefronts, and roaming bands of street punks. But Kensington was also the ideal location for snatching an Italian. Grabbing one close to Port Richmond's perimeter allowed Bielakowski to send a message without painting his own doorstep red. When confronted, he could shrug his shoulders and say street taxes were a dangerous business, particularly in a barbaric land populated by savages living off the government tit.

And prong three was another call to Big Bern Jaracz. Twenty-five shotguns were not enough.

4.

ANGIE SPINA WAS THE PITCH-PERFECT party girl. She sipped champagne with a giggle, swapped words with ooh's and ahh's, and flipped her hair as if she had dance club Tourette's.

So convincing was the performance that Marcek Bielakowski never considered the possibility she was hustling him. Granted, Angie was camouflaged in cleavage bait and a ruler-length skirt, but her riff on the nuns at St. Maria Goretti High School was too good for the rest of her cut-and-pasted dialogue. And when a drunk bumped the champagne from her hand, she stayed steady-eddy, not even a *Watch it, bitch* or middle finger.

Yeah, there was enough. He should've known.

Marcek had first spotted Angie a month earlier at Roth's Fine Diamonds. Her olive skin and dark features caught his attention; her contempt for the sales job kept him from looking away. While he had plenty of gigs, he filed her face in case they ever crossed paths. And here they were at a Delaware Avenue dance club—Marcek doing the courtship-across-the-bar routine, Angie making it easy, waving him over and asking why he waited so long.

For the rest of the night, the two drank champagne, smoked Marlboros, and danced until they were soaked in sweat and pheromones. Last call moved them outside, where Marcek suggested Geno's for cheese steaks. Angie waved him off, telling him about a late-night diner on Fairmount Avenue. "I'm feeling like pancakes," she said. "And I don't want to be seen in my neighborhood with a medigan."

They parked a block away and stepped slow because her feet hurt. The diner's windows were steamed by a mash-up of Dylan bohemians, club kids, Seattle grunge, and shift workers starting or ending their workday. The owner—an Einstein-looking caricature with teased hair and overgrown mustache—hustled between the register and the kitchen. His emotions cycled so fast that he barked and smiled in the same sentence, encouraging some customers' shticks, dismissing others as forced or foolish.

Seated at the counter, Marcek ordered his cheese steak with onions and Cheez Whiz. Angie went with chocolate chip pancakes and a Diet Coke in a to-go cup. Waiting for their food, they thought of nicknames for the owner and imagined his life as a teenager. When conversation slowed, Marcek pointed at a T-shirt mounted above the cash register. *Heaven is where the police are British, the chefs are Italian, the mechanics are German, the lovers are Greek, and it's all organized by the Swiss. Hell is where the police are German, the chefs are British, the mechanics are Greek, the lovers are Swiss, and it's all organized by the Italians.*

"What do you think?" he asked.

"What, as poetry?"

"As, I don't know, advice."

"Life would be easier if knowing people were that simple."

"There's truth in those descriptions." Marcek tossed his chin toward the owner. "You want him tuning your engine or running a bank?"

Angie surveyed the room. Two college students in hooded sweatshirts read from the same Vonnegut book. A man dropped ice cubes from a water glass into his cereal flakes. Half a dozen skateboarders counted money on a tabletop before ordering. "There's truth in everything. That's why people like conspiracies—only they are smart enough to make the connections. But I guess that's the difference between cash and credit. Careful making more of it than it is."

"What about you?"

"Me? Two hours ago, you had me figured for champagne drunk, short skirt, heels, and sex in the parking lot."

Marcek exhaled half a laugh.

"Now I'm eating pancakes in a diner. Shoes are off and my makeup is a mess. Things change."

Missing her hint of transition, he said she still looked great.

"Okay, let's personalize it," she said, eyebrows up. "Tonight you hit the town thinking you never looked better. All slick and clean, face shaved and hair trimmed. Fast-forward and you have a cheese-stained shirt, onion mouth, and your deodorant is breaking down. Life gets weird enough on its own. Don't help it by making a bunch of predictions."

They followed the tangent another thirty minutes before walking back to his car and driving to Angie's South Philly row home. Conversation was an easy give-and-take, neither one blocking the other from making a meaningful contribution. As Marcek double-parked, she worked her drink straw instead of reaching for the door handle.

Checking his rearview mirror, Marcek turned off the engine. "Where'd you say you work?"

"Told you at the club." She sipped her soda, catching more air than liquid.

"Jewelry Row, right? Roth's on Walnut Street."

"Yeah, for the moment. My boss is an asshole. Don't laugh, but I'm thinking about becoming a legal secretary. Maybe even a paralegal."

Marcek asked why she thought he'd pan the dream.

She scratched a freckle on her thigh. "I don't know. That's just what most guys do, like it's a joke."

He wondered if she was being real or manipulating the moment. His take was a little of both and it didn't matter. "I don't think going for what you want is a joke. Everybody deserves that."

With the corner of her mouth curled in, Angie gave him a soft smile. "So, you're quitting the jewelry store?"

"Can't do school and work at the same time. My cousin is at a big law firm and swears she can get me hired when I graduate."

Marcek leaned close, looking through the passenger window to scan her home. "Any chance your dad's going to have a problem with me parked here?"

"He can't see us from Curran-Fromhold." Inches away, she liked his smell, even after the dancing and smoking.

"All that can't be cheap."

"It's jail," she said, swiping his arm like they were playing on a fourth date. "Don't you know Curran-Fromhold?"

He dug her giggle, thought it was cute as hell. When her face was closed, like on the drive to the diner, she wore weariness beyond her years. All that disappeared as she let the light through. "I know CFCF—I'm talking about school. You said you're thinking about going back, and I said a school like that must cost good money."

She took a quick look at her home, not speaking until she resumed eye contact. "Why don't you ask me?"

He didn't know what she meant and said so.

She placed a hand on his forearm. "We've seen each other before to-night." When he didn't squint or flinch, Angie knew she had him cold. Silly boys always thought they were running the game. They only got what she was willing to give, never more. "My Dad's at CFCF because he likes to steal. Ask him what he does for a living and he says *I steal shit.* When I started at the jewelry store, he got that look in his eyes. You know the one, right? Yeah, you do."

The jig was up. Marcek had tripped hard coming at her with misplaced assumptions and blind bravado. Under different circumstances, either one was enough to get himself killed. "All night you've been dealing from the bottom of the deck."

"Don't start feeling sorry for yourself. If I wasn't interested, we wouldn't be here."

Marcek asked what gave him away.

Before answering, Angie motioned for a smoke. He pulled a pack of Marlboros from the glove box, lit two, and handed one over. Knowing how men responded to getting turned around, she was surprised he didn't toss the burning stick into her lap.

"I see things pretty clear," she said, exhaling a smoke ring that faded into the windshield. "Plus my boss was robbed a couple years ago so we're constantly checking the street, looking for anyone casing the shop. While you weren't obvious, you stuck around a few seconds too long. My first thought was you were good-looking enough that I didn't mind."

Feeling a rise in confidence, Marcek realized how subtly she was tugging his string. "And the second?"

Angie pinched a shred of tobacco from her tongue. "You and my dad have the same look when you're prepping."

Marcek cracked his window for some air. Everything Angie did was more than he expected. "So where do we go from here?"

"Like I said, school's my future. And like you said, it's expensive. The only change now is we both know the other isn't a lowbrow."

"So that's our path," said Marcek, feeling like the cheating husband whose wife has taken a lover.

"Are you going for the store?"

"I don't do smash and grab. I like it coming in or going out."

"So what, then, the wholesaler? The buys from New York?"

He shook off the suggestions. Product never held much appeal. If anyone in the chain got nicked, the whole operation was vulnerable. While diamonds were the best on a bad list, he still preferred cash, even if that meant smaller piles. "There's probably a half-dozen ways to make money off your jewelry story, but it has to be worth the effort. And it can't smell like an employee. Otherwise the cops will run names, find your old man's sheet, and shine the light in your eyes."

Angie reminded herself to step easy. She was circling the guy who was circling her piece-o-shit boss. Every part of that equation was an ambition she didn't want to jeopardize. "Let's figure out a way to make this work."

Looking at her looking at him, Marcek was struck by the twist. Twenty-four hours earlier his mom had peppered him about finding a woman. *Get a sweetie,* she said, rubbing his cheek with a dishwater hand. His response was he didn't frequent places populated by nice girls. She gave him a gentle slap and said it was okay to settle for pretty and smart.

"Your boss take in a lot of cash?"

Angie nodded. "His best clients are criminal defense attorneys that get paid with drug money. My boss skips the tax if they use it instead of a credit card. But I hope you're smarter than jacking him on his way to the bank. First off, he packs a gun. Second, he deposits right across the street. You'd have no chance."

Drove Marcek crazy how easy she doled out the advice, telling him what he shouldn't be doing. Her confidence was sexier than the panties he imagined her wearing. "I'm not robbing the jewelry store or stealing it straight from your boss. All too obvious."

"Well, how else are we going to make it happen?"

"We?"

"Isn't that the point?"

Marcek put a hand on her knee for no other reason than he wanted to touch her skin. "I'm getting the money. And you'll get your share. But the easiest way is tagging a high roller before he makes his jewelry pickup. All I need to know is when one of these whales is coming in and from what direction."

"Oh, so that's the big plan?"

Having no answer, he leaned across the armrest and did what he'd been waiting to do all night. The kiss was how he imagined. Soft, slow, and a sweet treat.

5.

OUT THE SHOP'S FRONT DOOR, Anton Bielakowski turned east for the half-mile walk to the warehouse. His journey was backdropped by a repeating sequence of brick and stucco row homes decorated with faded awnings, American flags, and porches covered in green indoor/outdoor carpeting. Breaking the architectural monotony were intersections sprinkled with owner-operated convenience stores, hair salons, and old-man taverns sporting last year's Christmas lights.

Four miles northeast of Philly's skyline, Port Richmond was a neighborhood no one had any compelling reason to visit or pass through. Most Philadelphians couldn't give directions or find it on a map. The neighborhood's eastern border was the Delaware River; the western was a debate involving Aramingo, Frankford, and Kensington Avenues. A majority of residents were second- and third-generation Poles employed by the nearby oil refining facilities along I-95. Of those born on the far side of the Atlantic, three dozen had participated in the Polish Resistance.

Distracted by what waited for him at the warehouse, Bielakowski forgot his first delivery, backtracking a half block to Mrs. Kaminski's home. Before dying, her husband had been Bielakowski's enforcer for much of the seventies and eighties. The man said little, never traveled, and enjoyed his work—the perfect hammer.

The sausage maker wasn't surprised when the widow opened her front door before he knocked. With the passing of her husband and all seven children gone to the suburbs, nothing remained to entertain her eye.

"Hello, Mr. Bielakowski," she said, reaching out to confirm his presence. She wore a white sweatshirt decorated with dancing pumpkins and glossy black pants. A few more pounds on her midsection would have challenged the clothing's coverage. "I saw you walk past and thought you'd forgotten. Now I can see a heavy burden on your face. Come in for a drink. Relax a moment while we tell stories about Jozef."

Bielakowski attributed the liquor he smelled to her loneliness. For the first part of Mrs. Kaminski's life, men went mad for her curves, declaring love outside her bedroom window while she still lived with her parents. Before getting serious with Jozef, she could've had two dates every night, never with the same boy twice. During her middle years, the kids snuggled in tight, soaking up all the hugs and kisses she was willing to give. Only recently had Mrs. Kaminski discovered anonymity. Shopping for one, she was invisible except to other cart-pushing widows and the checkout girl.

The sausage maker smiled as kindly as his temperament allowed and handed over a package. "Can't stay today. I have a few more stops. And my wife is waiting."

The widow wasn't offended. Bielakowski's face had her recalling Jozef's transformations. As he headed for the door after kissing his family good-bye, she saw something rise in him—a commitment to violence against men of no immediate threat. The same look was now on her doorstep. "Give me the other package," she said, "the one for Mrs. Wisniewski. No sense fussing over weathered hens when you have business."

"I wish Jozef were here to walk with me. The older I get, the more I recall our times together. He was a good friend."

It wasn't just Jozef Kaminski that Bielakowski missed. He'd outlasted his entire generation and was gaining ground on the next. His soldiers now included the grandsons and great-grandsons of his deceased partners. While they were competent, some couldn't speak Polish, and a few had married women outside the neighborhood. He still had the resources to run his operations—loans and collections, the overage house, money laundering, and a numbers game that stretched to the Bahamas—but he sometimes wondered if Port Richmond had passed him by. Was he indulged because times were good? His relationship with the neighborhood had always been give-and-take—they succeeded together by each protecting the other. Did the newer generation still buy into this arrangement? Did they understand the commitment? And if not, were there enough old-timers to see him to the finish line? These questions, he knew, would be answered soon enough. "It's divine grace to survive your foes," he said. "And a hellish curse to outlive your friends."

The widow stepped onto the stoop, tugging the bottom edge of her sweatshirt. "We've heard the rumors," she said, flicking her chin up and down the narrow street. "And seen your friend Bern making his deliveries. These people trust you, Anton, they always have. But at some point, the next generation must assume their roles. Either they'll fight for Port Richmond or they won't. The burden is not yours until you die."

Plucking each word like a loose bass string, he said, "No one comes into my neighborhood. Remember appeasing our German friends? *Give them a little and they'll leave us alone.* And we appeased our way right into the Bialowieza and the ghettos. Years of sleeping in the dirt, our people eating rats and rotten cabbage while they burned our farms. No, never again. I won't step back. When I'm dead the next generation can let the Italians, Russians, and Armenians run wild. But while I'm alive, Port Richmond belongs to us. Our money isn't paying anyone else's bills."

She placed a dry kiss on his cheek and said good-bye, sure her husband was looking down, praying for not another word. Though never the brightest of the Port Richmond crew, Jozef understood the organic components of longevity. When others were quick to describe Bielakowski as a rock, Jozef shook his head, arguing his boss was water. Years pass, the sun rises and sets, water crashes against rock, and everyone cheers the rock. But be patient. Watch. Bit by bit, the rock is broken down and swept away. The water goes looking for another rock. No exceptions.

Bielakowski stepped off the stoop and within fifteen minutes had passed the final home on Port Richmond's last populated block. He crossed beneath the highway to a lot once used by Delaware River coal haulers for impromptu baseball games. After working a hot summer's day, the men played six-inning games while drinking buckets of locally brewed pilsner. The field was now pockmarked with patches of blacktop, bottles, dead gulls, busted concrete block, and fast-food wrappers.

Through the back of the lot and down a crumbling access road, Bielakowski arrived at an abandoned warehouse protected by chain-link and warning signs. Stepping through a gap in the security fence, he paid more attention to snagging his trousers than to the threats against unlawful trespass. Familiar with the warehouse's structure, he opened an unlocked side door and started up the southeast stairwell. Each landing faced the Delaware River, so by the third switchback Bielakowski could see barges working their loads and fishermen motoring in either direction. At the sixth floor, he exited into an open layout with load-bearing pillars every forty feet. The warehouse's outer walls were banked in broken panes, allowing sheets of natural light and a cooling cross-breeze. The concrete floor—clear of trash and debris—was speckled with pigeon droppings and paint.

At the far end was a small, unpainted wood table. Atop the table was a knife. To the side was a metal-framed chair bolted to the floor. Tied to the chair with coarse rope was a man in his midthirties wearing a white sleeveless tee. His hair was jet black, and his stomach was flat. A bandana was tight across the man's mouth. His eyes were open.

6.

CLUTCHING A PATIENT'S FILE, the nurse backed through the waiting room door to call the next appointment. Three years had passed since she'd retired to South Florida for what her husband emphasized was the *goooood life*. She would have preferred staying in Wisconsin near the grandbabies but acquiesced out of loyalty and the urge for one last adventure. Eight months into retirement she returned to work because everything in Florida was double what they'd expected. Just a few days a week, her husband had promised, and no longer than a year. Fast-forward three birthdays and she was still driving from their Delray Beach apartment to the medical practice in Boca. All Florida meant for her was forty-hour weeks, swollen ankles, and varicose veins.

The nurse double-checked the file and gulped extra air. She had to be loud or the patients bitched, like it was her fault they were deaf. "Mr. Bonhardt," she yelled, tugging a hair off her lower lip. "Please follow me."

An old man wearing sandals and socks muttered at his watch as Sonny Bonhardt rose and trailed the nurse down a hallway decorated with starving-artist watercolors. The appointment was his hustle's last piece of due diligence. After poring over every available corporate report and medical journal, all that remained was tapping into the gossip doled out by pharmaceutical reps to their physician clients. If that meant faking an affliction, so be it.

The nurse stopped at the scale and grunted for Sonny to step up. Given her body language and lack of eye contact, Sonny could see she was struggling. Not chugging-booze-during-lunch kind of struggling, though not much better.

"Two hundred pounds," she said, with a moody staccato. "You're a lucky one with that high metabolism."

Moving from the scale to the row of exam rooms, Sonny heard his doctor's voice bleeding through a closed door. It was a low-frequency baritone that harmonized well with medical terminology. Inside his own room, the nurse wrapped a cuff around his upper arm, pumped the bulb, released the pressure, and asked what brought him in.

"Feeling blue," he said.

The nurse tore the cuff free. "Your blood pressure is a little high. More than a little actually."

"I'm a work in progress."

"Anything adding stress to your life? Maybe a change in circumstance?"

"Like I said, blue."

"Suit yourself, had to ask. I'll let the doctor know we skipped the intro stuff." The nurse blamed the short answer on his accent. After three years in Florida, her impression was that East Coasters like Mr. Sonny Bonhardt were a prickly lot. She preferred the more accommodating Midwest snowbirds.

Settling for what information the file offered, the nurse was surprised at his recorded height and age. Like a veteran carnival barker, she started each appointment with a guessing game of basic proportions. Seeing Sonny in the waiting room, she figured him for six foot two and fifty-five years old. The file had him two inches shorter and almost ten years older. She blamed the discrepancy on his broad shoulders and Robert Mitchum hair.

Sonny watched her study his medical file. Halfway down the second page, she paused and reversed course. "Korea," he said.

"Oh, my . . ."

When their eyes met for the first time, Sonny realized she'd been hiding her prettiest feature. Their coloring was a shifty, almost magnetic, green and he wondered how bright they must have burned when she was a young woman, fresh and anxious.

"A Communist carved my name on a bullet," he said. "Three actually. Two bullets nicked me and splashed into the mud. The third was either luckier or meaner, like a bee aiming for the tongue. It got inside and decided to make a home in my shoulder blade. I've been carrying that piece around probably longer than you've been alive."

"I'm fifty-seven."

Sonny knew the expectation of a woman offering her age, even one who ignored her appearance to the point of neglect. He smiled easily and spoke as though her affections were in play. "Fifty-seven?" he said. "Then I must compliment you on your skin. It's beautiful."

When she blushed, he tapped the knuckles of her right hand. They both chuckled, agreeing that while neither was fooling the other, the game was still fun.

Most of Sonny's war story was true except for the bullet count and his suggestion that Korea was responsible for all the scars. There *was* a metal fragment in his shoulder. And it did come from a skirmish on a nameless hilltop on the other side of the world. All that happened just as he'd explained. But the other scars on his torso weren't from any war, or even a gun. Sonny had learned that folding them together avoided the buzz created by an honest explanation. The rubbery-looking eight-inch scar running from his last rib was courtesy of an alley fight on the soft side of fifteen. The other, a much smaller scar below his heart, was courtesy of an ice pick that had him seeing white light and reaching for God's hand.

"Carrying around that bullet must have changed your life, always reminding you of the war."

"Probably not the way you think."

Her tilted brow was his invitation to continue.

Sonny lowered his voice. "When I was in the field hospital, the doctors thought I needed my last rites. They called the chaplain over, who was this soft-spoken black guy from Alabama. I was so damn thirsty I could hardly whisper, but I managed to ask him if I was dying. Instead of saying yes or no, he told me a story."

Most appointments, the nurse fled as soon as the weight, pulse, and pressure were recorded. Her own life wasn't in a place where she could muster much sympathy for other people's travails. That morning, she appreciated the chance.

"The chaplain," Sonny said, encouraged by her interest, "told me about a tiger chasing a monk. The tiger had run this fellow to a cliff's edge where his only choice was climbing down. The few roots on the rock face were weak and wouldn't hold long, and another tiger was waiting at the bottom. As the monk clutched to the rock wall—pinched between two man-eaters—he noticed a small, perfectly formed strawberry growing from a nearby crevice. The monk reached out, plucked the strawberry, closed his eyes, and ate it in one bite. He'd never tasted anything so pure."

The nurse slapped her thigh. "My God, what kind of story is that for a dying soldier?"

Sonny was accustomed to the reaction. People's expectations for their last moments didn't include an Alabama preacher talking about monks, tigers, and pieces of fruit. They wanted their sins washed away in preparation for the journey to heaven, where fine-looking people in togas were playing silver harps and awaiting their arrival.

"That story changed me," he said, leaning back into the chair. "It took a few weeks of healing to understand. The point is, we're all dying. Maybe it's from some bastard's bullet in your shoulder, or a tumor, or old age, or two tigers drooling over your bones, but that Angel of Death comes for us all. The chaplain was telling me how to live, regardless of whether I had fifteen seconds or fifty years."

The nurse's upper body swayed, gaining momentum with each new cycle. "Thank you, Mr. Bonhardt," she said, tucking a handful of hair behind her ear. "Maybe I was meant to meet you today."

A sucker for underdogs, Sonny took her hand. "You know the best way to find strawberries?"

She shrugged, though not enough to shake him loose.

"Stop acting like the tigers don't exist. See them or not, they're everywhere."

7.

TEN FEET SHORT of the bound man, Bielakowski stopped to pull antacids from his shirt pocket. His bleeding ulcer had resurfaced, an affliction he treated with Rolaids, milk, and a doglike pain tolerance. After unwrapping and popping two, he tapped the packages beneath his left arm. "A special delivery for you."

The man fought like a snared animal hearing the trapper's approach. While the rope and chair moaned, neither surrendered. Bielakowski shrugged as though all was according to plan. "Give up hope. It's useless. You know by now my men can tie a good knot."

The summation spurred another burst of energy, this one lasting half as long.

Bielakowski sucked on the antacids. "Stay still and I'll get to it. You've waited long enough. Last night you and a twin named Toscano visited a strip club called Fancy Tina's. You discussed weekly tributes with the owner before enjoying private dances. Toscano picked a brunette called Raven, but you've got a thing for blonds and went for Cheryl. As you know, she likes Canadian whisky and has a panther tattooed on her hip."

When the man shook his head, Bielakowski raised a hand. "The tequila you drank was drugged. Raven took Toscano home. Cheryl invited you to her apartment. Your next memory is waking up here, roped to the chair, with that knife on the table."

Bielakowski wiped chalky residue from the corners of his mouth, using the pause to appraise his captive, reading him for comprehension. "I want to remove the gag. We have matters to discuss, but I don't want you screaming. Not because anyone will hear or care—Port Richmond isn't concerned. Screaming only makes our time more difficult. Show you understand."

The prisoner assented with a blink, and his gag was pulled down. "They'll find me," he said, trying to catch his breath. "Toscano saw my girl. Other people know I was in Kensington. They'll come looking."

"Kensington is not the Italian Market. And the trail is already cold."

"My car . . ."

Bielakowski spoke like a reassuring grandparent. "The car was taken to a junkyard. Your girlfriend Cheryl jumped a plane this morning. Visiting family in Florida, I think. Your people have begun making calls, but so what? Toscano last saw you on a couch in a strip club's back room. I suppose they could strong-arm some of the bouncers, or slap the girls around. Then again, I know the Irishman who owns that dump. He doesn't like being bullied."

The man's expression was reduced to rhythmic blinking.

A distant horn floated in on the breeze, adding a touch of civilization to the bleak surroundings. "You know who I am?"

"You're Bielakowski." Spit flew with the hard B.

The host stepped to the knife. As he'd instructed, it was a traditional Eastern European design—lead tape balancing the handle, a subtle curve to the blade. He flicked the back, spinning it like a soda bottle at a teenage kissing party. A subtle friction echoed off the concrete, the single sound filling the space.

"Kensington is no-man's-land," said the captive, breaking away from the knife's hypnotic rotation. "Open territory."

Bielakowski pressed a finger onto the knife's center point, the tip aimed at the Italian's face. "Rea is communicating his understanding of power. First in Fishtown with the men putting their boots on the bar. And again last night—mouths open and hands out." Bielakowski felt his blood rising. "Was that you in Lou's Tavern?"

"No, not my job or style."

Studying the hostage's face, Bielakowski was unable to parse any subtle nuances. His conclusion was that the man was well versed in deception. "Your whole generation—all barbarians. No measure or restraint. Machine guns on the highway and bombs in the neighborhoods—what is that? Who does these things? Even your attorneys—men paid to protect you—hold press conferences after you've been arrested, preening at the cameras and screaming your names. This is not style. It's war and suicide."

"Rea won and Anticcio is dead. Everything else is earning a living."

"I guess you figure that sounds right."

"I don't know about right anymore. That's just the way it is."

Bielakowski paused while he tugged at his ear. "You know about nihilists?"

The man shook his head.

"Me neither, not really. But the other day, I was watching PBS and heard that word. Some professor was saying these people—nihilists—don't believe in rules. Morals, either. They just do whatever the hell they want. I call them kind of people assholes. And I think I'm looking at one. Rea, too, now that I'm thinking about it."

"We're all greedy pricks. Okay? You, me, Rea—what else you going to say to change any of that?"

"Fair enough," said Bielakowski, reinforcing his words with a long blink. "Let me explain so you have an answer for St. Peter." He noted the man's tattoo, a black cross on his shoulder. The simple design reminded him of Russian prison markings, a stark contrast to the cartoon characters and pet names preferred by Americans.

Bielakowski lowered his voice. "For years our businesses didn't conflict. Many times—with my overage houses and your unions—we even profited together. But now Rea pokes me. Next, will I see him in my shop? You're here paying for that arrogance. And if your life isn't enough, others will suffer until we're left alone."

The hostage shook sweat off his nose. "If you were going to kill me, you'd have already done it. Getting me here was harder than blowing my head off in the strip joint."

Something in the man's assumptions made Bielakowski smile. His cheeks receded far enough for light to reach his silver-capped molars. "That's how *your* kind handles these matters. There are better ways." And then, like a match on a moonless night, Bielakowski's grin flamed out and his teeth retreated to their darkness. "I'm told your name is Martin."

"Yeah, Martin. Martin. It's Martin." He repeated the word as if it was a calming mantra.

"You run a high-stakes game in Jersey. Some time after this business with Monte, you allied with Rea and made a name as a good earner. When the dust settled, you survived with a niche on the numbers side."

"Then you know I'm not muscle. I wasn't in Kensington to collect."

Bielakowski hated how the Italians parsed their words, like children arguing over tag technicalities. "I'm not interested in what you weren't doing. It's enough you were caught in Kensington. And now you're here because I want information."

"This is so fucked up. I'm not even who you think I am."

Bielakowski grabbed the knife and checked its sharpness against his thumb. Theatrics weren't his bailiwick, but some moments needed extra salt. "You were marked the moment you wandered into Fancy Tina's. The only question is the length of your final verse."

The host noticed a quickening in the Italian's jugular. "If you cooperate—tell me what I want—I'll cut your throat clean. You'll die feeling like a warm blanket has been draped over your body."

Martin swallowed hard, the dry part of his tongue catching on the roof of his mouth. Gagging, he said, "And if I tell you to fuck off?"

"You know my name and still speak to me like I'm covered in eggshell. Study my face. Is the answer that elusive?"

Martin fought to string out the conversation. "You told me best-case scenario was a neck smile. I'm asking how much worse can it get?"

Tapping the wrapped packages beneath his arm, Bielakowski said, "I'll pry your mouth open, stuff it with blood sausage, and pinch your nose until you suffocate. Then I'll cut your head off and toss it out the window into the Delaware River. Maybe it floats downstream to South Philly, or maybe the crabs get it, or maybe it gets sucked into the prop of a coal barge. The rest of your body will not be treated much better. We'll leave it for the rats."

Martin rolled his head forward, to the side, and all the way back. As he stared at the ceiling, the room was silent except for sounds from the river and watershed. It was singular to that moment in time and space, like him and the Pole.

"Of course," said Bielakowski, his voice rising, "I could do none of that. It might be simpler to sell you to the Armenians."

"No, please . . ."

"They'll hold you hostage and send pieces of your flesh to Rea until he delivers a briefcase of money or drugs. I'll let you predict his response."

For Bielakowski, the pause that followed was not unexpected. He'd learned to be patient with men envisioning their end. Evolution had massaged human psychology into seeking pleasure and avoiding pain. While the selection was usually handled by quick-acting instinct, there were times—pressing moments with consequences—when a man needed an extra minute to sort through the mire.

"I've heard you own a butcher shop," Martin said, breaking the silence with blooming panic in his voice. His eyes were still up at the ceiling. "That you work in the same place your dad built."

Bielakowski tapped the knife. "I'm not a butcher. I'm a sausage maker. Same difference as a stonecutter and a stonemason. The rest of what you say is true. I have other lines of business—which I'm sure you've heard of—but I'm a sausage maker first. My own son shows little interest in wearing an apron. Says it doesn't appeal to him."

Tears welling, Martin closed both eyes. "I have a son." The moment was proving too much, making a last look at the boy all that mattered. "I want to see a picture. It's in my wallet. My boy's school picture. I can lean over a little and you can slide it out."

"With this boy, maybe you should have chosen a safer line of work. Or picked the Vietnamese or Puerto Ricans to shove. It's a shame we only think of the ramifications after we've made our decisions."

Martin paused a full minute before speaking again. "I've got something to trade," he said, his voice steadier, more assured, as though he'd drawn the right card. "It's worth more than my life."

"If it is money you're offering, I've got all I need."

"I'm not talking about money. Or drugs. Or girls, either."

How many desperate offers had Bielakowski heard in his lifetime? Every man choking on a gun pledged the world's treasures, and almost none of the promises were worth the ten seconds of presentation. Indulging the moment of nostalgia, he said, "So tell me, here in this warehouse amongst the pigeons, what is more valuable to me than ending the life of Rea's best earner?"

Martin rolled his head around and locked eyes with the host. "I'm a cop."

8.

A MINUTE PASSED before the doctor knocked and entered with an out-stretched hand. He was a tall, lean man with hound skin, long earlobes, dark hair on his fingers, and moist lips. Cautious of germs, Sonny declined to shake, pointing to his own palms as though they were sore or blistered.

The doctor said he was glad to see Sonny and buried his nose in the file. He flipped through five pages of notes, pausing after the first and third sheets to lick his fingers. "My nurse wrote you're feeling a little blue."

"That was a lie."

"Okay," he said, looking up. "What's the real reason for today's visit?"

Sonny had given serious thought to initiating the discussion. At stake was lining up his biggest score of the last decade. "I think," he said, care-ful to stutter, "that I'm broken."

"Excuse me?"

Sonny pulled himself to the front of his chair and cleared his throat. "The bedroom was an issue this morning."

"What?"

"The bedroom."

"No—I heard what you said. I don't understand what you mean."

"Come on, Doc," Sonny said. "I saw the demographics of your waiting room and all the Buicks in the lot. I'm talking my libido."

"Hmmm, yes, I see now," said the doctor as though he'd nailed a six-letter stumper in that morning's crossword puzzle. "Sexually perform." The doctor ran a hairy knuckle across his forehead. "You're saying you couldn't achieve a full erection?"

"Bingo."

"Maybe it was a matter of attraction? Or mood?"

"I'm dating a thirty-five-year-old Russian model."

The doctor's nod showed he understood. The pursed lips covered the envy. His wife worked the Florida gala scene in size twenty-two dresses and blocky shoes that resembled Dutch clogs. "Has this ever happened before?"

"Never, Doc."

"Never?"

"This morning and that's it."

The doctor's face was both sincere and doubtful, a look he'd worked on since medical school. "A man your age, a pattern of dysfunction is nothing to be ashamed of."

Even roleplaying, Sonny bristled being compared to his age group. "I'm telling you, it's never been an issue. Divorced three times and all of them would take the stand."

"How many times a month do you and your girlfriend have sex? More than five?"

"Double." Sonny wanted to shock the doctor off his standard procedure.

A dozen questions rushed into the doctor's brain, none appropriate for a medical consultation. "It's probably just a one-time event. An anomaly due to stress or an upset stomach. For now, I'd recommend a wait-and-see approach. Let's give this situation some air and distance, see if it develops into a pattern."

"I know you're a busy guy, but indulge me a second."

"Okay."

"Let's assume this happens again and I insist on medical intervention. What are my options now and, say, a year from now?"

The doctor slid Sonny's file beneath his arm. "If the dysfunction becomes a reoccurring theme, you'll undergo a thorough medical exam, which includes blood work and a good look at your prostate. If all that comes back clean, we'd prescribe a medicine that's injected into your penis."

Sonny figured the doctor was used to a certain reaction. He frowned, dropped his chin, and stared at the floor. At the end of a twenty-second pause, he looked up. "You'd put a needle in it?"

"Actually, you'd give yourself the shot. Prior to engaging in intercourse, the syringe goes into the shaft and the medication is injected." The doctor's voice softened. "Look, while not ideal, it's the same method we use with paraplegics, so it works. And it's safe. I've heard from my older patients that when it comes to the syringe, the thought of the needle is far worse than reality."

Sonny was ready to push. "Jesus, Doctor. That's the best you have— a needle?"

Medical school trained the doctor to break patients down with reality and build them back up with hope. "Don't be too pessimistic. There's a development on the horizon, could be a game changer."

The Promised Land, thought Sonny. A little more leading the witness and he'd have the critical date. "What are we talking about here? Surgery or something? A lotion? A pill?"

"Yes, a pill."

"That's terrific."

The doctor removed his reading glasses and placed a hand on the doorknob, his go-to moves for letting a patient know an appointment was fading to black. "Problem is, the FDA hasn't given its approval. For now, the syringe is pretty much our only avenue."

"What's the time frame?"

The doctor frowned. "You fought a war for the government. It could be a month or a year, or they could reject the entire application and send the pharmaceutical company back to the drawing board."

"That's the official line, the story they feed the masses so the stock market doesn't get rattled."

"I'm not following, Mr. Bonhardt."

Sonny rose to his feet. "This FDA business is old news for anyone reading *The Wall Street Journal*. There's a pretty little pharmaceutical rep coming in here once a week with free lunch. I want her sales pitch on this miracle drug. Tell me what she's whispering in your ear."

The doctor turned the knob. "I understand the pressure you're under—"

"Damn it, don't do that."

The doctor dropped his voice and raised his eyebrows. "When you lose that part of your identity, that part of your *manhood*, it's a blow. And then you come here and I start talking about needles and prostate exams and it sends you swimming. That's hard. I don't mean to sound insensitive, but I've seen it a thousand times."

"Focus on what I'm saying, okay? Once the drug company receives approval, how long until the drug is publicly available?"

The doctor eased up on the door handle. "In my experience, it's dangerous to chart medical treatment based on a drug still in the approval process."

"Oh hell, Doc, open your hand and let that bird fly, okay? I'm looking for a time frame, that's all. No promises or hard dates. Give me a range and we'll go our separate ways, I promise."

The pharmaceutical rep had warned the doctor about rising hysteria. He'd scoffed at her—chalking it up to typical sales talk—but maybe she was right. Perhaps Sonny Bonhardt was a foreshadowing of things to come. "The pill," he said, taking another step down his vocal range, "is indeed a miracle drug. They're calling it Viagra, and there's tremendous pressure to get it into the marketplace. I've been told there are facilities and warehouses geared up for immediate manufacturing once the government gives a thumbs-up. Florida is the highest priority. You're talking millions."

"What, millions of dollars?" Sonny already knew the size of Viagra's market but liked hearing the numbers.

"Yes, I suppose, though I meant people," said the doctor. "My Pfizer rep says I'll be writing prescriptions six to eight weeks after the announcement."

"You're saying six to eight weeks after approval and the pharmacies will have the drug?"

"Yes, Mr. Bonhardt, but I can't overemphasize the need to relax. Your problem won't get any better worrying about when the FDA is approving an application. If anything, stress will compound the problem."

"Okay," he said. "No stress. I got it. Hearing about this Viagra puts my mind at ease."

In the parking lot, Sonny called his girlfriend before she could split for work. When her voice mail answered, he said, "Hey baby, sorry for running out. It wasn't you, okay? I'm heading for Philly and will make it up when I get back. Let's sail down to the islands. See you, babe."

Blessed with the discipline to compartmentalize events, Sonny Bonhardt set aside the Viagra heist for his next pressing piece of business. In two hours, he was catching a flight to Philadelphia to meet the head of the Polish Mafia. Sonny owed the man two good ideas.

9.

WHENEVER HE HAD THE TIME, Tyler Lehr recalled each detail of the crimes he'd witnessed. The memories were organized into sensory checklists that rolled forward in one-minute increments, what did he see, hear, smell, and so on, until all the observational data had been evoked and refreshed. The process was his morning and evening prayer, a habitual recitation in anticipation of one day becoming the U.S. government's primary witness against the Philadelphia mob.

To accent his factual framework, Lehr dripped bits of color into the black-and-white summations. Juries were persuaded by the most eccentric crumbs. He knew which victim shit his pants before dying, or begged for his mommy, or wept tears until his ducts were dry. And he knew, sure as he sat tied to a chair, that his own death would produce a similarly distinctive note, one that Anton Bielakowski would never forget.

Staring at the ceiling, images of his son pulsating in his brain, he wondered if his next three words would be that magic moment. Lehr rolled his head forward and, flat as a funeral song, said, "I'm a cop."

The old man didn't stir. Lehr hoped the stillness meant Bielakowski was at least considering a different path. "This can work. Let me explain."

"What is your birth name?"

"Lehr," he said. "Tyler Luke Lehr. Nick Martin is my cover."

Bielakowski repeated the new name. "An Irishman. I don't see it."

"Black Irish."

The old man blinked long enough to suggest he wasn't outright reject-ing the explanation. "For the moment, let's stick with your cover name. Tell me about your family, Mr. Martin, your real family."

Nick Martin recalled a ten-year-old bureau briefing on Bielakowski and the Polish Mafia: *Anton Bielakowski excels in all elements of organized crime and—despite his age—should be considered extremely dangerous. In the 1940s and '50s, he made a name kidnapping prominent businessmen in Phil-adelphia, Trenton, Harrisburg, and Delaware. Rising in stature, he expanded into racketeering and—with an unknown accomplice—developed abilities for laundering large sums of cash. He is suspected of laundering for criminal or-ganizations as far north as Providence and is believed to maintain a network of banking connections throughout the United States, Eastern Europe, Swit-zerland, and the Caribbean. He survives because he makes few, if any, mis-takes, and when he does make one, he handles the situation with brutal efficiency. Continually underestimated by younger adversaries, Bielakowski has fought off every challenge to his position. He has been linked to killings— both ordered and personally performed—in each of the last six decades but has never been indicted. Measured, disciplined, and consistent, he is respected within the criminal underworld for implementing his determinations with conviction and little, if any, collateral runoff. Bielakowski's use of violence is pragmatic rather than psychologically or emotionally driven, which makes his aggression all the more perilous. His criminal family has never been infiltrated because of its symbiotic relationship with the neighborhood of Port Richmond and the attending cultural and language barriers. As such, determining his exact number of associates is difficult because he draws upon the resources of the neighborhood—both in material and manpower—during times of need. They protect each other.*

Despite the consequences of revealing his own background, Martin didn't have a choice. He'd invested too much to die in a Port Richmond hothouse. "The program," he said, speaking thoughts he'd only ever imag-ined, "didn't allow for married guys. I've got a twelve-year-old boy in Atlantic City. Different last name than me. I see him a couple times a year and I'm no longer involved with his mother. That's it. My parents are dead, and I'm an only child. High school in Central Jersey, a couple years in the Marine Corps, and four years of college in Maryland."

"Are you FBI or with the city?" Bielakowski was constructing a foundation of facts instead of relying on the spin of a trained liar.

"Federal," said Martin. "Deeper than anyone has ever gone. I've been on the streets since coming out of the Academy in 1988."

"Am I the focus of your efforts?"

"No."

Bielakowski waited for a tell—a twitch of the right muscle in the wrong way. He saw nothing. "Do you have any co-workers infiltrating my operations?"

The question was a riptide. Outing another agent was the ultimate betrayal. "I guess we're done with the foreplay."

"It's nut-cutting time."

"The answer, to the best of my knowledge, is no. But I can't make any guarantees. As far as I know—"

"Stop. I don't accept qualified answers."

"That's the thing. When they dropped me in, all ties were severed. No computer, no office softball team, and no access to other operations either within or outside the FBI. I get nothing but two sit-downs a year. I barely exist except for my Social Security number in somebody's office vault. The U.S. Attorney doesn't even know about me."

Bielakowski tilted his head, studying his captive from a fresh angle. "Do you think I need your help?"

"If I say no, I'm negotiating against myself. And a yes has its own implications."

"My reality isn't going to be tainted by what you say," said Bielakowski. "All of my adversaries have had their share of cheerleaders. None ever imagined defeat."

"Maybe Rea is different."

"They were all different. And when I finished, they were all the same."

Martin sensed a crease, an opportunity to drive in an anchor point. "But you've never had the Italians pressing your borders. They have more men and resources than you've handled before. That's a fact. I've spent years with them, working to gain entrance and now from the inside. My whole life has been memorizing the details—all the mistakes, all the weaknesses, all the little parts of the puzzle."

A pigeon flew in a nearby window as though it wanted to hear Biela-kowski's response. When the old man told Martin to continue, the pigeon made a half-circle and exited at the far end.

"Rea's ambitious," said Martin, careful to tap down his mob-influenced pronunciations. He wanted to appear neutral, showing that the affect was part of an easily discarded costume. "He's off-the-charts motivated to be the next big thing. For brains, he's smart enough. We're not talking Ivy League candlepower, but he's not falling down any uncapped wells."

"What about his relationship with the motorcycle gang?"

Martin knew it was more than a throwaway question, more than a casual inquiry to verify his access and authenticity. Many of the old-schoolers were intrigued by Rea's relationship with the War Boys. Some thought it was the deciding factor in his victory over Anticcio. The bikers weren't a recent creation—they'd been around in one form or another for forty years—but their affiliation with the Italian mob, and specifically Rea, was a newer development.

"The War Boys are a wild card," said Martin. "Rea was the first to see their potential, especially with the meth."

"We don't deal drugs. There was a time the Italians didn't either."

"Tom Monte was more into cocaine than anyone realized," said Martin, finding a rhythm. "And Rea has made no bones about dope. It's too much of a moneymaker. He figures gambling is on the decline because it's going online and offshore. Even prostitutes are switching to the Internet. But drugs are a street business, and meth is the best."

Over the last year, Bielakowski had grown increasingly troubled by the bikers. Gun for gun, Anticcio should have never lost to the likes of Rea. That he did meant the War Boys were a factor. "Explain why he wants the meth."

Martin could talk for twenty hours on Rea's businesses, and maybe someday would get the chance from the witness stand. Until then, he'd leverage the information for his life. "It's not that the drug itself is better or the demand stronger. The power of meth is that it can be sourced locally. Cocaine comes from South America and the Colombians. Heroin and hash come from Turkey and Afghanistan. Even most weed comes in across the Mexican or Canadian borders. Meth can be made anywhere. As long as you have enough raw materials—off-the-shelf cold medicine is a key ingredient—it's easy. The War Boys figured this out before anyone else. Their problem is they're organizationally crude with limited distribution. That's where Rea comes in. Together they can source, manufacture, distribute, and defend the trade. They haven't perfected the relationship, but they're pretty damn cozy."

In return for the briefing, Martin received a subtle nod, which he took as a win. Survival wouldn't be delivered by the cavalry charging through the door or a SWAT team in the window. Microevents—as delicate as a wink or breath—dictated his future. Martin steadied his thoughts and reminded himself to be patient.

After a few moments, Bielakowski said, "Go on."

"His men like him enough that nobody's shooting him in the back. Rea promotes all the old-fashioned greaseball shit. His crew is half-convinced Hollywood will be making movies about them someday."

Bielakowski understood the power of historical glory. Rea was inspiring his soldiers to achieve the inflated greatness of previous generations. "Young men want the lives of their grandfathers. And the old men would gladly switch places."

"There's more—"

Bielakowski didn't give him the chance. "Did you ever meet Monte?"

"Saw him a couple times. We shook hands once, never talked business. He was a suspicious guy. That's the reason for my program. It takes time."

The old man looked toward the windows and around the room before returning his captive's gaze. Nodding ever so slightly, he said, "In ten years, you never got more than a handshake from Tom Monte. And here comes Rea—on top a few months—and he's got you running jobs. A cop out on collections. That would have never happened with Monte. Had you gotten closer, he'd have sniffed you out and put you down. Rea lacks those instincts."

Martin figured it for a test, whether he was a go-along, get-along yes-man. Raising his voice, he said, "Rea had enough to beat Anticcio, which I'm guessing was a surprise. Even though he's a little caught up in the title, he's not assuming it guarantees his success. You're seeing that with the tax."

Bielakowski worked two fingers in a circle for him to continue.

"On the surface, coming north of Spring Garden looks thick, like he was rushing to make money. Here's the thing—Rea planned the entire dance. That production in Lou's was scripted to get the troops focused on an enemy outside the neighborhood because all they've been doing the last twelve months is shooting each other."

Bielakowski was disappointed for not diagnosing the maneuver sooner. Rea was unifying his family by rallying them against an adversary the younger Italians no longer respected or feared. "Where are you in this scheme?"

"Top producers have always been valuable commodities, even when we don't have the pedigree. Wars only increase our importance. I make money and I'm level-headed, so I'm rising in rank."

"How did you begin?"

Dehydrated and exhausted, Martin struggled to recall those long ago details that now felt as if they belonged to another man. "The plan," he said, "was to start small. We figured that if I built the right résumé they'd come looking for me. My first racket was a sports book in Cherry Hill. Once that had wheels, I started handicapping at the racetrack. That took almost four years. With those plates spinning, I sponsored a weekly poker game for high rollers and wannabes. Nothing major, just enough to introduce and integrate. Another couple years until I finally got close with a guy from South Philly who was connected."

"Who?"

"Jimmy Zoots."

Bielakowski shrugged his shoulders. "I know the man."

"Then you know Zoots isn't the cousin of a guy. I'm running with a made man, paying my dues, collecting chits. You know the routine."

"Building your case."

"Yeah, right, building my case. And then Monte gets arrested."

Bielakowski asked why that wasn't enough for him to get pulled.

"I had nothing to do with that. Some mobster already doing time gave Monte up for parole considerations. I heard about the arrest same time as everyone else."

"So the plan changed," said the old man. "They kept you available for the upcoming power struggle."

Martin saw an opportunity, the second Bielakowski had provided. "History repeats itself," he said. "Unlike the suits at the U.S. Attorney's Office, we knew the mob wasn't dead. There was still plenty of talent on the bench, and the money didn't evaporate just because of the plea deal. We figured Anticcio would step forward and his campaign wouldn't go unchallenged. The bet was on Rea."

"How did you get aligned with Rea? I remember Zoots being with Anticcio."

"That move was a calculated risk," said Martin, wondering whether he was earning trust or delaying the inevitable. "My gut said Rea was going to be the aggressor and win any shootout. Didn't hurt he needed manpower and was open to building his ranks with outsiders like the War Boys. When I proposed defecting, he knew I was a big earner and saw the move as confirmation."

"Confirmation of what?"

"His destiny."

Bielakowski wobbled a half step before steadying himself against the table. "Greed was the weakness that plagued Anticcio, Monte, and before them Anastasia. And that craving will cripple Rea."

"Obsessions provide leverage. They are an exploitable weakness," said Martin, remembering his psychology lectures at the Academy.

His belly groaning, Bielakowski popped two more antacids. "The criminal mind isn't that complex. It comes down to what it has always come down to—chasing dollars."

Martin shook him off. "Knowing and proving are two different things. You make it sound like the cops can drop money into the street and stand by with lassos. Look at me, I'm living proof it's more difficult. I did six months in Ocean County lockup to keep it real. And now I'm here, with you, and greed had nothing to do with any of this."

Bielakowski spread his arms like a tent preacher. "We all choose the chairs we sit in. Some part of you is getting exactly what it wants."

Martin lifted his chin like a belligerent child. "They seduced me. How they sold it, I never had a chance."

A whistle from a passing barge filled the next fifteen seconds. Both men used the break to process what they'd heard and reset their boards.

When the barge's call dissipated, Martin spoke first. The onus was on him to make a case against the status quo. "I'm close, you know," he said. "A little more time and I can get the indictments. Rea would be off your border and out of the tax business."

"How far north will the indictments reach?"

Martin hated the old man's technique. Each question took him in a fresh direction, eliminating his ability to massage the narrative. "You talking North Philly?"

"North Jersey," said Bielakowski. "And New York."

Martin shook his head. "Philly is my focus. But Rea has mentioned using me as his liaison with New York."

"When you bring the indictments, will other families be included?"

"Bit players, none of the management. So far, Rea has handled most of the diplomacy stuff, and there hasn't been much dialogue. I think the other families are waiting to see if he can hold power." Martin did his best to make the partial truth sound complete. The honest answer was that being Philly's go-between with New York was his idea, not Rea's. If he could infiltrate both criminal enterprises, they'd commission a bust of his head for the Hoover Building. It was an ambitious play, the type necessary to make his ten years worth the sacrifice.

The sun's edge dipped below an adjacent building, cutting natural light away with each passing second. Twilight and then darkness would soon define their environment. Bielakowski looked over his shoulder at the sun's position. "Our time is growing short. My wife is expecting me."

The old man had made his decision, Martin was sure of it now. The knife won. It was the easiest of the options. Captured and restrained, his whereabouts unknown, a dead Martin came at no additional expense. The thought had Martin pawing at his wallet, fighting for one last chance to see his son's picture. If he asked the old man to pull it now, it'd be seen as surrender, as if nothing he'd said was valuable. He curled his fingers into a fist and pressed against his restraints, the fibers in his shoulders stretched to their breaking point. "You've been asking me questions," he said with a rising voice. "Give me a last chance. One more run to explain what I can do. Please, on my kid's life, I'm begging you."

Bielakowski told him to stop sounding like a pleading whore. His decision didn't hinge on the pledges of a man in the midst of a countdown.

Martin couldn't help thinking of the lengths any other mobster would travel to acquire what he offered. Perhaps that explained why Bielakowski outlasted them. "Forget what I can do. Let me say what I want and everything else is yours," he said, blinking fast from a final surge of adrenaline. "First, I want out of this chair. I want to live."

The comment didn't register on his captor's face.

"And second," he said, "I want to finish off Rea. I've given it my life. Let me get to the end and I won't hold anything back. I won't kill a man or hurt a civilian, but everything else is yours. As long as I'm FBI and I'm allowed to close my case, you own me. I swear it. You own me."

"Save your oaths," Bielakowski said with a wave of his hand. "How many promises have you broken to get yourself in this warehouse?"

A silence built between the two. Bielakowski used the pause to weigh his options and double-check for false bottoms. The offer wasn't perfect, or even as good as Martin believed. His disappearance and reemergence could be a problem. Rea might think his missing associate had been arrested, flipped, and put back on the street. If that idea took hold, Martin wouldn't survive the next twelve hours. But even with that possibility—or likely outcome—the opportunity to have a federal agent inside the South

Philly crew was still worth the move. If war was on the horizon, Martin could tilt the scales in his favor. If the fighting never materialized, Bielakowski could sit back and wait for the indictments against Rea.

While his men might wonder why he freed the Italian, Bielakowski was a pragmatist. Rule number one was survival. Silly rituals or hyped notions of duty were distractions for other men, not him. Staying alive and protecting Port Richmond were the only guidelines, and he wouldn't deviate now that he'd been gifted such treasure.

"Okay, then," Bielakowski said, picking up the knife. "Let's remove the ropes. And then we've got to come up with a good story for your car. Maybe I should smash your face so you can claim you were robbed."

10.

WHEN HIS PLANE TOUCHED DOWN early, Sonny Bonhardt ran the numbers and figured he had enough time to visit the old neighborhood. He checked into his hotel on Broad Street and hailed a cab for the five-minute ride up the Benjamin Franklin Parkway. East on Fairmount Avenue to North Twenty-third Street, he peeked through the windshield, handed up a hundred, and exited without change.

Still a block from Eastern State Penitentiary, he needed the distance to take in the abandoned prison's looming gun towers and stacked granite. Throughout the prison's hundred years of operation, the surrounding homes—some as close as fifty feet—were occupied by guards and beer makers from nearby Brewerytown. When the last prisoner transferred out in '71—and all the breweries closed—the local population transitioned to city workers, graduate students, and Olympic-hopeful rowers training on the Schuylkill River.

As much as anywhere, Sonny considered the prison neighborhood his home turf. He'd lived on its streets after fleeing his last foster home, scavenging to survive before discovering local bartenders would give him a nickel or beans-and-bread for sweeping floors and cleaning the johns. The rest of the day, he passed time by tossing rocks at the prison walls, daydreaming his father was inside, hearing and understanding the *tap*

tap tap as his son's code. Sonny pictured his old man as a stand-up guy, the kind who wouldn't have abandoned him unless there wasn't a choice. The kind who'd know what his rock tossing meant and track him down after being released.

One frigid day, fifteen minutes shy of the noon whistle, a prison guard on his way into work barked at Sonny to stop tossing *dem fucken rocks at dem walls* or he'd get a boot in the ass. Instead of emptying his hand and wandering away, Sonny reared back, threw one high at the granite wall, and asked the guard for whatever he didn't like in his lunch pail. The guard's answer was the back of his hand.

The blow—short and well practiced—dropped Sonny to his knees, where his suffering doubled with the guard's humiliating laugh. Just because there wasn't another person in the world shedding a tear for his pain didn't mean he'd given up on himself. Before the guard strutted ten feet, Sonny grabbed a dozen stones and fired them like buckshot from a scattergun. For all the anger in his heart, he wished they were. A jagged piece caught the guard at the base of his skull and drew blood.

Knowing the guard's reaction, Sonny figured his best chance was finding cover in the woods. Running west toward the Schuylkill River, two blocks of blurred stoops was all he needed to know he'd never make it that far. No decent food for a day left him little chance of outstriding the guard.

At the corner, Sonny faked crossing Fairmount and headed north into the heart of the neighborhood. He could hear the guard's boots hitting the sidewalk, mismatched echoes of his own soles. Just past Aspen Street, the guard narrowed the distance, grabbed Sonny's collar, and flipped him onto the sidewalk. His shoulder hit first, followed by his left eyebrow, which split wide.

"Little pisser," said the guard, huffing as he kicked Sonny toward the nearest stoop. "Like tossing rocks, do you? Maybe you won't be so worried what's in my lunch pail when I knock them teeth out of your head, eh?"

The guard closed his hand around Sonny's neck. Living on the streets half his life, Sonny caught his share of beatings, most from boys his own age or teenagers striking fast and quick. Injuries sustained in those altercations were rarely enough to send him to the hospital. But looking into the guard's eyes, Sonny knew he was dealing with a different species.

The guard pulled him close. His breath smelled like rotten herring and black bread. "You know how some of the fellows in the prison make their point? They'll have a man mouth the railing and kick him in the back of his head."

"Please . . ."

"Now with the politeness?" The guard's words were packaged inside another laugh. "Open up that hole and put it on the first step."

Sonny swung both elbows and whipped his legs forward to brace against the stoop. The guard had little trouble slamming Sonny onto his belly and dragging him forward.

Seeing the guard's aiming point, Sonny narrowed his mind. He figured the most important factors for surviving were picking the right spot of stone—like maybe a raised ridge was better than a depression—and the aftermath. Would he have the strength to walk ten blocks to the hospital? How much blood would he lose? What would the kick do to his jaw? And beyond that, when the bleeding stopped and he was back in the orphanage, who would ever adopt such damaged goods?

Sonny opened his mouth and took the rounded edge of the stoop between his lips. The discord between enamel and stone vibrated up his brain stem. Expecting the next sound to be the guard's heel peeling off the sidewalk, Sonny flinched at words mortaring in from across the street.

"That's enough, you son of a bitch," said a man's voice on a closing trajectory. "Hell's wrong with you, Dickie?"

"Piss off," answered the guard, standing tall in his uniform jacket. "I was just putting a scare in the boy. I wasn't going to boot him."

Wanting to dash, Sonny was held down by muscle spasms and nausea. Diagnosing himself with a busted rib, the boy focused on his rescuer— a short, stout man with a great-sized belly wrapped in a black bartender's apron. His hair was thinned into a horseshoe pattern; an iron pipe hung from his right hand.

"Nonsense you were." The man's voice had a forced resonance, as if his vocal cords had been nicked and required twice the air. "I was watching from the tavern window. That'd kill him, sure as anything you could do."

The guard matched the bartender's volume. "Don't come charging at me, Bonnie. This here is none of your business."

"Anything happening in front of my tavern I'll stick my nose in."

"We're not in front of your tavern," said the guard, pointing at the ground. "We're across the street. And you didn't see my head." He touched his wound, hoping to produce damning evidence. "Anyway, he hit me hard enough that I saw stars."

The bartender tossed his chin in Sonny's direction. "For Christ sake, I'm trying to keep my patience, but he's a boy. You got enough licks to even the score. Time to tie it off."

"Aw, he hasn't even started paying for my blood."

The barkeeper rolled the pipe on his shoulder like a batter after one too many brushback pitches. "You're about to find out how much I hate bickering. Get yourself to work. Could change my mind, though I'm think-ing I don't want you in the bar for a week. Go drink at Schmidt's or the Hellcat. For all I care, stay at home with the wife and kids."

When a few seconds passed without a response, the bartender figured his argument had taken hold. Leaning on the pipe, he extended his free hand to Sonny. The guard grunted, "Fuck you," and kicked at the offer-ing. True to his word, the bartender whistled the pipe into the guard's left arm and delivered a second blow to remove any doubt. The snap of bone was muted by the guard's wool uniform.

"I warned you," said the bartender. "The pipe's a finisher."

Tobacco dribbling down his chin, the guard cursed the bartender and damned his bar to ashes. *We're not through, not by a long shot.* When he pledged revenge a fourth time, the bartender chased him away with a couple of quick swings.

Pressing both hands to his injured side, Sonny mustered enough strength to rise. He wanted off the street and out of the neighborhood before the cops showed. Not that the bartender wasn't in the right, or didn't have the grapes to handle the questioning. Sonny needed to maintain a runaway's profile. "I'll be on my way," he said, backpedaling toward Fairmount Avenue. "Thanks for what you did."

The bartender stood with one foot on the curb, the other in the street. "Don't go running off. Follow me and I'll stitch that cut. Wait too long and it'll never heal—look like an oyster sitting above your eye."

Feeling the blood trickling down his face, Sonny knew he had little choice. He couldn't wander in that condition without attracting the wrong kind of attention. He nodded and followed the man across North Twenty-fifth Street into Bonnie's Whiskey Room. Through the front door he found exactly what he'd expected from the narrow little tap house—walls of exposed brick, fifteen stools at the scrolled bar, a nickel-framed mirror behind the bottles, and three fans hanging from a pressed tin ceiling. Wood shavings and peanut shells covered the scuffed red oak floor. A pool table weighed down the back room.

The bartender pointed to a stool while he slid behind the bar. "The name's Bonhardt. Horace Francis Xavier Bonhardt. Friends call me Bonnie. You can do the same." He finished the introduction by tipping a nonexistent cap.

"I'm Sonny."

"You got a last name?"

"Just Sonny. Beginning, middle, and end."

Bonnie put a cigar box on the bartop and rummaged through its contents with fingers fat enough to suggest cloven hooves. "Fair enough," he said, softer now that he was distracted. "Seeing you out there, I figured you're the runaway I've been hearing about. Not too fond of the orphanage?"

"I prefer going my own way."

"No argument from me. I've never been one for bosses," he said, holding a needle before his eyes as if he'd drawn it from a stone. "Little devil took advantage of my eyesight. Okay then, now for the bad news. All I have is black."

"What?"

"Black thread," he said, holding a spool. "All I have for stitching your eyebrow is black thread. Going to make you look like a pirate, but it'll hide the bone."

Sonny didn't care if he used hot tar. The point was to close the cut and stay out of the hospital. Without waiting for further instructions, he slid his elbows across the bar, tilted his chin up, and pulled back his hair.

Bonnie cleared the blood with a splash of water and went to work. His right hand stitched while the left held Sonny's head still. "Not that it's much of my business," he said, "but you ought to reconsider who you're throwing rocks at. Prison guards are thin skinned."

While the needle would have consumed most people, Sonny focused on Bonnie's other hand. He could feel callused skin and smell the pipe's lingering metallic residue. It wasn't that the boy avoided human contact; it just didn't cut across his path that often. And when it did, the exchange usually made him flinch and flee.

"The eyebrow will heal fine. Not much we can do about the ribs." Bonnie stepped back to admire the stitch work. "Young kid like you, they'll heal soon enough. And you don't look like a stranger to bruises."

Sonny pitched forward to catch his reflection in the mirror. Grazing the stitches with his fingertips, he said, "Maybe you could spare some bread if I scrubbed your toilets real good?"

"When's the last time you ate?"

"A rotten apple this morning. That's why that guard caught me. It cramped up my whole insides. Before that, I don't know, maybe a day or two." Sonny felt shame for the bones he'd pulled from a Green Street trash can the night before.

"Forget the toilets," he said, pouring Sonny an unrequested glass of water. "Before I saw you with Dickie, I was getting ready to cook steak and eggs. It's just as easy to dress two plates. You like your meat rare or cooked clean through?"

The kid didn't have an answer. He'd never had steak. "Make mine like yours. I'll eat whatever you come out with."

Bonnie turned for the kitchen, humming an Irish drinking tune. He liked easy-to-please patrons.

Sonny was alone at the bar—on his third run through the bartender's tune—when a slab of sunlight crashed the room. Wary of the prison guard's return, he was relieved seeing a man no older than twenty-five stepping through the tavern door. Well built with a stern look, the stranger wore thick-soled boots, a gray flannel work shirt, and nothing but a dollop of oil in his blond hair.

Unmoved by present company, the stranger settled two stools down and withdrew an ivory-handled penknife. He scraped his nails with deep, even strokes, mindful of keeping the droppings off his pants. All Sonny needed was a sideways look at the squared-off chin to know the two had never crossed paths.

"Ah," said the bartender, emerging from the kitchen with steaming plates. "I see you two have met. Good, good." He set down the food plus several pieces of mismatched cutlery. "Don't steal the fork," he said, breaking into his own routine of cutting and swirling.

The stranger leaned over to appraise Sonny's steak. "Too little fat. The butchers in this neighborhood don't know horsemeat from horseshit. I think there's a little of both on your plates."

Cursed by a quick-setting loyalty, Sonny wanted to lash out in the bartender's defense. His first steak looked better than anything he'd ever eaten.

"You act like horsemeat is such a bad thing," said the bartender, smiling to show he was not similarly offended. Two bites in and golden yolk was already smeared on his chin. "I'd be half the man without hoof in my diet."

The stranger looked at Sonny. "Who's the kid?"

Bonnie was bald enough that facial expressions extended into his scalp. "I thought you two had met?"

"You said that."

Sonny took note of the man's accent. It wasn't full-blown off the boat but prominent enough to turn t's into d's. Probably German, Sonny figured, or maybe one of the Slavs from the city's northeast neighborhoods.

Bonnie set down his utensils and used a bar towel to clean his face. "Okay, this here eating my gourmet is Sonny. No last name, just Sonny. Doesn't like foster homes or prison guards and doesn't seem to back down given long odds. I'm not sure what else there is to know because we haven't gotten that far yet. And those stitches are my work, so don't tease." Shaking a thumb in the stranger's direction, the bartender said, "Sonny, this is Anton Bielakowski. He is a serious man. Someday we'll catch him smiling, but I'm not holding my water."

Bielakowski leaned across the stools with an outstretched hand. He matched the boy's grip and added a little extra to let him know there was more. Turning back to Bonhardt, who was spinning his plate for better access, he said, "Where can we talk?"

"Right here. The solution to our problem is two stools to your left. When I saw him this morning, I knew why I went to Mass and said all those prayers."

Bielakowski turned his palms up. "What are we talking about?"

"A runner."

"Shit, really?"

"No fooling."

"Underwriting a kid that age is risky. We've got enough handling the payouts and calling the right cutout numbers."

"It's my choice. And I want him. Nobody else will do it anyhow, so what's the damage for trying?" Bonnie looked at Sonny. "Kid, you got any idea what we're discussing?"

"Yeah, you're talking about me running your numbers."

"See?" The bartender wagged a finger in Bielakowski's direction before turning it on the boy. "All right, Sonny, here's the breakdown. I want to use Anton's policy bank because he offers the best payout in the city. Sounds easy, right? Well, the sand-in-the-ass part is I'm too far out. Their runners are whining about the distance."

"How far is the run?"

"Port Richmond."

Sonny had never been to Port Richmond. Or Fishtown. Or even Kensington. But he knew numbers was a serious job and all the moving parts made money. "I'll do it."

Bielakowski took a deep breath as if getting ready to speak, held it for a moment, exhaled, and inhaled another. "Hell, either it works or it doesn't. My old man already has his reservations, so if this fails, it's a short fall."

"I'm not failing."

"Okay, kid. We'll see. While you're working, your piece is ten percent. It's good pay with no second chances. Late, slow, missing, dead, whatever. Those numbers come in when they're due. You start here and maybe we'll build up the route to Port Richmond."

Bonnie spoke up. "Make sure you're sure, kid. This ain't baseball with the boys. What are you, fourteen?"

Hoping to strike a nonchalant pose, Sonny picked up his fork. "I can handle myself. The numbers will be delivered no different than with fellows twice my age."

"Could work better with him," said Bielakowski, almost to himself. "Old and slow gets jacked all the time, and the lazy ones make it easy by taking the same streets. Maybe no one will figure him for a couple weeks. By then he'll have the gig figured okay."

"Hear that, Sonny-boy?" said Bonnie, balancing a fork full of smashed egg and steak. "Be smart and you'll make money. Be a dummy and that prison guard will check you into bed every night."

Bielakowski pushed away from the bar, brushed his shirt clean, and made sure his pants hadn't caught on his boot tops. "It's settled, then. We'll take your numbers with Sonny as the runner. Dad likes using the last three digits of the total mutual handle. Everyone can grab those easy enough from the paper."

The bartender raised a hand good-bye. "My regards to your father," he said. "And when Sonny drops off the numbers, give him some of that famous kielbasa. You need to keep your partners in good health."

"Forget the kielbasa. Nothing is better than our blood sausage. Everyone gets stronger eating kiszka. A pound a day and Sonny will be an ox." The Pole sealed the deal with handshakes before exiting into the sunshine.

Sonny relaxed into his stool. Life had tossed him heaters before, but nothing like what had just occurred. A steady job meant money, which meant food. Not grub he'd been given, or begged for, or pulled from a trash can. He'd have honest-to-goodness food he bought with his own dough.

As the bartender ran a finger across his plate and licked it clean, he winked at the boy lost in his thoughts. "Don't worry, kid. All that talk about getting jacked is Anton's way of making sure you understand the stakes. Nobody touches a Bielakowski runner. I didn't say it in front of him, but his old man's reputation is why I'm using their policy bank. Biela-kowski Senior is a scary old Polack that protects what's his. You'll be covered against anybody who knows better. Just watch out for the lowest scum and you'll be okay."

Sonny nodded though he wasn't all that concerned with his safety. What the bartender interpreted as fear was Sonny distracted by his first grocery list. He'd start with cake and work in milk and meat when he got tired of the bakery case.

"One more thing," said Bonnie, "before we go partners, there's a loose end that needs trimming."

Sonny figured the bartender might shake him down a few points. Everyone grabbed more when they had leverage and sometimes when they didn't. While he hated getting hustled, he wasn't taking any principled stands, not this time. Anything the bartender let him keep was better than the fold hands of the last few years.

Bonnie cleared his throat to no effect. "If you're my runner, I can't have you sleeping on the streets. Too unpredictable. Cops could scoop you up and I'd have no idea. Or you'll catch pneumonia and I'm stuck with the day's take."

"Well, you can forget me going back to the orphanage or a foster home. They'd never buy this routine."

"Easy, easy." Bonnie used his hands to tap down the fuss. "As far as I'm concerned, if you're tall enough to put your money on the bar, you're old enough to make your own decisions. I'm talking about a different deal, one where we each get a little of what we need."

"I'll hear you out."

"If you sweep my bar every night, you can sleep on the pool table.

That's it. I live upstairs and will lock the front door so you can't steal my booze. In the morning, before work, we'll eat breakfast together."

Negative reinforcement had taught Sonny to be wary of cherry deals. His world was a zero-sum existence where gains came at someone else's expense. With every new foster family, the other kids were generous the first day or two, giving him tours of the playroom and letting him test-drive each toy. Then, after they realized his stay was long-term, Sonny became a competitive threat for the home's resources. Goodwill was replaced by suspicion followed by hostility and violence. "What's your family going to think? Could look like I'm taking what belongs to them."

Bonnie grabbed both plates and headed for the kitchen. He paused halfway. "At one time," he said, looking over his shoulder, "I had a wife and baby girl. I lost one during childbirth and the other right after. I'm alone, so nobody on my end is getting jealous about an orphan boy."

"Pitts."

"What?"

"Pitts. That's my last name. Sonny Pitts. It's sad sounding, so I don't say it much."

"Jesus, it makes Bonhardt sound like Belgian royalty."

Sonny agreed about everything. The name, the job, the sweeping, and the pool table. He was on his way.

II.

MARCEK'S PROTOCOL WITH a new woman was letting a few days pass before calling. Some pals, wary of being labeled starry-eyed, swore by thirty-six hours. He stretched the shallow-water thinking to forty-eight. Angie's protocol wasn't any more impressive, waiting a week to call back. All that changed after the dance club, Greek diner, and confession on Christian Street. That first night, Marcek dialed Angie's digits five minutes after driving away, her chocolate chip pancake–taste still fresh on his lips.

"I loved tonight," he said.

"Me, too."

"I want to see you again."

"When?"

He fought sounding tentative. "Today."

"Good. Me, too."

Every night ended with plans for the following day. No *maybe* or *if you have time* or *I'm hanging with friends*. All *yes yes yes, more more more*. Their time together was simple and tender, eating in cheap Chinese restaurants or walking through the city's old neighborhoods and squares, sharing hopes and fears and all the minutiae soon-to-be lovers prattle about to keep the conversation going.

One night, in line for a movie, Angie and Marcek started comparing their respective favorites—television shows (*Friends* v. *Cops*), ice creams (chocolate v. black raspberry), music (Mariah Carey v. anything else), cars (BMW!), booze (Jell-O shots v. Yuengling), Philly sports teams (Flyers v. Eagles), etc. Twenty minutes after the show started, still standing in the lobby, they decided to skip the flick and grab coffee. That evening, at his apartment, they had sex for the first, second, third, and fourth time. Like many inaugural experiences, it was a little awkward and too short, but they got better with practice.

It wasn't a month later Angie identified their mark. He must have bought on her day off, because she knew nothing until her boss pressed the jewelry invoice into her belly. "Call this client for pickup," he said, "and make sure the appointment is in the next twenty-four hours. Two days out is a no-go. Unacceptable under any circumstances." That was the boss's way of saying he'd already spent the money, probably at an Atlantic City casino.

Before calling, Angie stole a moment near the cash register and phone memorizing the purchase details. She'd have no shot at a second look because her boss stored all off-the-books paperwork in his briefcase— away from staff and the IRS. The ticket totaled eighteen grand, a number that wasn't fluttering anyone's eyelids, except Marcek said ten was the floor, and fifteen was better than fine. Higher priority was that the buyer worked in Center City and was paying in cash. Done and done.

Despite thinking she was being low-key with the invoice, something about Angie's activity drew the boss's attention. He grinned with a closed mouth and started around the counter in her direction. She rolled her eyes and skipped straight to dialing.

Quick for his age and size, he needed two unanswered rings to close the distance, grab her hand, and push the phone into the cradle. "Hey, Ang, no calling up here. Go back and use the private showroom."

She knew why, asking anyway to hear his weak game. Since her first day on the job, she'd witnessed how he hustled the counter girls toward the private showroom, like being alone was their sole requirement for coupling with a fifty-five-year-old who'd eaten himself into diabetes.

Still holding her hand down, he leaned in and pressed harder. " 'Cause you're too shy out here," he answered. "Clients like flirting, makes them want to buy more. That's good for everybody because when I win, you do, too." The point was *It'd be worth your while to give me what I want.*

Angie snatched her hand away and spun on her heels, tracking the counter toward the rear wall. When earrings transitioned to watches, she looked back with her finest fuck-off look, letting it go before he incorporated the rejection into a twisted mating ritual.

Through a security door and down a half-lit hallway, Angie hotstepped into the private showroom—a glorified closet decorated with shag carpeting, fleur-de-lis wallpaper, and a desk draped in black velvet. With two guest chairs, the space was so cramped she couldn't take a step in any direction without bending around a piece of furniture.

Behind the desk, thighs against its edge, Angie dialed just as her boss entered doing an awkward lower back twist-and-stretch with his elbows chin high. She was glad for an answer after a single ring. Percolating urgency in every extremity, she wasted no time explaining the purpose of her call. The mark—a Center City lawyer named Billy O'Bannon who bought a Rolex for himself and a bracelet for a woman not his wife—said tomorrow after lunch worked because he could flip an expected retainer. She nodded at her boss to let him know the money was on its way, and maybe buy an extra peaceful second as he processed the news. Didn't take, though. Like a horse left too long in the gate, he was anxious for action, stepping close and wedging himself between the wall and her back.

He waited until she hung up the phone to coordinate a hand in her ass-crack with a whispered "Girl, you're crazy hot. Let's do this." She fought smashing the phone into his bridgework, knowing violence of that order would close the shop and land her a preliminary hearing.

Roth's clumsiness gave her an out. When he closed his fingers to pinch her bottom, she jerked her pelvis forward and snapped her head back. The nose blow was enough to pause the momentum and give her room to slide toward the doorway. "Damn, Derek, get off me."

His look was more shock than pain, like the family dog had nipped him. "Ah, hell, Angie," he said, working both sides of his nose. "Christ sake, you hurt me."

"Where do you get off pushing up between my legs?"

He pinched snot from his nostrils, checking it for blood. "You do that on purpose? You try hurting me?"

"What do you think?"

"I think you're a little bitch."

"What would you do if someone pinched your balls?"

"You offering?"

"Piss off."

"Oh, come on, Ang. Wasn't like I meant anything. We were just joking around, having some fun. You know, like kissing cousins."

"Joking?"

"Yeah, baby. Joking is all that was."

Hand on the doorframe, ready to run, she said, "You joke like that with your cousin's asshole?"

He ran his fingers across the velvet, smoothing its wrinkles and resetting the edges. "So that's the way it's going to be." The head butt was one thing. Slapping down his olive branch was sedition. Shop etiquette dictated forgiveness.

"I don't like you touching me."

His eyes narrowed enough to stop any blinking. "You think you're some kind of hot thing, so let me tell you how your story ends. Ten years from now, I still own this shop and two dozen counter girls will have passed through. Some will think they're better than me, like the way you do. Some—the smart ones—will see it for what it is and give a little extra of themselves. But you? The one with all the answers? You'll have a fat pasta ass and three or four rats sucking your titties flat. Your life will be so awful that you'll look back at Roth's Fine Diamonds as the good old days. I've seen pieces like you before, and this is the best it gets. Look around and make a memory."

While not fond of the forecast, Angie was more concerned with mutating Derek's work fantasy. Fearing the combustible nature of that variety of shame, she turned toward the back of the shop, clocked out, and retraced her steps before the boss could block her exit.

Passing the private showroom, she kept her eyes straight and pace controlled. The wrong vibe would only antagonize his battered ego. Two steps past the doorway, half-expecting a chase scene, Angie heard him yell, "Be back in an hour or keep walking." Maybe he thought she was taking an early lunch. Or maybe he just didn't give a damn.

Out on Walnut Street and wary of using her cell phone, Angie turned west for a pay phone three blocks away. Finding a couple of dimes in the bottom of her purse, she dialed the number and held her breath through four rings. "Hi."

"This you?"

"I found what we talked about."

"Slow down . . . where are you?"

"At a pay phone near work. He can't see me."

"You alone?"

She overread the word choice, hearing doubt where none existed. "What's that supposed to mean?"

He ignored the defensiveness, asking what she had.

Angie hesitated, knowing her answer was a graduation. "Marcek . . ."

"Yeah, I'm here, Angie. I'm right here. Take your time."

"There's fifteen thousand coming in tomorrow. The appointment is just after lunch." She wasn't sure why she low-balled the number.

"You okay?" Hearing the answer he needed, Marcek asked about the mark.

Angie hit the details straight and quick, explaining that the buyer was an Irish lawyer named O'Bannon. He usually bought a significant piece whenever he found a new girlfriend, which was two or three times a year. O'Bannon was partial to diamond earrings and bracelets but never rings because of the connotation. Angie said he usually combined the purchase with a little something for himself, like cuff links. This go-around was a watch.

Marcek had heard of the lawyer. O'Bannon was the kind of criminal defense attorney that pulled microphones from reporters' hands so they couldn't walk away. While he possessed decent trial skills, his niche wasn't cross-examinations or closing arguments. O'Bannon's brilliance was once a year securing lead chair in a high-profile trial where the defendant was too poor to pay. The best cases involved race and the Philadelphia Police Department so he could swap his retainer for airtime on the nightly news.

Marcek asked, "You usually around when he pays?"

"I'm in the shop, but the routine has him giving the money to my boss. O'Bannon comes in, flirts with me or one of the other girls, runs a finger down the display cases, and then heads for the back room. That's where his purchase is showcased on the velvet and money exchanged."

"Have you ever seen the cash?"

Angie thought maybe Marcek was doubting the job or her appraisal. "Of course I've seen it. He pays with cash. Every time."

"Just casting a wide net, okay? Now, I need to know more about the money. Small or big bills?"

"Lots of tens and twenties. My boss is always bitching that O'Bannon is worse than the strippers."

"How's the dough come in?"

Angie said she didn't understand, so Marcek explained he needed to know if O'Bannon used an envelope, a rubber band, or his pockets.

"One time," she said, "he came in singing about a big trial. I remember him waving a stack of money and saying we should celebrate."

"No envelope?"

"No. The money was folded, almost too thick to bend in half."

"Did he pull the dough from his pants or his suit coat?"

Angie tried remembering back to the lawyer's jaunty entrances, when a caricature artist would have painted him as a cat burping up bird feathers. "Honestly, I'm not positive," she said. The rising register betrayed her anxiousness. "Maybe it was his suit. Yeah, I think that could be right."

"Not for sure, though?"

She wished they were face-to-face so a headshake could stand for her answer. "I mean, I can't swear to it."

"One more thing," said Marcek, not seeing much point pressing her. His line of work assumed human inaccuracies. "How does he get to the shop? Does he walk from his office? Maybe you've seen him get out of a cab? Or maybe you've called a cab when business is done?"

Angie knew O'Bannon's car all too well and turned hopeful Marcek was thinking about carjacking him. She wanted maximum infliction of pain. "No taxi. He drives a blue Mercedes, which he parks in the tow-away zone. Before he heads to the private showroom, the asshole tosses me the keys and tells me to watch for meter maids, like I'm his little guardian angel."

"Fair enough. You've given me a good sketch. Usual finder's fee is fifteen percent."

She said okay, not knowing what was expected or quite understanding the formality.

"But you've done more than finding. And taking this O'Bannon dude isn't like I'm knocking off Tiffany's. So I'm figuring we split the take."

"Really?"

"Down the middle. Let's meet up after I roll him. We'll do the split, and I want to see you before I head out of town."

She sat on the conversation's longest pause. "Where you going?"

"Boca." He wanted her to come, but it had to be her choice. "I'm needed in Florida for a couple months," he said, not sure how long he was supposed to stay. His dad had been vague on the details. "There's work for me down there."

"That's a place I've always wanted to go."

"You've never been to Florida?"

"No."

Marcek couldn't help himself. "Interested?"

12.

SONNY WONDERED IF THE ALARM clock was synched with the hotel's wake-up service and why he bothered with either. His mind refused any sleep beyond five hours, often insisting on less. Not that he didn't need or wouldn't appreciate more—it was just that some part of him, a dark spot formed long ago, was always on guard.

Regardless, after a year of planning and two trips to Japan, Sonny was ready for the payoff. Every fall, he met Anton Bielakowski at Molly Ollie's Tavern on Cherry Street. The purpose was for Sonny to sell—and Bielakowski to buy—an idea. Two if Bielakowski was so inclined, or all three, as was happening with greater frequency. After the transaction, when the proposals were culled and price negotiated, they reminisced over a meal and bottle of wine.

Sonny dialed the hotel's front desk to cancel his wake-up call and order steak and eggs. By most standards, it was early for sixteen ounces, but Sonny stayed at the Ritz because the hotel committed to cooking his request at any hour. Ten years earlier, the Four Seasons was his choice until its kitchen balked. Sonny took the rejection personally, thinking it wasn't so much the meal but the class of people ordering it. His response merited a visit from the police and cost him donation checks to the

Philadelphia Police Athletic League and the night manager's personal account.

With time to kill before the food arrived, Sonny prepped the shower and spent a few moments staring at his reflection. While public confidence was not an issue, bathroom mirrors challenged his esteem. Only recently had he found some measure of psychological relief from his scarred skin. Instead of ugly markers, Sonny began seeing them as proof the living world—after three chances—still wanted him around. That had to count for something.

His first wife used to say the scars were rivers on a map. She traced the re-formed tissue with her finger, reassuring Sonny she accepted them as a part of the greater package. His third wife, a religious French Canadian, had an equally warm take. She said the scars were God's work, like he'd taken a personal interest in designing Sonny only to get distracted during finishing touches. It was the second wife, the one Sonny recalled in moments of deepest doubt, who stoked his inadequacies. One night in bed, as Sonny started explaining how he earned his back scar in Korea, she rolled away, saying she assumed he'd been burned as a baby and was happy to leave it at that. Sonny kicked off the sheets, packed a bag, and spent the night in his divorce attorney's parking lot.

At Bonnie's Whiskey Room, if a married guy carried on about wife troubles, Bonnie would say *The opposite of love isn't hate—the opposite of love is disdain, and if that's what she holds in her heart, the party is over.* When Sonny's wife said she didn't care about his scars, he knew in two seconds what Bonnie had preached for twenty years. The party was over, indeed.

Shower steam shrinking the bathroom mirror, Sonny stood high on his toes to examine the rib scar beneath his right elbow. Even though it was a gruesome meld, the memory surrounding its acquisition made him grin. On his fifteenth birthday, anxious to test his grit, Sonny went out of his way to cry foul during a back-alley dice game. His target *was* cheating. He was also half-mad from World War I mustard gas and turpentine consumption.

Sonny compounded the blunder by assuming his adversary would refute the charge. The cheater, uninterested in words, smashed his booze bottle and jammed the exposed edge into Sonny's ribs. When he tried withdrawing for a second stab, with every intention of killing Sonny, the bottle held fast, in turn making Sonny panic and run for the tavern. Bonnie took one look at the protrusion and figured the kid was screwing with him. The growing puddle of blood on the floor told a different story.

Sonny didn't joke about the second scar. He felt like, with as close as he came to dying, making light was thumbing his nose at the Lord's generosity. He wasn't born again or any of that, but he also didn't dismiss the Good Book as wasted ink on a page. The scar, two inches below his left nipple, convinced him, once and for all, that he wasn't cut out for the rough stuff. He'd be the idea guy, the one who handled the big-picture planning, above the fray and living decades longer than if he toted a gun or blackjack.

Anton Bielakowski was with Sonny for that moment of clarity and probably saved his life, though neither recalled it in those terms. Bielakowski's old man sent them to collect from a grocery near Temple's campus. The grocery's owner—a mouselike man with short arms—didn't owe on a lost bet or illegal loan. He was in the books for three dozen ropes of kielbasa. Anton was a semiregular on the collections circuit, so the assumption was that between him and Sonny, they could handle a man who spent his days pricing cans.

The only part of the operation that went right was the ride over. The rest was a box of bullets in a hot car. Anton's responsibility was clearing the store. Sonny took point. Chin up and eyes wide, he started by shoving the smaller man into a display of oranges. After explaining the purpose of their visit with a few prepackaged, tough-sounding lines, Sonny added a bit of flair by rapid-firing three oranges into the wall and shouting, "Now give me the money you little shit." The ripe fruit splattered and filled the room with an almost visible aroma of citrus.

Years of orphanage living should have taught him about inflated expectations. He should have been wary of the grocer, like maybe he wasn't reaching behind his back for a billfold. But Sonny, by nature, was an optimist who underestimated the darkness of men's hearts. When the grocer withdrew an ice pick and stabbed him in the chest, he was genuinely surprised.

To the grocer's credit, he didn't go for any extra thrusts. One was enough. He let go, stepped back, and stared at the wooden handle. An error had been made and each man began plotting a strategy for surviving the consequences.

Bielakowski said they should leave it alone—like a finger in the dike. Sonny understood the logic but couldn't stop himself. Wrapping one hand atop the other, he pulled the ice pick out and waited. The first sensation was a droplet of blood down his chest. The second was a hiss pitched somewhere between baby-bird tweets and a kid whistling through a missing tooth.

"Heaven's mercy," said the grocer. "It got you in the lung. That's air blowing out of the hole. I did it this time. I killed Bielakowski's kid."

Sonny would always remember that twenty seconds. Not because the grocer had mistaken him for Bielakowski—that'd happened before. And not because the grocer said he was going to die—what the hell did a dummy that'd stiffed a mobster over sausage links know about dying? No, Sonny would never forget because it was the first time he'd ever been speechless. Holding a hand to his chest, Sonny tried screaming for Anton to get the car and take him to the hospital. All he could manage was the chest whistling and two fingers pointed outside. Problem was, Anton Bielakowski was done paying him any attention.

Facing the grocer with his back to Sonny, Anton said, "Money, asshole. Get the money."

The grocer looked back and forth between the two collectors, struggling where to focus.

Anton Bielakowski solved the dilemma by striking him with an open hand. "You hear me now?" The grocer backpedaled into the counter as Bielakowski stepped forward for a second slap. "We came to collect. Nobody's leaving until that happens. So go into whatever hole your nuts are buried and get the money."

"But your friend, he's dying." The grocer peered around to see Sonny leaning against a display of onions. "Please, please take him to the hospital. I swear I'll get you the money. Just don't let him die. Not in my store."

Bielakowski pivoted his stance, a foot aimed in each man's direction. "Him dying is on you. Your ice pick, your decision to stick him. Collecting the dough is on me, and my old man won't see it different. I don't want Sonny dying, but I gotta get the money."

"Wait. You . . . you're the Bielakowski?"

"I'm Anton."

"Who's that?" said the grocer.

"Him?"

"Yeah, I thought he was the Bielakowski boy."

"No, that's Sonny."

"Sonny? Oh, thank God."

Sonny missed the exchange, his descent gaining too much momentum. His left lung sagged inside his ribs while both arms hung like untied shoelaces. The whistling had slowed only because his breath had weakened. His life depended on getting to a doctor, but Anton was slapping around a guy for what amounted to a night's drinking tab.

The grocer sat on the counter, swiveled his legs, slid off the back side with a thud, and stayed low. Anton followed, wanting to make sure the grocer wasn't going for a hidden sawed-off or snub-nose. What he saw was the grocer using a putty knife to pry up a floorboard. After getting it loose and tossed aside, he reached between the joists and pulled free a flour sack.

"There's what you owe for the kielbasa," said Anton, "and what you need to make good with Sonny. After paying me, you stuff whatever's left in his belt."

It was when the grocer opened his mouth and Bielakowski shushed him with a finger that he saw the coolness in his eyes, a void that said the fight was over but not the damage if that's how he wanted to play it out. The little man nodded his compliance, paid Bielakowski, and knelt by Sonny's side. Shoving a handful of bills into the dying teenager's jacket, he crossed himself and said a prayer.

Sonny had two more memories before passing out. The first was Anton

Bielakowski lifting him up and carrying him through the grocery's front door. The second was Bielakowski sliding a hand inside his jacket. "I think you may die," he whispered. "Let me hold your money so the hospital scum doesn't steal it. They're all thieves, you know."

A ringing cell phone brought Sonny out of his street adventures and back to the Ritz hotel room. Scrambling to find the phone, he recognized his son's number. "What's up, buddy?"

"Dad?"

"Yeah."

"I need help."

Sonny paused. "I thought you were in recovery."

"Stop, just shut up for a second. Didn't you hear me? I need help."

The script was a familiar one. Either Sonny agreed to wire money or Michael revved red and hung up. His son didn't allow for any peaceful, guilt-free middle ground. Problem was, Sonny was short himself until the Bielakowski meeting. "Bad timing. I haven't gotten paid yet this year."

"It's bad, Dad. Different than before, I swear on my life. What word don't you understand? I need fucking help."

So many things Sonny wanted to say but didn't because they'd all been said a dozen times. "Doesn't matter. I won't have a cure until I get back to Florida. Let me call you in a couple days. We'll get this straightened out."

The response was unequivocal. The dead silence of a disconnected line.

13.

WHEN NICK MARTIN WAS CONTEMPLATING zero gravity, a veteran federal agent summed up the mission as *a damn simple job*. Dangerous, sure—
the mortality rate for undercover work rivaled helicopter tail-gunners in
Vietnam, and those boys averaged fourteen minutes. "But, hand on the
Bible," he said, "this business is a small space with just a few rules. Be a
people person. And make them money. That's all because it's enough."

So that's what Nick Martin did.

His primary success was a multimillion-dollar sports book he built from
scratch. Launching with no clients or connections, he made customer
service his calling card. Day or night, whatever the game, Martin was
available. *Yo, I know it's three in the morning, but can I get a dime on the
Packers?* Setting the line wasn't the hassle. Vegas pros handled the spreads.
And rotten streaks straightened themselves out given enough time and
patience. No, people were the rub. Some weren't so bad; Martin actually
liked a couple. But the big middle—the hump in the curve—were degen-
erate lowlifes who'd hock their kids' toys for one more rush. He hated
ninety percent of his clients. Anyone would. Ninety percent of the ninety
percent hated themselves. *Come on, Nick—you know I'm good for it.* A
year of hard knocks to learn most weren't.

His second moneymaker was a weekly poker game that ran a full night and into the next day. Players chatted Martin up before and after, sharing stories of the can't-miss hands that did. He understood gamblers never remembered easy wins, only the lucky bastards raking in big pots on the draw. Regardless, he treated them all like they'd flown in on a private jet, hugging and shaking and kissing and feeding them to the point of dizziness. As the last one stumbled out into the midday sun, he paid the staff and grabbed a coffee before delivering an envelope to Rea's main guy.

Week in, week out, month after month, that was the routine. A rat running full speed on the wheel, plus meals with the crew and extra hustles to keep his reputation as an overachiever. *Be a people person. Make them money. Real simple.* Problem was—after ten years of treading water with gamblers, gangsters, and grifters—Nick Martin was surrounded but alone. And like a prisoner nearing the end of his sentence, he allowed himself to begin missing what he'd gone so long without.

Which explained Fancy Tina's. First two nights he had a halfway decent excuse, driving by on his way home from a road-widening project in Levittown where the contractor was getting lazy with his Komatsu PC300. A sparse line of pine trees separated the heavy equipment from a residential neighborhood. With a couple of assistants in gas company uniforms, maybe the loader could be driven through the backyards to a waiting trailer. A Komatsu in decent condition could fetch forty, fifty grand.

When he returned for a second look, the equipment was gone. Jobs were like that. More than sometimes, actually—good opportunities were short-lived. Maybe the contractor realized he was pushing his luck. Maybe another player was quicker to the payday. Maybe another Levittown street needed widening. Who knows? For every dozen proposals, Martin moved on one or two. And even with those best of breed, he batted less than fifty percent because of bailing or stepping back. In his position, he couldn't afford to be wrong. There wasn't time to get pinched while Rea's world moved on. His hustles had to work.

So night three—with the Komatsu gone and Levittown off his route—he had no more excuses of convenience for swinging by Fancy Tina's. Being there meant he was looking for the woman, the stripper with the hip tattoo. The one named Cheryl. The one he liked. The one who'd poisoned him.

He stayed in his car, positioned to see the front door and rear employee entrance. Going inside didn't seem the best idea, given his recent history. No telling how ownership might react. *Hey, boss, you remember the guy we drugged? No, not that one—the one we handled for the Pole? Yeah, he's back, sitting near Stage Four, sipping a club soda. Trouble? Yeah, I'd guess that's what he's looking for.* So Martin sat low and watched. First night he waited an hour before driving away. He saw a dozen girls, none looking like his Cheryl. Same on night two. Smoking with the windows up, he figured night three would be the same. Give it an hour and drive home. Solitary. Alone.

One hour turned into four, and that's when his persistence paid off. Hair pulled up and dressed in a teal sweat suit, she exited the rear entrance thirty minutes past closing. Her eyes were down, and her left side sagged beneath an overloaded shoulder bag.

He straightened himself and checked his teeth in the rearview mirror. A full ashtray and nothing to drink was tough on the scent front. Before he could look for gum or a mint, she was at his window, blocking his door.

She tapped a ring on the glass. When he rolled the driver's-side window down, she said, "You him?"

The stripper was how Martin remembered. Still blond, still with lips and eyebrows made wide with makeup. Her hair was light, almost fragile, like a little kid's. Last few weeks, Martin wondered if maybe the drugs clouded his mind's picture. Waiting three nights, he even considered the possibility she wasn't real. Just a dream, a couple of dancers swirled into one vision by the trauma. "I ever tell you my name?"

"I don't think this is a good idea."

"Nick Martin. That night, not sure we got to last names."

A pause to fish smokes from her bag. "I doubt you're here to hurt me. Or you're just real dumb going about it."

Martin flashed his lighter out the open window. As she bent to the flame, he shook his head. "Everyone was doing a job. I thought we were getting along pretty well before I fell asleep."

She must have seen something in his eyes, an assurance. "Then I'm still Cheryl."

"No last name?"

Ignoring the question, she told him how a bouncer spotted his car. *We've got a creeper, ladies.* Nobody figured him for the guy from a few weeks back, the one who got the special treatment. She did, though. No reason except she was paid to make men chase her, make them want. Most stopped after an empty money clip and clothes smeared in body-glitter. For whatever reason, during the few hours they spent together, she'd figured this one for a different variety.

"How much they pay you?"

"Doesn't matter."

Martin lit his own cigarette. "The plan—after the retrieval at your apartment—was to kill me. Hope you got the going rate for felony murder."

She wrapped an arm around her belly and used it as a ledge for her smoking arm. "You talk like a cop."

He dismissed the truth with a clogged, quarter laugh and wave of the hand. Yeah, she was a smart one. "Just words, baby."

"Anyway, I don't think they were planning on killing you."

"I could agree, but we'd both be wrong."

Cheryl tapped her ash and smirked. "Looks like everything turned out. I mean, you know, I see all ten fingers, so it couldn't have been too bad."

Martin didn't ask who hired her, or how it worked. He knew. Biela-kowski told Fancy Tina's owner to be on the lookout for a South Philly shakedown. Whoever was the unlucky soul assigned to collect was getting a pill. Night-night, greaseball. Arriving for her shift, Cheryl wasn't briefed on the politics or motivations behind the assignment. Fact was he picked her. If Martin was into gingers or dark hair, they'd have drugged him, too. Women on the clock, separating men from money—what difference did it make who did the paying or who earned it? Good for her. "Bygones. No hard feelings."

"Okay, so everybody forgives everybody."

"I've got something I want to ask you."

Cheryl shifted her weight. "I'm not like that. Dance in the club, sure. But I'm not for hire. Not like you think."

"You don't know what I'm thinking."

"Sure, doll."

He told himself it was okay, that he was close to the end, that he deserved a moment that wasn't a lie or a twist. Something real and all his own with a woman he wouldn't be ruining. "I'd like to cook you a meal. Sit-down with plates and the whole deal."

"I don't need to be rescued, okay? Like I'm some kind of runaway or victim."

He resisted getting out of the car, knowing it'd tilt the dynamic toward what she feared. "This ain't about me throwing you a line. I'm the one asking for a favor."

Unsure what to say, she peeked in his backseat and did a light scan of the parking lot, more to stall than anything. "Lonely, huh? Good-looking as you are, didn't figure finding dates as your problem."

He wanted to explain, wondering if opening up to Bielakowski had broken the seal, left him vulnerable to leaking on himself. "Without going into the details, I don't have the kind of timeline to invest in a long-term romance."

"You sick or something?"

"I'm just looking for a girl to have a nice meal with. I don't know her friends or have to meet her family, she don't get to know mine. That simple."

"Except we ain't strangers."

"Nobody's strangers after the first word. This is the best I can do."

She stepped back with the kind of side-to-side sway that reminded him why he was attracted in the first place. The girl had it going on. "All right, you gave me enough to consider this as a possibility. How do I get ahold of you?"

"I'll be back in a week. Right here, after you get off work."

"Late dinner?"

"Yeah."

"Figure you cook pretty good Italian?"

"I'll cook you anything except Italian."

She backpedaled all the way to her car, fifteen spaces from him. "See you then, doll."

14.

ANXIOUS FOR THE MEETING at Mollie Ollie's Tavern, Sonny arrived early and took a stool at the bar. The bartender—in a pressed shirt and buttoned vest—looked up from cutting lemons and greeted his first customer with a *heyhowareya*.

"If the coffee is fresh, I'll take a cup."

"That pot has been burning all morning. I'll brew a new one."

Sonny skimmed a newspaper as he waited for the bartender to return with a steaming mug and sidecar of cream. Preferring company to silence, Sonny asked his name and if he had any interesting stories. From his years in Bonnie's Whiskey Room, Sonny appreciated a good yarn and wasn't bad sharing a few himself. His personal favorite was sailing three hundred pounds of Jamaican ganja into the Florida Keys only to get spooked and dump it at the dock. A close second was the Bahamian prostitutes seeking sanctuary on his sailboat because a born-again governor ran them off the island. They had a high time partying together in international waters before the locals forced the governor to motor out and negotiate peace.

For the next twenty minutes, he and the bartender took turns riffing, their voices rising with each exchange, until Sonny spotted Bielakowski through the tavern window limping across Cherry Street. His friend looked ten pounds lighter and fifteen years older.

The bartender saw the shift in his guest's face and asked if everything was okay.

"No," Sonny answered, "I'm a long damn day from being okay."

Sonny blamed the hip surgery and cursed the doctors who pushed and pushed and pushed until they split Bielakowski's thigh, sawed off his femur, and installed the polished metal. He'd seen it with a few of his Florida buddies, men who emerged from surgical anesthesia as lesser versions of themselves, blurred images of an overdubbed video.

From behind, a whisper interrupted Sonny's internal rant. "I know," said the voice. "I know."

The old bastard had him cold. Sonny tried clearing his face in the time it took to push back and shoot his cuffs. Off the stool, he turned and faced his friend. "Well, Peter Pan you ain't."

The speed of Bielakowski's feigned punches caught Sonny like a hiccup. The first was a right cross an inch from his button, followed by a left to his liver and an uppercut.

"Fuck that leprechaun," said Bielakowski.

Sonny was liberated by the two-second sequence, a déjà vu moment that had him recalling his friend's close-quarter skill set. In their youth, Sonny begged him to take a sanctioned fight. The sausage maker's response was always the same. Between the family, the business, and the family business, he didn't have time for slap fights in shorts.

In the unique silence of an empty bar, the men hugged and exchanged a few pats on the back, newer physical expressions of their evolving relationship. Fifty years of rarely touching changed in the spring of '93 after Bielakowski's daughter died from ovarian cancer. Sonny arrived at the viewing, and before his overcoat was off, the grieving father pulled him in for an embrace reserved for wars and funerals.

Sonny dropped a twenty on the bar for the coffee and five hundred for privacy. Down a hallway and past the toilet was a back room with a few tables pushed against a high-back wooden bench. Mollie Ollie's specialty was hand-dipped beef, so each table came stocked with napkins, spicy brown mustard, and homemade horseradish. A corner fan oscillated air over paneled walls decorated with Bednarik and Frazier photos.

Without comment, Sonny took the bench and gave his friend the more forgiving chair.

Bielakowski sat down and transferred all the condiments to an adjacent table. He wore the same brown pants as the previous day along with a clean pale-yellow button-down shirt. The front pocket contained two pens, a notebook, and a fresh roll of antacids.

Sonny started. "You still lighting candles at St. Adalbert's?"

"Two this morning."

"One for each of us, just like old times."

"No, both for you. My wife has me covered."

Sonny smiled at the irony of Anton Bielakowski praying for his soul. Either one of them making it to heaven proved the system was rigged. "How did last year work out?"

Bielakowski shrugged. "Good enough that I've come back to the well."

Truth was, 1996's ideas were some of the best yet. With the overheated stock market and emergence of online trading, Sonny saw an opportunity for modernizing the pump-and-dump stock scam. Dozens of boiler rooms were already hip to pushing prices with phone campaigns, but Sonny— after studying the technicalities and flow of information—believed two nerds with AOL accounts could do ten times more hype on electronic message boards than any team of smooth-talking Long Islanders. He also saw that with computers instead of phones, cleanup was easier, the circle of accomplices fewer, and multiple campaigns could be created and disassembled independent of one another.

"I hope you made money on the stocks while the sun was high," said Sonny, rubbing a smudge off the table. "And that you're ready to move on to other opportunities."

Sonny and Bielakowski worked well together because both men honored risk's relationship to time. All the best rackets soured sooner than most participants were willing to admit. Victims squawked to the patrol cops who talked with detectives who chatted with assistant district attorneys. Promises were made to seek justice, oaths taken for revenge.

Most criminals ignored the rising danger because money was like vapor rub beneath their noses. Adrenaline and greed pushed them to seek more and more, stuffing their pockets while grand juries were impaneled and indictments drafted. For Sonny and Bielakowski, first in, first out, and leave the scraps. Their results were difficult to argue with.

As Sonny started in on his presentation, Bielakowski raised a hand, coughed hard, and shouted for the bartender. Saying he needed to settle his throat, he ordered vodka and a second for Sonny. They sat in silence until the bartender returned with two glasses on a serving tray.

Finishing first, Bielakowski gave a contented sigh. "I will have another when we've finished. Vodka makes me strong," he said, staring into his glass. "Go ahead with the business. I always look forward to hearing what you have."

Sonny cleared his throat a second time, crossed his legs to the outside of the table, and picked a piece of lint off his tailored trousers. "You still own any fighters?"

"I've got two guys in the ring this week at the Blue Horizon."

Sonny knew the phrasing was his friend's way of saying he'd fixed a match. "While boxing has been good to you, its time has passed. Numbers have declined since Tyson crapped out and the networks dropped their weekly cards. Sure, there's still money in that game, but it's all bunched at the top."

"Beats owning a horse."

"The next big thing is coming out of Japan. It's called mixed martial arts. Think of Bruce Lee fighting a wrestler, or a street fight with three-ounce gloves and kung fu kicking. Lots of blood, terrific action."

"Sounds barbaric, like a cockfight. There's going to be problems getting that sanctioned. State athletic commissions will resist."

Sonny didn't flinch at the challenge. He'd spent twelve months vetting his pitches and was confident they could withstand the scrutiny. "You have the people who can overcome those obstacles. Yeah, maybe the bigger boxing promoters will work the back channels, but they'll eventually see the light. You want in before that happens."

Bielakowski enjoyed his partner's theatrics and was impressed by his due diligence. No one delivered moneymakers like Sonny Bonhardt. "This explains the postcard from Tokyo."

Sonny nodded. "I saw two events over there. Forty thousand screaming Japanese, and half were women. Each paid fifty bucks, the fights were on pay-per-view, and everything for the next six months was sold out. What I'm proposing is you front-run a U.S.-based promotional team. Bring that fighting here by creating your own version of Don King for mixed martial arts. You'll print money and have the perfect outlet with the vendors for laundering other proceeds."

While Bielakowski wasn't taken with undermining boxing, the laundry angle had appeal. He was drowning in cash, and there were never enough soap-and-water mechanisms for cleaning it all. "They're not like us, you know, those Japanese. It's a warrior culture with all that ninja and samurai business. How do you know that type of fighting will translate here? Maybe Americans will thumb their noses, like with soccer."

"Because," Sonny said, leaning forward to make the point, "half those fighters in Japan are Americans. These are guys who aren't good enough to make it in the boxing ring. Maybe they played football, or wrestled in school, or grew up idolizing Chuck Norris. The point is they love fighting, and the Japanese treat them like rock stars. Our guys are going there and Brazil because they don't have the opportunity here yet."

Bielakowski had owned fighters since the fifties and knew boxing was in a full dive. The reason wasn't that Americans had grown soft. Anyone with a cable subscription or VCR could see that the public's bloodlust had grown beyond what the sweet science provided. A combat sport allowing knees and elbows might be enough. "This I like," he said, pointing at Sonny like a teacher praising a student. "The business is good. And the laundering puts it over the top. Big shows will have enough moving parts to mask my money."

Sonny was ready for the negotiation. "Toss out a number."

"It's a six-figure deal."

"What's the first digit?"

"One."

"I was thinking three," said Sonny. "It's damn near a legitimate business as long as you're smart injecting your own cash and keeping two layers between you and the corporate entity. Recruit the best young boxing promoter, stake him in Japan for a couple weeks to learn the game, and get him back here lining up events and signing the fighters to U.S. contracts."

"Two."

"Two and a half."

"Two and a quarter."

"Deal."

No handshake was necessary. Within twenty-four hours, the price would begin its journey through a series of wire transfers under a multitude of account numbers until it landed within the friendly banking structure of Grand Cayman. The first half of the transfer formula was all Bielakowski, designed to protect the origination point and the sender. The second half was Sonny's criteria for sheltering his identity, the source of the money, and its eventual destination. They reviewed the process annually and altered at least two steps to avoid recurring patterns.

Bielakowski retrieved the notebook and antacids from his front pocket. Sonny asked how his ulcer was doing, and Bielakowski mumbled that something other than a bleeding stomach would kill him first. He opened the notebook and scribbled on the thin, moisture-sensitive onionskin paper. The writing was an undecipherable mix of symbols and Polish/Russian hybrids that didn't include any real dates or numbers.

When he finished, Bielakowski set his notebook aside. "Anything else?"

"One more," answered Sonny, who had retrieved another coffee while his friend worked. He wondered about Bielakowski's stamina and capacity for processing additional information. Their negotiations depended upon the shared experience of dozens of other projects. If Bielakowski couldn't make those swift recollections, the next proposal would be difficult to conceptualize. "This one's a little unique," he warned.

Bielakowski knew what Sonny was implying. Not like there wasn't some truth to it. A minute hadn't passed in the last five years when he'd been pain free. Distractions like that took a toll. His wife with the little notes in his pocket was seeing it, too. But Bielakowski knew something they didn't—the experience with Martin had energized him. Since cutting the ropes off the FBI agent's wrists, Bielakowski felt like he'd sipped from the fountain of youth. At home that night, Bielakowski switched through the television stations until he found the broadcast of a local evangelist. He watched the preacher walk among the believers, laying hands on the sick and crippled until they shouted in relief. Bielakowski felt a bond with the recipients, a knowledge that in that singular moment, nothing in their ill bodies had changed, no metamorphosis had occurred, yet everything was different. It wasn't molecular or cellular, though Bielakowski was somehow feeling more alive. "Don't worry about using the brake with me," he said. "I'll keep up."

"Hey," said Sonny, "all I meant was I've been researching for months and it took me a while to wrap my head around this one."

Bielakowski held up his hand to show no offense. "If we flipped spots I'm not sure I'd be so accommodating."

Sonny stirred two sugars into his coffee and set the spoon on the adjacent table. "That's why I'm in the lab and you're on the street." When Bielakowski nodded, Sonny said, "Idea two is telecommunications."

"Jesus, more of this phone business? I miss the days of stealing cargo at the port." The sausage maker wasn't shy about playing the grumpy old man card, though he'd learned not to exclude modern business ideas. Their first couple of years at Mollie's resulted in one or two deals for every five pitches. Sonny would leave pissed and sell the rejects to New York or Miami Cubans. Bielakowski caught rumors of how much they'd made on the ideas and got smart quick. The last five years he'd bought almost all of Sonny's proposals, if just to keep them from the competition.

"You remember those times?" Bielakowski asked. "One night we'd get dresses. Another it'd be cantaloupes and Chilean grapes. All while dodging the cops and Italians."

"You ever pinch a truck loaded with five million?" asked Sonny, reeling in his partner. Dredging up the good old days was for after the presentation, during drinks at the Palm or Striped Bass. "I liked this one last year, but was waiting on the government to clarify some of the regulations and oversight."

Bielakowski signaled to proceed.

"It's all about the Universal Service Fund."

"Never heard of it."

"Of course you haven't," agreed Sonny, sliding into a steady, if not slow, tempo. "But you pay into it. We all do. On every phone bill there is a fee charged and dumped into the Universal Service Fund. This pool is hundreds of millions of dollars. Congress approved a law saying the fund has to pass the money to struggling little phone companies in the middle of nowhere so all Americans can afford a phone line."

"Subsidies for monopolies?"

"Wealth distribution," said Sonny, pausing to let the waters swirl. "Phone service in New York and Philadelphia is cheap because of all the users. Not the case in Kansas or New Mexico or Alaska. These rural phone companies get fat annual checks to offset maintenance and infrastructure costs."

Sonny hesitated, giving Bielakowski time to make a point or ask a question. When he grunted his displeasure at the coddling, Sonny pressed on, explaining that the first step was creating corporate shells in target states and fronting them with state-level telecom lobbyists and consultants. The suits were akin to the casino shills that protected the mob's identity in the early days of Vegas. They'd give Bielakowski operational legitimacy and a grace period from serious inquiry. Once the figureheads were in place, these patsies would buy hinterland phone companies for the purpose of peeling off the USF payments via invoices from other Bielakowski-controlled fronts. When the telecoms got audited, the trail would be a paper maze, and the only living, breathing people to take the rap would be the local management team.

Bielakowski said it reminded him of his dad busting out restaurants that couldn't repay their loans. He'd assign a guy to take over, double all the food and liquor orders, sell everything out the back door, and let the creditors fight over the ashes. Anton asked Sonny if he remembered a

Greek place they busted together on Fairmount Avenue. When Sonny shook his head, Bielakowski asked how much the Universal Service Fund sent to the telecoms.

Sonny spent a few minutes describing his research, how he acquired the numbers, and why he could vouch for their accuracy. "I've whittled the buyout candidates to ten and tagged patsies for each market. On an individual basis, the telecoms take in between four and six million from the fund. Skimming half is realistic."

"Best guess on how long it can run?"

"Two years. I think in year three the roof timbers start buckling and your patsy finds himself alone and trying to figure out where everyone has gone."

Bielakowski shouted the bartender back for a second go with the vodka. He'd been craving a follow-up since the first one stopped burning. Booze for him was a good-time accelerant, not something for drowning sorrows or blanketing a depression.

As they waited for their drinks, Sonny said, "It's one of the best proposals I've ever come up with. No one else has even brushed against it yet."

"Better than the 1–900 stuff?"

The porn con was a sore spot for Sonny, probably more sensitive than Bielakowski realized, making him question the man's point. Maybe it was nothing or maybe it was Bielakowski's way of acknowledging he'd screwed up. Two years earlier, Sonny devised a brilliant scam for manipulating the billing of online porn. Assured no charges would accrue until they proceeded beyond a certain point, porn-seeking computer users provided their credit card numbers for access to a free, complimentary website tour. Sonny's bit of programming magic was disabling their ability to backtrack or disconnect. To leave the website, they had to go forward, thereby activating the charge. Sonny knew the con was solid gold when he pitched it to Bielakowski for three hundred grand.

"You never should have resold that," Sonny said. "It was your right, but you got my hometown discount. If I had known you were hand-delivering it to the Mulberry mutts, shit, I could have done that myself and earned double."

Bielakowski had already admitted to himself he'd messed up selling to the Gambino crew. Not because he'd hurt Sonny's feelings or strained their relationship. He was kicking himself because the Gambinos pulled in four hundred million before they got greedy, stuck around too long, and were indicted. He would have bagged half and bailed before Visa sniffed out the billing practices and started an investigation.

Back to the order of the day, Bielakowski held up a peaceful hand. "The 1–900 thing is water under the bridge. A mistake? Sure, I'll concede the point so let's stick to what's in front of us. This Universal Service Fund is good. Seven figures good? No, not that sweet."

Flying up from Florida, Sonny's goal for the sit-down was anywhere between six and seven hundred grand. A little less might be okay if he trimmed incidentals and his luck turned at the track. The light side of five hundred was a cherry-bomb-in-the-pants-type problem. Much of his yearly nut was month-to-month expenses like the high-rise condo and marina slip. But those obligations, while important, weren't mission critical to his long-term health. The same wasn't true for his bookie and Vegas marker. The only reason Sonny had been allowed to float as much as he had, as long as he had, was because he was savvy enough to buy time without creating a panic. That said, everyone in the gambling business had a breaking point, and the bookie and casino had reached theirs. No more extensions. No more silver-tongued brush-offs.

The two and a quarter from the MMA deal covered most of Sonny's gambling, minus some of the accrued interest, so the tally from the USF scheme would dictate his next year's standard of living. "Maybe not a million-dollar idea," he said, sacrificing little by coming off the unrealistically high mark. "It's damn good, though. I just handed you the movie script for *Butch Cassidy and the Sundance Kid* with the title roles cast. Follow the script, stay out of Newman and Redford's way, and the rest will be easier than shooting crows off a carcass."

There was little mystery to Bielakowski's next step. Whenever he liked an idea and fretted the upfront, he tried offsetting the initial premium by dangling back-end action. Other business partners accepted the deferred payoffs to curry favor or because they believed it was the better deal. Sonny ranked them all as suckers. Trash can dining educated him on the importance of upgrading his immediate future, even at the expense of future earnings.

So Sonny declined Bielakowski's profit-sharing offer, saying he was still too greedy for patience. Besides, sweating the back-end meant vesting himself in operations, a work category he'd sworn off. He was the idea guy, a cost always paid up front. Bielakowski pushed, offering an extra ten points. Sonny's headshake was the final shovel of dirt.

There was a light knock on the doorframe as the bartender returned with the vodka. Bielakowski made an eager reach, held it high, and insisted Sonny do the same. Sonny said a toast was premature. A firm price was required before celebrating.

"To my friend, Sonny Bonhardt," said Bielakowski, vodka dripping down his outstretched arm. "The first man—the only man—to sell me a half-million-dollar idea."

With the toast hanging in the air, Sonny understood the message. It was a half million or nothing. He raised his own glass in acceptance of the terms.

Pleased with the outcome and the company, both clinked glasses and downed the alcohol. After a moment to savor the distilled vapors, Bielakowski asked, "Are we done? Anything more to consider?"

Sonny moved his hands across the table like a roulette dealer closing his wheel. "Done for now, although I'm already working on our next one. Probably won't wait until next year. More of a short-notice move."

"Sounds like a traditional operation."

Sonny smiled. His friend hadn't faded as much as he'd feared. "You'll love it. An old-fashioned truck jacking. Not ready yet. When it is, we'll have a couple weeks' notice."

"Please call. Perhaps it's one you'll consider for a back-end arrangement."

Sonny nodded in understanding, not agreement. "You want to grab dinner later? Or maybe we just eat now?"

"The vodka here is cold, and no one is bothering us, although it's missing your white tablecloths," said Bielakowski, a thumb tilted toward the mustard and horseradish. "And you may have to dry your own hands in the restroom."

Since Sonny had relocated to South Florida, Bielakowski teased him about becoming a hotshot high roller. Clothes, women, gambling, sailing the islands—the whole package was included in the jab. Bielakowski—in the same house, with the same woman, working the same job over the same butcher's block—was the other side of the mountain, the dark half. He was the dutiful immigrant who rejected the trappings of success in favor of an austere existence.

As though he needed to demonstrate a willingness to go all in, Sonny stripped off his suit jacket, tossed it on the nearby coat rack, unfastened his cuff links, and rolled up his sleeves.

"Stop. Enough," said Anton. "There's only one working man at this table, so let's not pretend. Done with the clothes? Good, then I have a favor to ask."

Retaking his seat, Sonny assumed the sentence was a mistake, an unintended jumble. Bielakowski wasn't the type who professed need or vulnerability. "The great man with hat in hand? This is turning out to be a historic day. First a fair deal, and now requesting a favor. The stars are aligned over Philadelphia."

"Don't," said Bielakowski, his word infused with more determination than desperation. "You may not like what I'm asking. But that's why they call it a favor. I'm an old man, Sonny. My body and mind are—"

"Come on, let's—"

Bielakowski dropped his clenched hands on the tabletop. "We've known each other too long to behave like insecure young brides. I'm not offering my condition so you can disagree and we can hen over why I'm not as bad as I think. I'm fucking old. End of story. Not picking-out-burial-hymns old, but the music is fading. Hell, if I was a dog, I'd sleep with one eye open."

Sonny laughed, in part because Bielakowski resembled an aging hound. And in part because ironic laughter was the best he could offer.

Waiting for the chuckle to fade, Bielakowski said, "I need Marcek out of Philly. I want him in Florida with you."

Sonny couldn't recall a Bielakowski fleeing the city. Their move was to retract, pull into the safety of Port Richmond until whatever storm passed. He highlighted the point while also making clear he wasn't in the safe-house business.

"It's true that the local conditions are in transition," said Bielakowski.

"Usual bullshit?"

"I thought so at first."

"And now?"

"Unpredictable. Like any ruler who ascends with violence, Rea's vulnerable to insurrection. To strengthen his allegiances he must rally his family against a common enemy."

Sonny raised his eyebrows and pointed a finger across the table. Bielakowski answered with a nod.

Since his move south, Sonny wasn't privy to Philly's criminal nuances. He had cocktails with a few of the retired Italians every couple of months, though didn't know the intricacies of their business, or of any changes with the Poles. "So get Marcek back to the neighborhood. That's always been enough. They don't have the muscle to overrun Port Richmond."

"True," said Bielakowski, "our boundaries are secure. But this goes back to my age more than anything, and your particular skill set. Marcek has learned everything he can from me, and I'm convinced that's no longer enough. He needs you now."

Sonny wondered whether his friend intended the flattery. "I'm no example. Most days I gamble away or spend on the boat."

"I'm not talking about your vices. It's the ideas. I want him watching how you do it." Seeing Sonny's face, Bielakowski added, "And don't worry about getting cut out or training your replacement. Marcek could be your shadow for five years and still not offer your magic. But I need him appreciating men like you, what you deliver."

Sonny leaned back to distance himself from the idea. "Jesus, Anton, I don't know. How can I win with that? It's not about Marcek. I like him enough, but not everything in life can be taught." The request wasn't like explaining the tax code or charting the best route to Bimini. Sonny wasn't sure himself how he came up with the ideas. Sure, there was a process, a routine that included a dozen daily newspapers, tracking law enforcement press releases, and skimming every magazine in the bookstore. The hard truth was he never knew what he was looking for until he found it. Sometimes he went six months and got nothing except ink-stained fingers. Then one afternoon he might sketch out a year's worth of ideas while killing a six-pack.

Bielakowski didn't view his request as a negotiation with options and outs. "If you were a sculptor, I'd understand the limits of making my son an artist. Some skills are not transferable."

Sonny nodded in agreement.

"But this is not that," said the old man. "An artist can certainly describe why he's drawn to a particular style. Or explain the task of chisel and hammer. Or why he chose one stone over another to express his vision."

Sonny remembered back to when he was fourteen and working his way into Bielakowski's organization. Numbers were his thing. Didn't matter if they were on a balance sheet or in a dice game, digits spoke to Sonny, telling him how they liked to be stacked and organized. Letters and words were a different hassle—they jumped the page like spooked tadpoles on a pond's edge. Despite Sonny's effort to camouflage the disability, Anton detected the ruse and took the problem to his mother, a woman who taught herself and half of Port Richmond how to speak and read English. She brought the street boy under her wing, recognized he was bright though learned differently, and had him comprehending Twain and Zane Grey within twelve months.

The time had come for Sonny to repay the good turn, a trickle-down fifty years in the making. "Describe my days with him," he said, resigned to the responsibility.

"He's with you when you're working up a proposal. Explain the process, what you're seeing and doing. I know it's part pixie dust, so save that lecture. Do the best you can."

Sonny asked about the money.

"Anything he runs, your cut is half. Right now he's partial to cash grabs between ten and fifty and averages one or two a month. He's expected to earn, whether it's Philly or Florida. My only rule is no street drugs. Forget the dope. Everything else is open. If he flunks out, send him home and it's my problem. Any ideas you come up with while he's shadowing will earn a premium at next year's meeting."

"I never had a chance."

"Don't start with the tears. He'll be down in a few weeks," said Bielakowski. "Now let's order some sandwiches. I want to tell you about my newest friend. He's an agent with the Federal Bureau of Investigation."

15.

NO ONE COULD ACCUSE Billy O'Bannon of sloth.

Between 9:30 A.M. and noon, the lawyer had four hearings in four courtrooms. His record at the Criminal Justice Center was ten, and six wasn't uncommon. Four was easy breezy, even with the martini hangover he'd acquired the previous evening buying drinks and telling stories at the Palm. The receipt in his pocket said he'd spent a grand, which meant a fine time even if he couldn't recall all the highlights or punch lines.

O'Bannon's first appearance was in front of a surly Irishman named Judge James "Jimmy Mac" McManus who'd walked a night beat while earning his degree at Temple Law. The hearing was over before it started because the Commonwealth's star witness no-showed a third time. The prosecutor, freshly promoted from preliminary hearings at the Roundhouse, requested another continuance and was denied. Ordering the defendant's release, Judge McManus offered his congratulations and an assured prediction they'd be meeting again soon.

Three floors down, O'Bannon's second hearing was his motion against the DA's office for refusing to provide a videotape copy of his client stealing windshield wipers from K-mart. If they couldn't give him a copy, the prosecutor couldn't use it at trial, and if the prosecutor couldn't show the tape, the case fell apart like wet toilet paper. The judge's interest was piqued, though not enough to dismiss the case; instead he hung a thirty-day window to rehear pending the DA's production of the tape.

Ten minutes and two cell phone calls later, O'Bannon was back upstairs for a hearing that never reached the merits because of his request for a Rule One continuance—courtroom code for a lawyer waiting to be paid. The judge, a former defense attorney, had no problem with the defendant cooling his ass in jail until his attorney received what was promised. The fourth appearance was the easiest of the bunch—a calendaring issue for a trial judge who didn't like working the last two weeks of November. Four cans kicked down the legal system's road as defense lawyers stalled and the ADA's shortened their daily stacks.

With his morning under control, O'Bannon's afternoon was shaping up. As long as his noon appointment didn't forget the retainer, he'd have enough money and time to pick up the jewelry and deliver it to his newest girlfriend. One look at the tennis bracelet and she'd blow him in the parking lot, which was all he could really handle because of the hangover and his wife needing him home before eight o'clock to watch the kids.

The closer O'Bannon got to the retainer, the more comfortable he became with collecting the oversized charge. The client was a Mafia grunt referred by Daniel Moss, the Italians' longtime legal counsel. When more than one associate got pinched, each needed his own representation to avoid a conflict of interest. Moss took on the highest-ranked and farmed out the rest to defense bar pals such as Joe Penny, Ed Delisle, and, most recently, Billy O'Bannon. Each lawyer understood that Moss controlled the defense team's strategy, so no one was allowed to run off and cut a deal with the prosecutors. Follow the rules, you got the cases. Go rogue, you got buried. O'Bannon had no problem falling in line. The cases were good money and he couldn't buy the free airtime he caught for representing a well-known South Philly hood.

For the most recent pool of clients, Daniel Moss told the other lawyers to get their retainers toot sweet because he was motioning for dismissal based on unlawful search and seizure. O'Bannon saw Moss's advice as an opportunity to hustle a couple extra bucks, no different from a trainer's tip on a horse. At the first client meeting, O'Bannon told the young soldier, "It's a ten-thousand-dollar case. But kick in another eight and I'll guarantee a win. And whatever you do, don't tell your partners, because if word gets out, you'll get ten years for tampering." He closed with a wink, but the soldier was smart enough to ask for more detail. On the spot, O'Bannon spun a story about a side deal with the court clerk who assigned cases to judges. O'Bannon explained that the right judge made all the difference, particularly one he roomed with in law school. All bullshit, of course, every ounce of it. Bullshit, bullshit, bullshit. But it had a certain appeal to a twenty-four-year-old kid facing five years in Graterford. If he was already on the hook for ten grand, what was another eight to seal the deal?

Cutting across City Hall's stained courtyard, less than ten minutes from his office, O'Bannon gave his retainer rationale a final review. Lies were a natural resource for the lawyer, though he wasn't calloused enough to shoulder them without periodic justification. His first and favorite argument was that the client deserved the inflated retainer for being so stupid. Nobody could or would fix cases for eight grand, and a criminal making his living on the streets should know better. Second, even if the legal team lost the motion, who says they couldn't win the trial? And if they lost? Well, in that scenario, the client was on his way to a state-run facility. *Let the bastard sue him for ineffective assistance of counsel from jail,* he thought. *See how that lollipop ride goes.*

His office was located on the fourteenth floor of 123 South Broad Street, where he shared a lobby, conference room, and receptionist with two other attorneys. O'Bannon's only personal staff was a paralegal named Rosie who'd been with him for a decade. Despite her decent looks and daily proximity, O'Bannon declared Rosie off-limits for him and the other lawyers because a replacement would cost a hundred grand in lost business and create a month of headaches.

After navigating the building's revolving doors and stepping into the elevator, O'Bannon's cell rang with Rosie's extension. He decided to postpone any law-talk until he'd made it upstairs and used the restroom. The Criminal Justice Center's bathrooms were the daytime latrines for

Philadelphia's criminal class and unacceptable, he believed, for a man wearing hand-stitched shoes and a tailored suit.

Once inside the firm's waiting area, O'Bannon's receptionist pointed her pencil quite purposefully in his direction as she spoke on the phone. Believing the call was for him, O'Bannon increased his speed, shook his head, and mouthed *I'm not in.*

Before he could disappear down the hallway, she put the caller on hold and spun her chair. "Your noon appointment has arrived," she said, spearmint gum dancing in her mouth. Answering phones for three criminal defense attorneys gave her a battlefield confidence, similar to a nurse in a mobile field unit who'd seen it all or wasn't surprised by what she hadn't.

"Yeah, they do that," said O'Bannon, distracted by her etiquette. "What gives with the gum?"

O'Bannon wasn't the receptionist's favorite lawyer or most hated. His attributes qualified for both, often in the same day. "He's already in the conference room," she said, spitting the gum into a tissue.

"You offer him something to drink, like we talked about?" They'd been coaching her on which clients deserved special treatment, though identifying the right candidates was harder than in most law firms. With a criminal defense practice, some of the shadiest were the best paying. The rub for the receptionist was parsing that economic class from the deadbeats who couldn't scrape together fifteen hundred for a preliminary hearing. O'Bannon went mad giving that demographic anything for free.

She bunched her lips to one side of her mouth. "It's not the one you were expecting."

Damn it, thought the lawyer, *always a complication.* Instead of getting paid, he had a walk-in chugging complimentary Pepsi in the conference room. "My noon is a beefcake kid named Costa. Big shoulders. Black hair, all oiled up. Who's sitting back there?"

"It's the same appointment, just a different guy."

"Somebody's here for Costa?" asked O'Bannon, leaning against the receptionist's chest-high counter, close enough to whisper. His intuition said it was probably Costa's old man, trading his life savings for an explanation of the lawyer's guarantee. "His dad here with the retainer?"

"Not so much," she said, enjoying his discomfort. One of the other lawyers mentioned O'Bannon wanted to skip the Christmas bonus, blaming the economy and city wage tax. The same lawyer neglected to mention it was a unanimous opinion. "It's his boss," she said. "The top dog."

O'Bannon's eyes flicked down the hallway. "Rea?"

"Yes."

"Alone?"

The receptionist nodded and released the call.

O'Bannon's first thought was that her Christmas bonus was taillights. He wasn't stuffing an envelope to reward this kind of bush league behavior. His second was that, with the head of the Philadelphia mob in his conference room, he had a better chance of growing a fingernail on his dick than collecting the eighteen-grand retainer.

With the law firm's design, O'Bannon couldn't reach his private office without passing the conference room's glass doors. Knowing a walk-by projected trepidation and/or cluelessness—both damning attributes for a counselor—his only real option was an immediate and unswerving introduction. "Call back to Rosie," he said, smoothing his maple hair before buttoning his suit coat. "Explain the situation with Costa—"

Hitting the hold button a second time with the type of refined exasperation reserved for trade masters, she said, "Rosie knows. She tried calling you. Watched her stand right there dialing your cell. You didn't answer."

O'Bannon hated staff getting the last word. He thought his signature on the weekly paycheck entitled him to more. "Okay, listen for a second. I'm not looking for input. In exactly five minutes, I want Rosie knocking on the conference room door with a file in her arms. When I wave her in, she's to remind me about a pending call with Judge Binns. Understood?"

The receptionist tapped her pencil twice on the message pad before shifting her gaze to the phone's blinking light. "Fine."

"Fine what?"

"With what you just said."

"You'll tell Rosie?"

"If that's what we just agreed to." The receptionist knew she scraped O'Bannon's temper by refusing to acquiesce with an unconditional *yes*. While that technique was an asset fielding phone calls from third parties seeking commitments, it was a maddening character defect in almost every other circumstance.

"Damn it, I don't need this attitude right now," said O'Bannon, turning for the hallway. Same as the lobby, the firm's corridors were lined with case-law books bought from an attorney needing money to fight a tax fraud indictment. At the discounted rate, the books cost less than wallpaper and classed up areas often occupied by soon-to-be convicted felons waiting for an appointment.

Reaching the conference room, O'Bannon instinctively paused before entering. Through the door's cut glass he could see Rea at the far window, his head tilted up as though the overcast sky were more interesting than the midday streetscape. His slacks were well tailored and recently pressed, the crease running an unbroken line to his back pockets. His blue shirt, tucked with care beneath a mahogany belt, provided a nice contrast against the burnished molding and windowsill. His hair was dark except for an unusual patch of awkward white a few inches above his collar. Though still, his lean figure radiated an intense energy and the lawyer's two-second take was that absolutely nothing about the man's slender physique suggested he was incapable of leading men into a street fight.

When O'Bannon popped the levered handle, his entrance was all shoulders and jawbone, like a boxer called to the center of the ring for prefight instructions. Corporate clients responded to reserved, controlled—even detached—counsel whom they judged according to Ivy League pedigrees and summer homes. O'Bannon's clients were the outliers. They wanted the pissed-off lone wolf who got off staring down the Commonwealth of Pennsylvania or the United States government. Law review credentials and sheepskin diplomas were all meaningless measuring sticks of a foreign society. They wanted someone who understood what it was like getting handcuffed by the cops and tossed down a stairwell, some-one who'd been victimized by the same system they were now fighting. They wanted one of their own.

"Mr. Rea, what a pleasure," said O'Bannon, his hand extended like the statuette atop a bowling trophy.

Rea stayed silent. A five-count passed before he pivoted without clos-ing the distance. He wanted another concession and got it when O'Bannon leaned forward enough to pull his back foot off the rug. Rea was almost playful in his acceptance, as if they were a couple of pals busting stones. "Little surprised, right?" he said, holding the grip.

"Actually it's good finally meeting you. It's just that I was expecting Mr. Costa."

"Costa couldn't make it," said Rea, quick enough to overlap the dia-logue. "Tickle in the back of the throat. I told him to take the day off. Turns out I didn't have anything on the calendar, so I volunteered to come down."

"I see," said O'Bannon, directing his guest to a chair upholstered in blue leather faded from too much afternoon sun. Rea accepted the offer, leaving the head of the conference table for O'Bannon.

Behind the lawyer hung an oil portrait of a nineteenth-century French general standing on a hilltop, surrounded by cannon smoke rising from the surrounding valleys. A second glance revealed more than a passing resemblance between O'Bannon and the Napoleon look-alike. "Nothing too serious with Mr. Costa's health, I hope? We have a very important hearing coming up."

Again laying his words over the lawyer's, Rea said, "You like it here?"

"Excuse me?"

"I asked if you like it here."

O'Bannon scanned the room. "Yeah, it's an okay office. Moved in almost three years ago and have a couple more on the lease. Wish the building had its own parking, but what can you do? We're close to the Criminal Justice Center and City Hall, which is worth something. I don't know, I used to be up near the parkway, but with all the homeless up there, I like this—"

Rea cut him off. "You're lost."

The bully plays were catching the lawyer off guard. "Wait, what?"

"Come on, your life is firing questions on cross-examination—this shouldn't be so hard. I'm asking if you like it here." Rea crossed his legs, fingers intertwined over his right knee. "Not this office. I don't give a shit about whether you like this office. And not this building or block or city. Fuck do I care if you like Philly, right? When I say *here,* I'm speaking in a metaphysical sense. Like, do you enjoy walking the earth? Taking air in, holding your wife's hand, playing with the kids, smoking a cigar with a nice bourbon. Or—and this is what I'm asking—maybe you don't. Maybe it's all too much hassle. Maybe you'd rather not own the routine of Billy O'Bannon anymore. Some guys, you know, some guys have this death wish kind of swagger. They want to die, they're just too chicken-shit to off themselves. You ever hear of that phrase *suicide by cop?*"

O'Bannon nodded. The glands beneath his armpits had opened. Beads of nervous sweat trickled down his flanks until they were either absorbed by his undershirt or redirected by seams of fat.

"Okay, good, we're reading from the same book," said Rea. His tone was increasingly animated; his body remained still. "Let's take a random guy looking to kill himself. Maybe he's self-loathing, or his old lady is playing around, or he's gotten in over his head. Who the fuck knows, right? Instead of eating a bullet or walking west, he looks to antagonize. He heads for the tavern and picks a fight with a goon twice his size, but that's not enough 'cause a beating is only half the job. So now he turns up the volume and hits the streets looking for a cop 'cause cops don't like fighting. That's why they carry the guns. This guy, he wanted to die with a bullet in his brainpan. He just couldn't reach the trigger. Follow?"

Another nod from O'Bannon, this one smaller, less sure what he was agreeing to.

"This fellow is an example of someone *not* liking it here. He wanted to move on and picked a cop for assistance. Happens all the time. So my question is, are you playing me for your cop?"

While the most optimistic parts of O'Bannon's brain had been preaching hope, the rest understood there was only one agenda behind the Costa-for-Rea switch. New bosses were hypersensitive to public perception. Adversaries had to believe, deep in their soul, that the don of the Philadelphia Mafia was the baddest mofo in town. If word got out that Rea's men were easy marks, or that he was slow protecting their backs, the hordes would charge the walls.

"If you're referring to the retainer, that's really between me and Mr. Costa. Attorney-client privilege—"

"You sure that's the right course?"

The lawyer shifted in his seat. "In hindsight, the quoted retainer was probably high. Given the circumstances, that is."

"By circumstances you mean Moss arguing at the podium with you perched pretty at the defense table? An easy eighteen in your pocket while another lawyer gets the case dismissed?"

"Search and seizure motions don't always go as planned," said O'Bannon, steadying himself on more familiar ground. "If Moss loses, we're going to trial. While my quote is high for pretrial motions, I'm committed all the way to appeal. Am I overpaid sometimes? Sure, just enough to balance when I'm holding the short straw or no straw at all."

A quick rap on the door interrupted Rea's rebuttal. As instructed, O'Bannon's paralegal had arrived with an escape route. Peeking her head through the doorframe, she said, "I'm so sorry to interrupt. Mr. O'Bannon, your conference call with Judge Binns starts in two minutes."

Rea spoke first. "What's your name, honey?"

The paralegal stepped inside. "Rosie," she answered, flashing a nervous—almost embarrassed—smile as though a singer onstage had picked her from the audience.

"Rosie," repeated Rea, his eyebrows tilted up toward his hairline. "You said the call was with Judge Binns?"

"Yes."

"We're in luck. Him and I go way back. Explain that Boss O'Bannon is meeting with Raymond Rea and we'll be done when we're done. Ain't that right, Bill?"

O'Bannon raised his voice, his only tool for recapturing control. "You'll just have to reschedule, Rosie. You know the routine. Explain that a client emergency has come up and offer my sincere apologies."

Rea chuckled at the hasty charade. "Lies are a slippery slope. Truth—even an uncomfortable truth—is better than begging for forgiveness."

"Rosie," barked O'Bannon, embarrassed for proposing such a veiled ruse. "Reschedule for this afternoon and we should be fine. Thank you."

The paralegal nodded, unsure of her next step. Her role only had one line. "Yes, of course," she said, offering the men coffee and water on her way out. Both declined.

When they were alone again, Rea took the reins. "Nobody's expecting you to work for free. This is still America. But the right retainer is eight grand, ten tops. Eighteen grand is taking advantage of a situation."

O'Bannon opened his mouth only to be cut off by a wave of Rea's right hand.

"I know what you're going to say. That now—given this discussion—you'll happily accept ten. Here's the problem. When I get called in, I don't negotiate to get even."

O'Bannon's eighteen grand was gone, and ten wasn't looking much better. Then the thought occurred to him that maybe Rea was there for something else, another chip in play other than money or respect. Why else make the personal appearance? With the descent of the discussion, couldn't hurt to take a shot. "I don't think you'd come all the way up here to save Costa some money."

"Good."

"Good, what?" said O'Bannon.

"Good that you're not as dumb as I feared. Good that you kept fighting for the angle." The stick-and-carrot program had worked. Rea had taken a blindfolded O'Bannon into the valley and was now guiding him out a more humbled man.

"What do you want from me?" asked the attorney.

Rea returned to the window. He was better on his feet. Motion defined him. In his experience, success was never born from staying still or stepping back. "You know a lawyer named Norman Deeb?"

With his bald head and penchant for tweed, Norman Deeb didn't fit the profile of a Philadelphia criminal defense attorney. As a Penn Law grad and former assistant U.S. attorney, he was different from the start and distanced himself further by never teaming with other lawyers on strategy. Well aware of the U.S. Attorney Office's ninety-seven percent conviction rate, Deeb played the better odds, converting his clients into cooperating witnesses. On the street, they were called stool pigeons. He preferred the term *free*.

"Mr. Deeb's got a new client," said Rea, looking left and right out the window to test his line of sight. He could see as far as the Walnut and Spruce intersection before the building's facade clipped his view. "The client is a young man who's been charged with involvement in the local meth market. Name's Tommy Paschol."

When a pause took hold of the room, O'Bannon asked what that had to do with him.

"You know Deeb. He hasn't tried a case in fifteen years. When clients walk in his office, they're not even offered a chair. Deeb makes a call and they head right to the prosecutors for a proffer and plea deal."

"I don't hear much bitching about him," said O'Bannon.

"You're not listening to the right people. I know all lawyers make deals—it's how you slinks work—but Deeb pushes his clients beyond just trading guilty pleas for reduced charges. He has them naming names."

O'Bannon had two plays. He could join in the conversation, injecting his cooperation at appropriate markers, maybe even garner some goodwill. Or he could go mute, hang the burden on Rea to make his case. He settled on a combination strategy, knowing his nature wouldn't allow all of one over the other. "And you're worried Deeb's lining up Tommy Paschol," he said, measured to not give it all away in the first sound bite.

"It hasn't happened yet. The preliminary hearing was just three days ago. But as they get closer to trial I see no reason why Deeb would stray from his playbook."

Like an underdog after a couple of quick scores, O'Bannon could feel the momentum shifting in his favor. "And true or not, you're thinking this meth dealer might say something to hurt you or another interest you maintain."

Rea turned back toward the conference table, hands working change in his pockets. "You familiar with a Port Richmond businessman named Anton Bielakowski?"

"Yes. Not personally, of course, but as a criminal defense lawyer, I know his reputation."

"He makes me curious. I've been studying him, how he's survived so long. You know, since he's been in this country, he's never seen the inside of a cell? Maybe for fighting or petty garbage in his younger days, but no serious stints."

"Quite an accomplishment if true."

Rea raised a hand like a witness taking the oath. "Oh, it's true. I've lived double digits behind bars. This guy is almost eighty and has spent more money on dry cleaning than lawyers."

O'Bannon's head swayed side to side. "It's my understanding he maintains a rather closed loop of associates. Specifically, Poles from Port Richmond. That's it. His men all maintain real jobs and separate lives, so nobody gets the reputation of a full-time hood. On top of that, those people are comfortable keeping a low profile with their money. If you don't act and look like a criminal, and you don't brag about your crimes, it's pretty tough to get pinched."

"Exactly," agreed Rea. "I like the way you put that—he's got a closed loop. I don't have that luxury. The family's legacy and my ambitions require a broader circle. This, on occasion, poses a threat. Like when scumball Tommy Paschol gets arrested and hires Norman Deeb for his attorney."

His mouth dry, O'Bannon regretted not asking Rosie for a bottle of water. His attempt to mimic and mirror Rea's behavior—a jury technique for expressing similarity—now seemed shortsighted. "I understand the concern. Is there something you need me to do? Perhaps I could call Deeb. He'd probably refuse to talk, but maybe I could get a feel for his direction."

"I just told you his direction. The next meeting, they'll hammer out the details of a deal." Rea was purposely vague. Best to let any proposals come from the lawyer's lips.

O'Bannon understood the dance. "It's not too late for Paschol to fire Deeb. Happens all the time. One lawyer handles the preliminary hearing, another comes in for trial. Hypothetically, you could talk with Paschol, persuade him that a different lawyer is in his best interests. Convince him he doesn't need to do time because a jury trial is winnable, just not with his current lawyer. Deeb out, new guy in."

"Yes," said Rea, "another lawyer is the solution, one who doesn't pimp out his clients to the prosecutors. Problem in this particular situation is that the defendant is part of another organization. He's a War Boy."

"Okay."

"There are certain lines with the War Boys I've been asked to respect. One is communicating directly with staff. No contact allowed. Can exceptions be made? Sure, hell, I don't know, but not before other avenues are exhausted. And that's what I'm doing here."

"Long way around the block for a man like you, considering the stakes."

"I've got time for another option. Not much, though."

O'Bannon now understood why Rea had come out so hard. He needed help, and Costa's retainer was his leverage. "Soliciting another attorney's client is an issue, though not impossible. Takes an experienced hand. I'd like to think there'd be some kind of appreciation for the effort."

Terms of the deal were Rea's specialty. Unless properly framed and inserted into a more deniable framework, they were the nuggets that always came back to bite the parties at trial. "Costa's new retainer is forty grand. Payable today. Plus, if this War Boy gets handled right, I'll consider bumping you up in the batting order for Moss's spot."

Daniel Moss, Esquire made plenty off his representation of the mob. Not from their fees—which often went unpaid—but from all the business flowing in from those seeking the same lawyer as the city's bad boys. "Make it subtle," said O'Bannon. "Too fast or abrupt and the rumors will start."

"Easy, cowboy," said Rea. "The word was *consider,* not *guarantee.* Moss knows where the bodies are buried, and I'm not kicking him out yet. Not before I see how you handle business."

"That loyalty got you into this mess." The conversation had wandered into O'Bannon's natural kill zone, where he could nurture doubt via innuendo and a thousand small razor cuts.

"What, you talking about Moss?"

"He's your legal counsel. Seems like for him, that means biding his time and waiting."

"Waiting for what?"

O'Bannon had to suppress his excitement. He took an extra breath and licked his lips to slow down. First he got the forty grand retainer, and now he had Moss on the ropes. "When you get pinched, Moss becomes the city's newest rock star. He'll be on the news every morning and night, making headlines and needing two extra girls to handle all the calls. After a week of headshots in the *Daily News*, he'll start popping up in Stu Bykofsky's gossip column while you're eating chipped beef in lockup, waiting for your trial to start again on Monday."

"You'd be any different?"

"Moss steps in for the client after they've gotten their tit in the ringer. *Call me if you're ever arrested*, he says, then shows up at your cell with a fee agreement and a gold pen. I'm more proactive."

"For example?"

"The War Boys. Moss should never have let that get so intertwined. He should have helped you create the appropriate structure for limiting liability. He didn't, and now you're exposed."

"Going forward, how would you handle the liability part?"

O'Bannon could smell the win. "Every few months we'd sit down and walk through the pros and cons of your relationships. We'd address legal implications, layers of deniability, and review certain conversations that may contain telltale signs of government involvement. Maybe we even talk about trends at the DA's office and what's cooking with the U.S. attorney."

Rea hated that he was almost impressed. "What does today's visit tell you?"

"You're letting the tail wag the dog. I understand the War Boys' importance to you—my new Costa retainer tells me that. But this Deeb situation is a harbinger of things to come. If you were a corporation and they a necessary evil for transacting business, you'd buy them, rip off their competitive advantage, or destroy them. Hell, what if a rival gets in their ear and flips their loyalties? Trust me on this, those bikers are fire on a boat."

The next likable lawyer Raymond Rea met would be his first. Whether it was Moss or the forked-tongue O'Bannon, he struggled being in the same room. Problem was, they often preached the truth. O'Bannon had the War Boy situation nailed dead to rights. Much of Rea's power came from selling meth, which meant he was beholden until he could replace the motorcycle club's manufacturing capabilities. He'd let the relationship get too loose, too obliging. The scales were out of whack. Proof was Paschol. Any other regime in any other generation would have killed the prick and whoever was sitting to his left and right. Instead, Rea was searching for a bloodless solution with an Irish mouthpiece.

As for O'Bannon, Rea decided to keep him on a string. Slick, yeah, but his willingness to push beyond what Moss ever offered was enticing. "Right now, don't worry yourself so much about my house. Handle Deeb's newest client and we'll talk."

Not knowing when he'd get another crack, O'Bannon wanted to propose one more inspired hustle. "I'm thinking there's another way for us to make money together."

"The retainer is more than generous."

"Stay with me," said O'Bannon, rubbing his face for an extra moment. Sure, Rea could funnel him extra clients, but after fifteen years practicing law he wasn't looking to double his nuisance cases. What O'Bannon craved was a move across the street to City Hall, where juries heard the multimillion-dollar personal injury cases.

"This has nothing to do with the retainer," said O'Bannon. "It's a hundred times bigger."

When Rea agreed to hear him out, the lawyer explained how many of Philly's largest personal injury cases involved victims with relationships to Rea. These connections could and should be leveraged for a piece of the settlement. For example, a month earlier, the power company settled with a card-carrying delivery driver for ten million after he was electrocuted in South Philly. Parked on a tight one-way street, the driver was delivering Sheetrock when he brushed some low-hanging lines with his off-loading crane. A couple thousand volts traveled down the crane and into his handheld control unit. Witnesses said his chest glowed like a lightbulb. He lived, but without his hands, feet, or ass cheeks. The hard part of that case wasn't proving liability or assessing the ten million in damages. The rub was getting the case in the first place. In the world of personal injury law, catastrophic injury cases against deep-pocket corporations were guaranteed lottery tickets. And that's where Rea had been dropping the ball. With his union connections, Rea should be harvesting those cases and funneling them to a lawyer willing to pay a referral fee.

Rea's response was exactly as O'Bannon had hoped. "Ten million? You're shitting me."

"As the lawyer on something like that, I can grab forty percent. If the case settles, I'll split it with you fifty-fifty. If it goes to trial, sixty-forty, plus expenses. For that electrocution deal, your take-home would have been two million."

Rea stood from the table. "I'm not agreeing to anything today. If a case like that ever walks in out of the blue, you'll have my answer. And I expect you to act accordingly."

"Of course," said O'Bannon, never doubting the outcome. Raymond Rea's type was genetically precluded from passing up such a deal. He'd be calling his union contacts with the new mandate before he was a hundred feet from the building.

"As for Mr. Costa's retainer, it'll be delivered within a few minutes of me leaving. The man will not speak and he is not to be asked any questions. Understood?"

"Of course," said O'Bannon, already planning how to call his wife with another excuse for coming home late. Sure, she'd let him have it with both barrels, but current events had him wanting to celebrate with his new girlfriend. Jewelry pickup, then drinks, dinner, some dessert, more drinks, and a room at the Ritz with a bucket of champagne and strawberries. No matter how sharp, his wife's harping couldn't override that menu.

Before departing, Rea had a final question, one he'd come up with while waiting for O'Bannon to arrive. "You have three defense lawyers working out of this office. As clients pay their retainers, that makes for a lot of cash coming in. What's stopping a hustler from waiting outside and picking your pocket or bashing your head in?"

"Deposit slips."

"They deliver the money to the bank?"

"Absolutely," said the lawyer, fingers interlocked across his belly. "Some of them pay at noon intending to steal it back at five o'clock. And you know what? You can always tell which ones, too. When I hand them the deposit slip their faces are like, *Shit, man, this dude's got us figured.*"

Rea rapped his knuckles on the table, as if checking whether anyone was home. "I don't want that with my delivery. No deposit slip. No bank. He drops the money and walks out."

O'Bannon chastised himself. Not the time to get too comfortable too soon. He assured Rea that wouldn't happen with the Costa retainer because he was personally handling the money.

"Be careful," said Rea. "Money attracts the oddest characters."

"No worries. I'm a determined sort." O'Bannon rose from his chair. "I'll handle the retainer, just like I'll take care of Tommy Paschol. When I play the charm card, I'm irresistible."

Better be, thought Rea. *Paschol's life depends on it.*

16.

GROWING UP, ANTON BIELAKOWSKI FIGURED his old man had all the answers. He could ask him anything—what to do with this, that, or the other—and the replies were quick and clear, a sharpened blade through dry grass. Method was the key; the old man kept it simple, knowing what he knew, drawing out reasonable lines when he didn't. The neighborhood said Bielakowski was cut from the same cloth, judgments guided by an unwavering confidence and worldview. No confusion. No debate.

And still Nick Martin stumped the hell out of him.

Why come back to Fancy Tina's? What was the point of waiting three nights and making a date for the following week? Was Martin rebelling, staging some kind of bizarre protest? Maybe it was a fuck-you to the club's owner, or he'd cracked from the undercover deployment, or was he waiting for Bielakowski's men to pass information? All were plausible excuses until he incorporated the stripper. She was the wild card, the Black Maria trashing the hand.

Half a day spinning scenarios convinced Bielakowski he wouldn't be threading the needle with a perfect explanation. The move was too unorthodox, too random. So he settled for the one conclusion that made the most sense. Nick Martin was reeling in the stripper as a future witness. Instead of being grateful for his life, the cop was expanding his evidentiary reach. *Hey, Cheryl, who told you to drug me? Did you know Bielakowski was behind the kidnapping? Who hauled me from your apartment? They were going to kill me, don't think they won't do the same to you.*

Ready for a resolution, Bielakowski started with the easiest task. A few days before her dinner date with Nick Martin, Bielakowski had the stripper delivered to the abandoned warehouse. Not bound, though not free to leave either. He explained how she controlled the meeting's length. Answer two questions correctly and she'd be on her merry way. Red buzzer beeps and things would get rough. Cheryl knew who she was dealing with, the ramifications for getting lippy. Not like she had anything to gain safeguarding a guy she'd already poisoned once.

"First," said Bielakowski, "what did Martin want with you?"

"I thought he was getting even, but that wasn't it."

"What, then?"

She looked at each man in the room, dismissing all for their inherent emotional weaknesses. "Lonely. The guy is just real, real lonely."

Bielakowski was more confused. What the hell was he dealing with? He closed his eyes and took a deep breath. "Okay, second, you want five thousand dollars and a one-way flight to Florida?"

"Or what?"

"Or do you want to die?"

Cheryl picked Curtain Number One. Nick Martin's loss was Tampa's club scene's gain.

The Martin problem was trickier. He was an undercover cop who'd survived ten years in the mob plus a night in the Port Richmond warehouse. Bielakowski conceded he'd underestimated and misplayed the man. Should have whacked him when he had the chance, not overthought all the angles. He tried imagining his father in a similar predicament. That ended any debate.

Bielakowski called his two best men. *Day after tomorrow, go to Fancy Tina's. Kill the sucker from the warehouse. Closing time he'll be sitting in the parking lot, waiting on that blondie who's long gone. Dump his body in the goddamn Delaware River.*

The Polish hitters baited their trap with the stripper's car, parking it in her usual spot—two rows from the back, beneath an overhead light. They took a position six spaces away in a beige Crown Victoria with tinted windows. As they waited, the men didn't eat or drink or talk. They sat still, holding pistols in their laps, watching for Nick Martin.

Martin kept the television on in the background as he cooked his meal for two, but he was just going through the motions. His body hadn't caught up to the decision building all week, right up to cutting the vegetables and marinating the meat. He couldn't take the chance going back to Kensington, must have been a little insane thinking it was even possible. Deserving time with Cheryl—wanting time—had nothing to do with it. What if the Pole heard? Or if Rea saw the stripper and started wondering about that night he disappeared, popping up twenty-four hours later, his wrists scabbed over, claiming kinky handcuff sex? Should never have stalked the broad. Whole fantasy was toxic enough to get him killed.

So close to the finish, he couldn't trip now. *Keep it on the road,* he whispered to himself. *No swerving.*

He pulled his trash can from the end of the counter. He dumped the potatoes first, followed by the veggies and even the meat. All of it had to go. The wine was allowed to survive only because he was using it to dull the pain of missing his date. Adios, Cheryl. Another time, another life.

Bielakowski let his cell ring twice before answering. The voice said the man from the warehouse never showed. "Should we track him down?"

"Let it go," said Bielakowski. "We'll have other chances. Better chances."

17.

"OH, SONNY, I'M A LITTLE light-headed," teased Tatiana, flipping back the bedsheet, smoothing her tousled hair, and heading for the bathroom. "I guess you did miss me." Passing a mirror, the Russian caught her boyfriend surveying her runway figure and rewarded him with a one-two hip shake. With the self-assuredness of a model, there wasn't an angle or ounce she was afraid of promoting.

Their evening had started two bottles of wine earlier when Sonny arrived home from Philadelphia. Dinner, the booze, and Tatiana were waiting for him on the condo's balcony. The food was takeout because she believed in spending time on her best assets. For their stay-at-home date, that meant an afternoon at the salon and shopping for a dress as sexy as a secretly passed hotel key.

Brushing her teeth in the bathroom, Tatiana was thrilled with her plan's execution and return on investment. Sonny held her hand throughout dinner, shared stories of his hometown, complimented her dress, and said they could skip dessert because he was having her.

She rinsed her mouth, added a touch of color to her lips, brushed her hair, and reached for the thigh-length robe hanging from a nearby hook. It was pale pink and decorated with Japanese cherry blossoms. She slid her arms into the cooled silk and considered how to best tie the strings.

If Sonny wasn't already asleep, she didn't want to discourage a second go-around with a CLOSED sign.

Returning with the silk lapels hanging loose over her breasts, Tatiana found Sonny out of the bed, scrambling to collect his clothes. She asked if everything was okay. After a few silent moments passed, she rephrased the question with the same result.

Sonny's mind was elsewhere, plotting a strategy for grinding the next few hours. After Tatiana had excused herself to the bathroom, Sonny called his son and caught a worst-case scenario. In all other aspects of his life, Sonny had a simple philosophy for dealing with past mistakes—he didn't pay them much attention. Michael, his oldest son, was the exception.

Like Sonny, Michael had an obsessive personality that teetered between genius and disaster. As a kid, he sold stolen bikes out of the family garage, sometimes collecting enough to post liquidation fliers on neighborhood light poles. Two years into puberty, Michael brokered low-grade grass between Puerto Rican youth gangs and suburban high schoolers. At twenty-five, he made his first million peddling Yellow Pages ads. Three "Salesman of the Year" plaques went hand in hand with a full-time coke habit and a stint in the state penitentiary for misappropriation of funds. Sonny picked up the court-ordered restitution, which was a few bucks shy of a hundred grand.

After his release, Michael did sixty days at an Arizona rehab facility, remarried, had a kid, revisited rehab three more times, and convinced Sonny to stake him in a used car dealership. Six months after the lot opened, Michael was back to earning big bucks and blowing it on bad habits. The only lesson he'd learned was being a little sharper hiding his footprints.

When Sonny called Michael from his bed and the line picked up, he could hear a Latin dance beat in the background. It struck him how there was always a soundtrack to his boy's struggles. Punk, hair metal, reggae, techno, hip-hop—the tunes changing as the crowd turned over. "Michael, it's me. I'm back from Philly. You in a club? Go outside for a second."

The music faded at the same pace as a closing fire door. "You're too late," said Michael, his speech breathy and rushed. "I'm a dead man walking."

Sonny pictured his son standing in a nightclub parking lot, his pockets full of dope and someone else's money. If the call was going to be productive, Sonny needed to know what direction his son was heading. On the back side of a binge, Michael was unreachable. Sonny would hang up and start fresh in a couple of days. But if he was still ascending and minus the voices, there was time.

"How much of that talk is the blow?"

Michael enunciated each word with a double-time cadence. "I told them everything would be all right if I could get to my dad. So that's what I was doing. Okay? I was trying, man, really working on making everything right. But I screwed it up. I'm, I'm screwed up."

Sonny tried keeping his voice down. Tatiana wasn't Michael's biggest fan, telling Sonny his son was a taker, the type who wrung the rag until there wasn't a drop left. Sonny would respond with a half-dozen excuses, including Michael's no-show father and bipolar mother. Tatiana didn't buy into the enabler propaganda.

Clutching the phone, Sonny concentrated on rolling his words right down the middle. Steady and firm worked best whenever his boy was ranting. "Take it easy for a second. Come by the diner tomorrow. I've been traveling all day and could use some sleep. You could, too."

"No good. Too late for that," said Michael, dragging out the last syllable before recharging. "Dad? Dad?"

"I'm here."

"Meet me in an hour. At the place you took me last year for my birthday. You know the one, right?"

Sonny was moving as he answered. "Yeah, the joint with the stiff drinks." He tossed the phone and dashed to the closet. They'd agreed—had sworn to each other—that whenever either dropped the SOS line they were to rendezvous on Sonny's sailboat at the Boca Raton Marina.

He pulled on pants, shoes, and a windbreaker before reaching to the top shelf for his gun. The pistol's diminutive size and lack of registration were its main attributes. He tried hiding it in the small of his back, didn't like the feel, and settled for a jacket pocket.

Stepping from the closet, he looked up and saw the blue eyes of his girlfriend. If she'd observed the whole routine minus the gun, Sonny could have explained the mad scramble with a mostly true story about Michael needing quick cash. Except he was sure she caught a glimpse of the metal.

"What the hell is going on with you?" she asked, reaching for the drawstrings of her robe and cinching it tight. Tatiana wasn't a simpleton. She knew Sonny didn't make his money in the ministry or serving the poor. But a loaded gun in the middle of the night was new territory, a discomforting deviation from the norm. When Sonny reached for her hand, she snatched it back and stepped away.

"Don't start," he said.

Tatiana had spent her twenties in a succession of unhealthy relationships with immature, possessive men. Then she met Sonny and found herself wishing he cared more, that he held her tighter, that he didn't let her float so loose and free. "I like you," she said, wiping a tear from her cheek, "and we've got something good going. But I'm not sure I can handle that." Eyeing his pocket, she said, "Secrets are okay, and you don't know all mine. But some are too dark, and I'm worried that's what I just saw."

Dozens of women were sprinkled throughout Sonny's life. Most were pleasant, a few not so much. All were physically beautiful, and perhaps it was the open competition for their affections that lured him in. The courtships began with good intentions—six made it to an engagement ring, and three wore white down the center aisle—but whatever the genesis, none lasted longer than a few years. Three ended less than honorably, in explosions of bottled resentment, infidelity, or emotional manslaughter. Others died a slower death, like neglected fruit left too long on the vine. In his sixth decade, Sonny was tired of being damaged goods, incapable of giving and accepting all the elements of an evolved relationship. He wanted to push through, to outlast the low points, to be a couple that trusted in love and believed in its safety net.

Softer now, Sonny said, "What you saw, and me walking out the door, has nothing to do with us. Here's the truth. You could ask me to stay and I wouldn't. Tears, tantrums, the whole emotional routine—wouldn't matter. It's a dog deal, worst thing I've done to you. But that's the way it's going down. All I'm asking is for you to draw the line out and give me some room. You don't owe me that, but I'm still asking."

Tatiana knew her choices. A man with the motivation to load his pocket with a gun wasn't opening the floor for debate. The absoluteness of Sonny's decision was the known variable. She was the question mark, the one with the ability to pull back or push forward. Truth was, while she didn't know Sonny well enough to write his obituary's first paragraph, she'd never made him for a killer and still didn't. He was just a guy with a problem.

Tatiana stepped toward him, eyes up, making sure he had enough sense not to look away. If he'd acted put out or distracted she might have pushed him aside and made for the door, silk robe be damned. He didn't, which made her heart jump.

Wrapping her arms around his neck, she said, "Fly away, birdman. The cage door will be open when you get back."

18.

GUN BENEATH THE SEAT in case he got pulled over, Sonny turned right out of his building's underground garage and accelerated with a heavy foot. The initial plan was to arrive first, prepare the sailboat for a quick launch, and cover the parking lot in the event uninvited guests followed his son.

The radio was playing a Coltrane set he'd heard a thousand times. While jazz had been Sonny's thing since meeting the saxophonist during his Strawberry Mansion days, he didn't like tarnishing the artist with the night's black cloud. He tapped the row of preset stations for a different riff—one he didn't mind getting dirty—and found enough ads and soul-killing oldies to make him punch the OFF button with a closed fist.

Minus tunes, Michael and Tatiana's conversations replayed in his head, making him ache for two fingers of Scotch and five minutes to enjoy it. Without handy booze, his thoughts turned to the half-smoked joint hidden between Alabama and Alaska in his AAA map book. Might be just the thing to take the edge off. After a cop-peek left and right, he put the unlit roach between his lips, caught a glimpse of himself in the rearview mirror, called himself an asshole, and flicked it out the sunroof.

"Damn kid," he muttered, "the things I do for you." A lifetime of heart-breaking screw-ups and still Sonny was willing to stiff-arm a Russian beauty, speed around Boca Raton, and toss away perfectly good weed. When it came to motivating behavior, nothing ran on the same race-course as Catholic guilt. Sonny often wondered if he'd experienced a more normal childhood, if his role models weren't barflies from Bonnie's Whiskey Room, if he hadn't sailed away from so many wives, maybe he could have been a better father and his son a better man. Michael was the backyard rocket that began each flight with such promise and ended nose-down in the dirt, broken and battered. A friend once told Sonny he was missing the point. The issue was no longer who shot Michael. That was old news. The bigger deal was who was driving him to the hos-pital. That somebody was Sonny. Always had been.

Turning left into the marina's entrance, Sonny looped through the crushed-shell parking lot on high alert. He'd once heard an old-timer say *No coincidence, no story*, a maxim he'd since heeded. Boring was best. Good jobs weren't supposed to look like a game of pixie sticks.

The security shack was unoccupied after ten o'clock per the board of directors' efforts to cut costs. With favorable weather conditions, the lot was sprinkled with three dozen cars left by sailors out for the night or liv-ing full-time in the marina. Illumination from the thin-cut moon and single light pole was too dim to make out a man's face from twenty feet.

Sonny parked in the last row, a few spaces from the marina's dumpster. His bumper was tight against a hedge of forsythias, giving him an unob-structed view of the entrance, the storage shed, and most of the parked cars.

Sitting in the quiet, the devil part of him wished he hadn't tossed the roach. Whatever fraction of goodness was left over understood the de-pravity of smoking dope while rendezvousing with a struggling drug addict. As he reached for his door handle, a flash crossed his side mirror and cold steel filled his ear hole.

"Michael said you'd park over here. Guess he doesn't lie about every-thing." The voice had a diluted Latin accent, like a Puerto Rican who'd lived in Brooklyn for a couple of years before returning south.

Sonny moved his hands to the top of the steering wheel. From the pressure and the voice's distance, he figured the piece for a double-barrel shotgun, one of those sawed-off numbers with the custom handle. His first thought was that the weapon wasn't the typical choice for a stickup—an amateur hustle dominated by pocket pistols. Shotguns were the professional's alternative, a weapon that required less-than-perfect marksmanship without leaving behind forensically traceable ammunition.

"Why don't you lower that before it makes a mess of my Cadillac," said Sonny. Taking in the limited data points, he formulated his first theory of the night. "And tell my boy to come out of hiding."

"He said you'd be cool," said the gunman. "Two for two." He backed the barrel off Sonny's head and tapped the metal roof. When the first tap went unanswered, he followed with two more.

"Come on, man. You can't whistle?" Sonny rotated his chin a quarter turn. "Tell Michael to get over here. No need to chip my paint."

"Old dude with big onions. Dig it."

Sonny opened his door. He'd been set up for a reason, and it wasn't so his brains could fertilize the marina parking lot. "While we're waiting for Michael to get his back up, why don't you tell me who you are?"

The gunman lowered his shotgun to Sonny's knees. He was wearing a loose-fitting black shirt, and his dark hair was pulled into a thin, braided ponytail. A scar cut a bald strip across his left eyebrow. Clean-shaven with groomed sideburns and deep-set eyes, he had the type of face where a smile made all the difference. "The name is Cassir. C-A-S-S-I-R."

"That don't figure."

"What's that?"

"I had you for Puerto Rican or Dominican. *Cassir* sounds like an oil sheik."

"Cuban, if it matters."

It did to Sonny. He hadn't been fond of Cubans since a beautiful one with long legs left him for a younger man. "That your last name?"

"Far as you're concerned."

Sonny was stalling, trying to figure why his son hadn't surfaced. Injured or scared were the obvious choices. "Name like that, the way you look, I'm figuring there's a lot of ingredients in the sauce."

"Mom's from Cuba. I'm told Dad's got a little Moroccan and French Jew in him. You?"

"Always been free to choose."

Cassir nodded. "Here's how we're playing the next few minutes. You're being easy, so I'm lowering my gun. You don't think I'm shooting you anyway. Michael's going to come out and we're going to have a civilized conversation. Like real gentlemen."

"How much he into you for?"

"That's number one on the agenda."

With a hand up for Sonny to stay put, Cassir turned on his heel and disappeared behind the dumpster. Michael emerged out the other end, Cassir prodding his ass with the shotgun. Michael had his father's sturdy build and long arms. He also sported a looser belly, hair he couldn't keep out of his eyes, and the gleam of an addict accustomed to rescue.

"Say hi to your pops," said Cassir, shoving him hard between the shoulder blades.

From reflex, Sonny extended a steadying hand. When Michael regained his footing and opened his mouth, Sonny shook him off. The last thing he wanted was an apology or more lies.

"I told you I needed help," said Michael, ignoring the guidance. Sweat had soaked all four sides of his Tommy Bahama shirt, and his left eye was swollen. "When I called you in Philly, my time had run out. I didn't have a choice tonight."

"Enough of the family reunion," said Cassir, stroking his ponytail like a swimmer squeezing out the pool water. "Why don't we head to your sailboat? I'm thinking a big shot like you has some beer."

Sonny told them to keep their mouths shut until they got on board. It wasn't in anybody's interest to get the cops called, a distinct possibility with Cassir and his shotgun. "Leave it here," Sonny suggested, half serious. "You won't need it on the boat."

Cassir winked, shook his head, and flipped his chin for Sonny to take point. On the far side of the parking lot, the crushed shell gave way to a strip of grass and wide-planked stairs leading to the boat slips. A light breeze was blowing offshore, just enough to keep the lines and lanyards chirping like little frogs.

Passing a dozen slips, Sonny was glad he'd left the pistol under his car seat. Shooting time had expired, and the gun would be a distraction during the upcoming negotiation. Cassir was another in a long line of black market shysters Michael had burned, and since Michael was still alive, the next hour was all about the numbers.

Boarding the fifty-two-foot Hinckley Sou'wester, Sonny made sure everyone knew where to step before unlocking the cabin. He flipped on the lights, pulled three beers from the fridge, and set them in the middle of the galley table. Not keen on fueling Michael's high, he also didn't need the boy crashing or going red hot.

Cassir set the shotgun on the dining table so he could use his hands to sit and scoot around the semicircular bench. Once settled, he grabbed the nearest beer, twisted off the cap, and took a long pull. "Word is you were some kind of gangster back in the day."

Sonny waved off the notion like an old man disappointed in the brisket.

"Come on, don't be shy," said the gunman, wiping his mouth with the back of his hand. "You one of them rumrunners?"

Sonny turned on the stereo before taking an open seat at the table to Cassir's right. He wanted background noise in case any big-eared sailors wandered by. "All you need to know is I've been dealing with assholes since I was seven. Time will tell if you're the biggest. Haven't ruled it out yet."

Cassir finished his beer with another long pull and tossed the bottle against the partition above the fridge. The sound echoed in the tight quarters as shards exploded and rained down on the surrounding countertops. "How do you like that?"

Despite the ringing in his ears, Sonny refused to flinch or break eye contact. For him, the display was a predictable young-bull-versus-old-bull moment. All gunpowder, no shot. Fifty years earlier, he'd done it himself a few times. Wasn't all that effective then either. "I think you're overplaying the part. Less is more."

Cassir's shoulder shrug and smirk indicated he wasn't taking the critique too hard. He grabbed the shotgun and used its barrel to tap one of the two remaining beers. "What, you guys not thirsty?"

Michael had responded to the flying glass by dropping down and covering up. Hearing Cassir's question, he looked up, grinned, and returned to his feet with too much forgiving levity for the circumstance. Sickened at the need to please, Sonny handed him a beer and waved at the gunman to do what he wanted with the last one.

"Enough of this getting to know each other. How much does Mike owe?"

"Two hundred grand."

"Fuck sake."

Michael took the number's disclosure as his cue, pitching nonsense about a financing crunch at the dealership and how he really only needed one hundred as a bridge loan to cover a late summer shipment but with the vig and then the air-conditioning unit in the showroom blowing up, and property taxes and, well, it just got out of hand, you know?

Sonny listened with closed eyes, a defense mechanism to remove his son's face from the folly. "It's okay. None of that really matters right now. Let me handle this."

"Oh, yeah, I just thought—no, you're right. I get it, man." Michael took a drink to either camouflage or minimize the irrelevance, crossed his arms, and leaned against the galley sink.

His attention solely on Cassir, Sonny said, "So two hundred is the number?"

"Yeah."

"Then I don't know who's the bigger idiot—Mike for borrowing the money or you for providing it. What kind of shylock does business with a drug addict, and for that kind of dough?"

Cassir twisted so he'd have the room and angle to slid his left leg onto the bench. "That wasn't my call," he said, scratching a bug bite on his ankle. "I'm just the Repo Man. My guess—if you're asking—is that he posted you as collateral."

Watching for any interplay between them, Sonny tacked into the wind. "Here's one I've been wondering about. Call it a hunch or maybe paranoia. How do I know this isn't a shakedown? Half of me thinks you two are drug buddies and I'm the mark. That there wasn't ever a loan. No two hundred grand, just a couple coke heads hanging in a dance club tossing around ideas for easy money."

"Damn," said Cassir, laughing in Michael's direction. "How many times have you screwed this guy? I've seen abused ex-wives less jaded. A Cuban shows up with a shotgun in your back, and your own father—your flesh and blood—is thinking it's a game of charades. That's some dysfunctional-ass family shit right there, man." Turning back to Sonny, he said, "Straight up, this thing here between him and me—and now you—is what it is. If you insist it's a robbery and that I'm not owed two hundred grand, I'll walk Michael outside, shoot him in the face, dump his ass in the canal, and follow up with you in a couple weeks."

Knowing the conspiracy was unlikely, Sonny was still glad he'd raised the issue. There was advantage in showing the gunman nothing could or should be assumed during the confrontation, including the bond between father and son.

Cassir put the shotgun across his lap with the barrel aimed at Sonny before flipping it in the other direction. "Fact of the matter is I was chasing him down when you called. Wanted to explain his options."

"Which are?"

"The money he owes is long overdue. Last week Michael was given an opportunity to work down the debt. A good-faith gesture, you could say. There's a car that needs to be delivered to New Orleans every week. He picks it up in Miami, drives over to Louisiana, drops it with a close friend of mine, and takes a bus home. He does that a few times, there's value to the service."

Sonny watched his son slide back to the floor, his head beneath the sink's edge, and wondered if the move was anchored by shame or pretense. "Look at me," he said. When Michael cleared his hair, Sonny jabbed a finger in his direction, then tossed a thumb at Cassir. "Don't ever drive a car for this guy. Okay? You mule his garbage, you'll either die or spend the rest of your life in jail. Half of those runs are sacrificial lambs anyway, gifts to get the police believing they've solved the riddle."

"Well," said Cassir, tilting his bottle at a forty-five-degree angle, "he must have heard you whispering in his ear, because he no-showed the pickup. Now I've got a guy who owes me money, won't lift a finger to pay it off, and a car still needing a driver. So you know how these things work. I'm embarrassed, and my boss is all over my ass about my accounts. Says your boy Michael is a threat to my future with the company. Oh, man, this gets me stressed. All this anxiety starts building in my neck and shoulders. I mean, you know Mike, he's a lovable guy and all, but would you stake your career on him? I had no choice. Had to put him on the top of my honey-do list, make him a *priority*. But here's the funny thing. You're going to laugh. Technically, tonight is my night off. This whole thing was penciled in for tomorrow. Then I'm out with my girl, having a couple cocktails, trying to relax away from the office, and lookie lookie here comes the cookie. Michael sneaking past the bar and out the fire door."

A sailboat motoring down the canal paused the conversation. As they waited for it to pass, Cassir's attention shifted to a piece of teak trim above his head. "Must confess," he said, running a knuckle over the wood, "I've never been on a sailboat. Nice. More of a motorboater myself. Nothing too fancy, just something to take the kids out for a day trip or maybe some fishing. Boat like this, all the fancy rainforest wood, what's it cost?"

"You're not getting my boat."

"Oh, I didn't mean that. Wouldn't want you sacrificing so much to save Michael. Besides, I'm not sure it's yours to give. Hustlers rent, never own. I was just wondering out loud because this cabin smells like a Rolls-Royce. My guess? I'd say a list price of a million dollars. Leasing, I'd speculate your monthly nut, including slip and insurance, is probably twelve grand."

Sonny felt out of rhythm, his timing off. The typical modus of collectors was cracking skulls and leveraging fear. In most organizational hierarchies, they were a disposable asset harvested for their testosterone-fueled willingness to serve as both hammer and shield. To that point, Sonny half-expected Cassir to blast off Michael's hands in the parking lot just to set the minimum table bet. Yes, there was the bottle incident and Michael's swollen eye, but those were starting to look like low-cost props. While he didn't doubt Cassir's willingness to go rough, Sonny decided the man also had discretion and some skills on the verbal side of the ledger.

Palms up, Sonny said, "I need a whisky. I'd be happy to pour you one or grab another beer from the fridge." When Cassir answered by shaking what little was left in his bottle, Sonny slid out and stepped over his son's legs.

Returning, Sonny handed over the beer and raised his highball glass. "To good health."

Unsure of his host's sincerity, Cassir chortled half-raising his own brew. "No guarantees."

"Oh, I don't know. With the exception of that shotgun, you strike me as a man I can do business with. You've only got one scar on your face, which tells me you don't do much fighting. And that tells me you're smart enough to know dead men don't pay their bills."

Cassir rubbed his eyebrow. "This one here? That's not even from my day job."

"I've got one on my brow, too. Can't see it any more with the wrinkles. A prison guard wanted to kill me when I was a kid. Split me open on the sidewalk. You?"

"Spare the rod, spoil the child was my old man's favorite poem. This here," Cassir said, pointing to the rubbery stretch, "doesn't make his top ten. Knocked the hair clean off my eyebrow and he was all *hahaha, that's funny-ass shit*."

"Sounds like a sweetheart."

"Next day, his move was to come into my room, try convincing me his methods were making me a man. I'd nod and say, *Yeah, Dad, you're right. I get it*. Whole time though, in my head, I was like, *How does getting smacked around make you a man?* Doesn't matter. I got even. He was my first."

The meaning wasn't lost on Sonny. Michael—never one with sensitive antennae—didn't blink.

Sonny tossed back what remained in his glass, wondering what was worse—no dad or one using heavy hands to inflict pathological damage.

"How about your guy?"

Sonny's uneven brow said he didn't understand the question.

"Your guy, the prison guard—the one that bashed you when you were little. I've said what my scar gave rise to, now I'm asking about yours."

Sonny's easiest play was spinning a story about how he too had killed his tormentor, how he'd plotted revenge until he was strong enough to plunge a knife through the guard's belly. He could run that yarn out an hour, until Cassir drank his last beer and Michael passed out cold. But even if it'd been true, a dated story of violence retold by an old man achieved nothing. Every word in the negotiation had to count, like dollars tossed into a contested pot. Anyway, as far as Sonny was concerned, the truth was almost as good.

"He's Mike's godfather."

"Wait," said his son, suddenly awakened and engaged by the declaration. "You're talking about Uncle Dickie? I never knew he tried killing you."

Hating an empty glass at story time, Sonny quick-stepped to the bar and returned with the whisky bottle. "I was a street kid running loose, trying to find where I belonged. One morning, I lipped off to a prison guard on his way to work. Should have known better. Should have figured the guards used those minutes to get their minds right so they could survive shift work inside a penitentiary. Good lesson, though. Taught me to respect timing."

Cassir spoke up. "So this guard smacks your around—that's a long way from becoming *Uncle Dickie*."

"He busted my ribs and was two seconds from jawboning me on a stoop. Might have been lights out—I was a hundred pounds and he was every bit two fifty. Anyway, another fellow stepped in and saved me." Sonny took a sip, lost for a moment in the long-ago memory. Despite his recent visit, the streets of Philadelphia seemed so far away. "Back then, before they had lottery, we made money running numbers. Turns out, I had an aptitude for the occupation. A calling, you could say. The fellow who saved me had connections. He introduced me around and lined up a route. We doubled the business every year until we controlled numbers for half of Philadelphia. I was eighteen and moving more money than a bank truck. Whispers started up about competition and me being a target, so I hired the nastiest son of a bitch I knew to be my bodyguard."

"You're talking Dickie—that's so upside down, man," said Cassir, his face open to play up the enthusiasm.

Sonny nodded with a sheepish half-grin. "Yeah, a little unorthodox, but once Dickie came on board, I never got robbed or even hassled. Not once. And he wasn't such a bad guy. We ended up working side by side for twenty years. Point is, for the men I answered to, business was all that mattered. Not feelings, not vendettas, not some goofy code of revenge or retribution. Get paid and move on. Everything else is expensive horseshit. And they were right. Dickie was a million-dollar move. Those first moments meeting a man tell part of the story. The rest plays out over time."

Figuring they were paging toward the evening's last chapter, Sonny poured another snort and pushed the bottle in Cassir's direction. "You catch the name painted on the back?"

"This boat? Missed it."

"*Eastern State*," said Sonny. "That's the prison from my neighborhood. The one Dickie worked in."

Cassir hoisted the bottle to his lips and drank with level eyes. "I thought boats were supposed to be named after prostitutes or the broad who took your virginity."

"It's a reminder. Living near a prison, watching men delivered and released, all disoriented, you get pretty wise about the consequences of half-ass hustles. My take was do it right, with the proper people, or get out."

The room fell quiet, all three understanding the time had arrived to hash out their deal. Cassir spoke first. "Wish we'd met earlier, could've avoided a lot of aggravation. At this point on the calendar, not many options. You pay like Mike says you can, he gets a new lease on life. You can't—or won't—well, we don't need to imagine."

Sonny tapped the table to make his point. "When the money is passed, it's a blank slate. Like Dickie and me, there's no lingering animosity. Not friends, not enemies. We're business acquaintances with no grudges or festering wounds. I see you in a bar, I buy you a drink and compliment your girl. *Hey, Cassir, looking good, man. And your lady friend, what a knockout.*"

"But we're not talking you and me, are we?"

"Principles apply to all of us. Me and you, you and him. It'll take three days to get the money. Once Michael hands over the dough, you two separate with one absolute truth. Your doors are closed to him. No more loans, no nothing. He calls, you hang up. He begs, you get in touch with me. Under no circumstances do you loan him money again. Or supply drugs."

"Dope ain't my thing."

"That car heading to New Orleans full of citrus?"

Cassir smiled. "Okay, now it's my turn. I'm here to get paid and you're talking three days. Extensions aren't on the house."

"Screw your vig. It's two hundred grand."

"Not what I'm saying. Two hundred is still the number. The change is you're now party to the deal. You want us to be professionals? You want your boy having a clean slate? You want another three days? Fine, you're cosigning the paperwork."

"Me paying should be enough." Sonny was neither thrilled nor surprised with the demand. He'd have preferred to pay on the spot, but his Bielakowski money hadn't yet cleared.

"My dad had another favorite poem. It's one line. A cat like you'll dig it."

"Do tell."

"Paying ain't paid," said Cassir, bringing the shotgun back onto the table. "If you had the money on board, okay, we're not having this debate. But that's not your proposal. You want amnesty and time. Hell, you're lucky we're having this chat. If Michael didn't have you on the line when I saw him at the club, he'd be renting a locker from the coroner."

"Three days," said Sonny, rising from the table. The liquor was in full effect, making him question why he poured and drank with such gusto. Seeing his forty-year old son sitting on the floor, arms wrapped around his knees, concluded the mystery.

"Three days." Cassir slid off the cushioned bench, straightened his ponytail, and moved past Sonny toward the cabin exit. Two steps into the fresh air, he reconsidered and stuck his head back inside. "Michael, no hard feelings. Like your old man says, just business."

Michael picked his head up, looking for whoever called his name. A greenhorn cop peeking into his pupils could've spotted the backslide into another drug stupor. "Yeah, man, totally," he said, smiling and nodding as though nothing was lost on him. "We're good. All good, bro."

19.

THREE HOURS SLEEPING on the boat wasn't enough for Sonny's system to flush out all the booze and grief.

He awoke at sunrise, still in his clothes, with his head in a hangover flight pattern. Marina personnel were already washing the adjacent sailboat, bitching about their boss and debating why women picked assholes over nice guys. The squeaky-voiced worker with the bucket and brush admitted he'd chase hot ass too if he was born good-looking instead of smart. His partner, the one with the spray hose and fat ankles, said he didn't think he was all that bright and proved it by squirting him in the crotch.

The previous night had ended with a disappointing sequence. After Cassir's departure, Sonny poured a nightcap and took a seat next to his son. He wanted an honest exchange, maybe a connection if Michael sobered up enough to recognize what they'd achieved. All he got was tasteless whisky and a rant about the federal government controlling the cocaine trade. Tossing a pillow and blanket in his son's direction, Sonny tried recalling if he'd ever known anyone so casual about dying. He fell asleep without a close second.

Next morning, during the thirty-minute ride to Michael's house, both stayed inside their own heads until passing a McDonald's. Michael gave a *whoa* and asked about McMuffins and coffee. Sonny lied, saying he didn't have any cash. When Michael didn't make a move to check his own wallet, that, as they say, was that.

Turning into Michael's neighborhood, Sonny said he'd call when the money was ready. He made clear Michael was handling the delivery because he'd had enough of the shotgun-in-the-face routine. Michael shrugged, saying he assumed that was the case. In the driveway, engine running, Sonny said, "I should come in, say hello to Holly and Mickey."

As though he hadn't heard, Michael stepped out and picked up the morning paper a few feet down the drive. Returning to the open door, sweat already darkening his hairline, he said, "Not home."

Could have been a dozen reasons why Sonny's daughter-in-law and grandson weren't home. Little Mickey had baseball practice, or they were spending the day at the beach, or mommy and son were at a classmate's birthday party. But Sonny knew none of those was the answer. "Ah shit, Michael."

"Gone a week. She packed up while I was at work. Took all the couches and beds, left the cat and a note saying they were moving to Pittsburgh. She has a sister up there that hates me. Won't answer when I call."

Sonny tapped the steering wheel and nodded, taking his time with the update. Truth was, he liked Holly and loved the boy and had no doubt they were better off. Hell, a homeless shelter and food stamps was a better life than hanging their hopes on his son. He also knew Michael was waiting for him to say Holly had no right taking Mickey and he should get a lawyer. All his deadbeat friends were surely chirping that load, blaming the victims for breaking free. But Sonny didn't believe it for a second and wasn't going to encourage the fantasy. Michael was an arsonist when it came to burning bridges, so tough shit for being on the wrong side of the river.

"Get your life together."

"I'm trying."

Sonny dipped his head, his voice following the lead. "For an addict, there's no room for *try*. That's a tax on all the people around you. Me, your wife, that sweet kid of yours. Not doing is better than *trying*. At least we'll have our expectations set. Holly and Mickey can make a life in Pittsburgh. I can stop guilting myself into a heart attack. If you want the drugs, if that's your heaven, go curl up in some juice house and melt your brain."

Michael wiped a forehead of moisture into his hair. "I'm checking into a facility. As soon as this Cassir thing is off my back, I'm getting clean. This is rock bottom. I'm there, Dad. Honest to Christ. I can't run anymore. I can't come home to an empty house. You get me the money, I'll drop it off and head straight for ninety days and sober living. You won't hear from me for a bit, until I get out and back on my feet."

Sonny reached for his son's hand. Maybe it was the lack of sleep or hangover or getting tapped for two hundred grand, but the emotion welled up. "I love you, kid . . . you know that, probably more than anything I've ever loved in my life. Me and you, it's obvious we're the same kind of cookie, so goddamn obsessive. Difference is, I'm addicted to the action, to piecing together my hustles. My neurosis requires a clear head. You're addicted to the off-switch, doping so you can tune out the noise. You need help going your way. I hope you find it this time. I really do."

As Michael returned his father's grip and leaned in for a hug, Sonny didn't much care if it was real or another move in the addict's playbook. The ten seconds of connection trumped any explanation.

Both pulled away sniffling. Michael gave his father a smile, closed his eyes, and tilted his face into the morning sun. "Going to be a beautiful day."

"Yeah, it's a pretty one. You should go fishing. Relax a little." Sonny hoped his son would hold the pose. He was watching his little beach boy again, the blondie who loved kites and pillow fights and was too kind to trap lightning bugs in a jar.

Michael opened his eyes, tapped the Cadillac's hood, and headed up the drive. He didn't look back until he'd unlocked the front door. By that time, his father was halfway down the block.

Sonny stuck to side streets, not wanting the noise or competition of the interstate. The rhythm of repeating low-slung apartment buildings focused his mind on Newton's Third Law of Motion—all actions, regardless of intent, have equal and opposite reactions. Not that Michael much cared, but Sonny's two hundred grand to Cassir wasn't a victimless outlay. Proceeds from the Bielakowski deal were just enough to cover his own gambling issues and keep water under the boat. Michael's bills had doubled his commitments so that two-thirds of the take was allocated before his suitcase was unpacked. Late summer was looking like tuna sandwiches and afternoons at the public library. *Oh, screw it,* he thought. He'd been worse off a dozen times.

Six blocks from his high-rise condo, he picked up croissants and nonfat lattes from Tatiana's favorite faux-French bakery. Sonny found it comforting to do nice things for her, especially when she was asleep in his bed. At home he slid his key into the front door, snuck into the kitchen, stashed the pistol, and put the croissants on a plate. Taking a seat at the breakfast table, he sipped a latte and started in on his daily stack of newspapers, beginning with *The New York Times.*

From behind his back he heard Tatiana whisper, "Morning." She was leaning against the kitchen doorway, sleep in her eyes, wearing the same robe. "Can't believe you're awake."

Sonny peered over his tortoiseshell reading glasses. "If you hoot with the owls, you've got to soar with the eagles, so says one of my ex-mother-in-laws."

"Everything okay?"

"Not for the three men I killed. We leave for Cuba within the hour. And that's the good news."

"Just three?" she said, wrapping a hand around the back of his neck and kissing his cheek. "I missed you. I was worried."

"That's why I bought the croissants."

She took the chair to his right and started pulling apart her pastry the way beautiful women dismantle their food. "If you want to talk, I know that's not our way, but I'm a good listener."

"I got you a latte." Sonny retrieved the drink, taking a moment to rub her shoulders before retaking his seat. It wasn't that he didn't want to share with her, per se. He just didn't talk business with any of his women.

She took the cup in both hands and pulled her heels onto the chair's edge. "Is Michael okay?"

"You're a smart one. Got me figured."

"Not hard," she said, taking a sip. "After you left, I started thinking about what would get you hopping out of our bed. It had never happened before. Should have figured it was Michael."

"It was him. I'd like to say it was a false alarm because I didn't need the gun, but there was a negotiation with a man who likes Michael less than you do. Everyone walked away with all their fingers, toes, and teeth, which was a success given the disagreement's launch point."

Tatiana started in on the second half of her croissant, offering Sonny a piece. "You smell like booze. I'm guessing Michael isn't clean and sober at the moment."

"We were on the boat. Michael showed up high and I wanted the other guy thinking I was getting loose. Mission accomplished. Probably didn't need the last two. Woke up this morning, dropped Michael off, he said he was going to rehab, and now I'm home with you."

"Rehab?" she said, her head coming forward. "You buying it?"

"Literally."

"Wait, what?"

Sonny picked up the paper. "Every few years, I'm gifted thirty minutes to imagine he's back on track. Today's window came at a record setting cost, so let me enjoy. I'm no dummy with the odds, but I also like being a believer. It suits my worldview. Otherwise, what's the point of the long play?" The question was delivered with a *we're done talking* wink and half smile.

Slapping at his paper, Tatiana said she was taking a shower. "I'm just glad everything turned out okay."

Sonny refolded the paper along its machined creases. "You want to take the boat out today? Looking like a nice breeze. Just me and you, what do you say? I'll have the marina deliver some food, and there's still wine from last time."

While Tatiana was doing her best to catch the sailing bug, she couldn't make the connection. It just seemed like a bunch of goddamn work and wasted time. The lines plus all the different sails and labor to *kinda* go in the right direction. What was the point when the cruisers and cigarette boats whipped into whatever hot spots they wanted for drinks and dinner? Onboard, Sonny waxed poetic about the bond between sailor, boat, water, and weather. The only part Tatiana bought into was the passion. All the accessories and philosophies were a lost cause. "I was going to grab a workout and meet some girlfriends for drinks. Casual afternoon and maybe dinner in South Beach. You can come—would be sweet having you with us."

"Have fun with the girls. I'll catch up on my reading, run some errands. Maybe I'll go out solo. Been thinking this might be my last year with *Eastern State*. Getting to be a handful."

Tatiana knew silence was often the most effective advocacy with men. They'd float trial balloons and wait for women to shoot them down in hopes of being proven right. She'd lie low, let the boat issue play itself out. "Enjoy the day. I'll have my phone if you change your mind."

"You coming back here tonight?"

"Sure, baby," she said, walking away. "As long as you swear to spend the whole night under the blankets."

Sonny returned to the paper. As a practical matter, the headlines and big issues never held much interest. His moneymakers were the side stories, single columns, and asides devoted to a three percent rise in a nowhere state's land prices, or which lobbyist was seen eating with what congressman. Enjoying the latte's caffeine surge, he thumbed page after page until he reached the Business Day section and stopped cold on a below-the-fold article.

He read the words twice before soft-stepping into the bedroom to confirm the shower was running and the bathroom door closed. Grabbing the cordless phone, Sonny headed for the balcony and dialed a number he used three or four times a year.

"Bielakowski's," said a female voice in the deep part of the register. It was a curious habit how some Northeast Philly women adopted the husky, dulled speech patterns of their men. "What can I do for ya?"

"Anton working today?"

"He's in the office. You want me to get him?"

"No," said Sonny. "When we hang up, go straight back and tell him his Florida friend wants a call. You got that? Quick with the message, now. He'll want to know."

Sonny stuck his head inside to double-check on Tatiana. She was partial to half hour showers, which usually drove him nuts but was fine under the circumstances. Anton Bielakowski's system for callbacks took anywhere between twenty seconds and ten minutes. While not certain, Sonny figured his friend used pirated lines spliced into the connections of residential neighbors, or he traveled a circuit of nearby pay phones.

Sonny, rereading the article a third time, jumped at his ringtone. "I'm here."

"Too late for a renegotiation and too early for a Merry Christmas," said Anton, no hint in the background as to his location. "My gut says you've found something in the paper."

Despite whatever precautions his friend had taken, Sonny was hesitant. No sense helping the government if they'd bypassed the safeguards. "At our meeting in Philly, that third deal I mentioned, you remember? Like the old days down at the docks?"

"Yes, I recall."

"Nothing certain. But if you have the chance, wouldn't hurt putting out some feelers. You'll need a significant buyer with a particular résumé. The product will be unique and very, very profitable. We're not talking televisions or toasters."

"Nobody is listening. Speak."

"You sure?"

"Goddamn it, Sonny—"

"Viagra."

A pause long enough to cover two full breaths. "I do not understand."

Evoking a hospital bedside scene, Sonny slowed his words and increased the volume. "It's a medicine called Viagra. Starts with a V. A pill for men who can't get it up. Makes your dick hard."

"Don't shout," said the sausage maker, tightening his grip on the phone.

"I hear you fine. Okay, now, these pills, do they make you high, too? That's not for me. Don't waste my time with drugs."

"Not high, just hard."

Another pause. "Hard? That's it?"

"Yes."

"Longer, too, or no?"

Sonny considered whether Anton was slipping or screwing around. "It's a medicine, not plant food. Viagra makes your dick sturdy enough to withstand a knife attack, just like you were eighteen again."

"How come I've never heard of this?"

"Because you're old and because it's still unavailable, but today's paper says the government is fast-tracking the approval process. For a timeline, the pills could hit pharmacies before our next meeting. They'll require a prescription."

"Stupid politicians," said Anton. "You've got to humiliate yourself with a doctor before getting help? How is it anybody's business what happens between a husband and wife?"

"Can we skip a debate where neither disagrees? For us, the prescription is a good thing. Take it from me, men hate going to the doctor to talk about sexual problems. It's embarrassing as hell. But if I can work out the supply problem, we'll be the alternative. Forget the doctor and his prescription pad."

Anton mumbled, "I'll make some calls."

Sonny expected a few follow-up questions. When silence ensued, he told Anton not to hang up.

"I'm still here."

"Don't underestimate the opportunity. You remember how many dresses fit in a truck trailer? We're talking pills. And imagine what a guy who hasn't been banging for five years would pay for a go between the sheets."

Anton's laugh filled the phone line. "Sonny, you got a way about you, always the heat merchant. The consistency is a good thing. But heat is just a starting point—how strong you feeling this? Government approves and the pills are out—you committed to an immediate go?"

"Something less. Still too many variables. Right now, consider me a heist liker, not a heist lover. Get a buyer and price first."

"Fair enough. We'll play it loose. Now, for the money, you want back-end action or payment up front?"

"Undecided." Sonny's personal balance sheet suddenly had growing debits. Despite his best intentions, the last twelve hours with Cassir and Michael even had him revisiting the whole notion of a family mausoleum. Nothing like a shotgun in the ear to get someone deep thinking about the big sleep. "I might want an ownership interest, or maybe a role in procurement. I don't know yet."

"Hands on?"

"Yeah. Maybe."

Anton wasn't done laughing. "Unretiring? Now don't go forgetting your dance in the grocery story. Remember? The oranges and ice pick and three weeks in the hospital?"

"Yeah, well, dishwasher, roof, and furnace all went out and the kids need new shoes. You know the story."

Anton figured Michael had reemerged. While Sonny never blamed his son, Michael's shortcomings were usually why Sonny chased scores beyond the two or three ideas he sold. Made him grateful for Marcek. "Fair enough. Your gig, you make the call. Stay in touch, and I'll get things on my end tuned up."

"Hold on." Sonny paused. "Everything else okay?"

"Why? What have you been hearing down there?"

20.

IN BIELAKOWSKI'S PHILADELPHIA, the word *ally* was a term of art, an elusive commodity that fluctuated in cost, quality, and availability. Explicit in the definition was a mutually beneficial collaboration. Implicit was an openness that invited disease.

Bielakowski believed in the second of the two. He led Port Richmond as though alliances were confessions of weakness, aiming points for opponents and rivals. Criminal organizations didn't fail because of investigative genius, the coordinated efforts of a frustrated community, or the manpower of the federal government. While those groups contributed to the attacks, they seldom initiated the spark. Most challenges started closer in, usually by those sharing your bottle and bread.

Throughout his tenure in Port Richmond, Bielakowski had kept his arms in tight, only extending when shielded by layers of deniability. The South Philly Italians were once much the same. They transacted business with third parties but never went all in with factions not bound by *omertà*. The passing of time and the Americanization of their family changed that tradition. Proof was Raymond Rea's alliance with the War Boys— a partnership that, before his reign, had been rejected for forty years.

The War Boys were a South Philly motorcycle outfit founded by soldiers returning home from World War II and Korea. Seeking the same camaraderie and adrenaline they'd experienced in foxholes, the ex-soldiers gathered in neighborhood garages to drink and build motorcycles. As their numbers increased, weekly races were organized, and soon a "social club" was formed, with a warehouse headquarters, elected leadership, and a patch to identify membership. Since almost all attendees had fought in Europe, the Pacific Islands, or the Manchurian Peninsula, the club's name came easily enough.

During those times, with most of the War Boys' membership employed and its collective energies focused on building bikes, the club's criminal activity was limited to fights with rival clubs and the occasional robbery. Only one homicide in fifteen years was associated with the War Boys, and that occurred when a South Jersey biker came over the bridge flaunting colors. A patrolman found him stuffed headfirst down a Passyunk Avenue manhole with his boots sticking two feet above street level.

This relative innocence lasted until the counterculture movement of the sixties, when the bikers discovered the business of marijuana and acid. While they were initially content with providing muscle and protection, all that changed when a club member came home from Vietnam convinced the War Boys' future was in distribution and sales. His name was Chuck Trella, and under his watch the bikers rose from neighborhood tough guys to major players in the Philadelphia scene. Chuck Trella's unexpected death in 1978 allowed the Puerto Ricans to front-run cocaine, but the War Boys regained the lead once Chuck Trella Jr. came home from the Gulf with the next big thing—methamphetamines.

Like his father before him, Trella Junior had a gift for recognizing value within a supply chain. He realized meth's sweet spot was anything outside street sales. Sure, local dealers still made dough, but heroin and cocaine proved management grabbed the real money. Applying those lessons to meth, Trella Junior was determined to control raw materials and large-scale manufacturing. The rest could be sold off or farmed out.

For that type of business relationship, Trella Junior looked to his cousin's cousin Raymond Rea, who willingly took on as much meth as the War Boys could cook. The Italians, while not dominant in the drug trade, maintained outlets in their own neighborhood and the slums of

West and North Philly. As long as each party stuck to what they did best and didn't get greedy, the match worked.

Given events of the last few weeks, Bielakowski conceded this alliance was a viable threat. One of his men was killed, and a second escaped an ambush inside a nightclub bathroom. The Poles doubled down, going after Rea's top-producing bookie during the World Series. Early one morning, Bielakowski's man delivered two dozen roses to the bookie's girlfriend. When she opened the door, the assassin said her boyfriend had sent the flowers and would she like to return the gesture? *Just tell me where he is and what you want delivered.* Forty-five minutes later, the bookie—clutching his morning Danish and the girlfriend's thong—exchanged his betting book for three new holes in his head.

Bielakowski wasn't rattled by the escalation or hesitant to see it through. He'd fill every South Philly funeral home with caskets, weeping wives, and hysterical goombahs if that's what was required. Prudent and resourceful, he had the financial resources to survive a prolonged disruption and the men—many anxious to establish their own legacies—to go blow for blow. Yet, despite these advantages, Bielakowski wasn't naive enough to underestimate the task. Balance of power was a fickle force and could tip if an undeclared third party joined the fracas.

To protect his flanks, Bielakowski needed reassurance from the one outfit that could make him an underdog. It was well known the Italians steered wide of the Armenians, which left the Russians and their leader, Kolya Drobyshev. Among his own people, Drobyshev was a *vor v zakone*, a criminal's criminal forbidden from cooperating with authorities. Both of Drobyshev's knees were tattooed with black stars to symbolize his rank, adherence to the Thieves' Code, and his determination to bow to no man.

In the Philadelphia underworld, little was known of Drobyshev's homeland background other than he'd survived the White Swan, a Solikamsk prison notorious for breaking the criminal elite. Even though the White Swan's guards were themselves masters of torture, they preferred other prisoners do their bidding. A favorite technique was the cell press, which involved two dozen prisoners in a twenty-by-twenty cell initiating the newest inmate. In such conditions, sleep was impossible, fear a constant companion, and rapes a daily threat. Drobyshev did two years in the White Swan and nine years in the Central Prison zone. He emerged weaker in body but stronger in conviction, knowing the state and its instruments could not break him.

Once freed, Drobyshev immigrated to the United States, where he—along with thousands of other Russians—settled twenty miles north of Port Richmond in the bedroom communities of Lower Bucks County. Drobyshev wasted no time building his criminal network, shying away from traditional operations like extortion and taxes in favor of higher-level financial scams and cargo heists. His one old-school indulgence was a burgeoning gambling operation that started with two customers in a small tavern and spread into Trenton, Allentown, and Scranton. The first time Drobyshev crossed paths with Bielakowski was when the Russian needed an overage house for heavy betting action coming in on a St. Joe's basketball game. Introduced by a trusted intermediary, Bielakowski agreed to back the bets for a high—though fair—fee. Despite the bet never hitting, both men were pleased with the transaction and agreed to consider each other's services again in the future.

The men's second interaction would not be for another six months, when a Russian girl was victimized by a brutal gang initiation. Carjacked a block off La Salle's campus, the college girl was forced to drive at knife point to an abandoned lot where she was assaulted, cut, and left for dead. She was found the next day, alive and scarred for life. The girl's family called Drobyshev from the hospital. *Get them, Kolya. Hunt them, let them know they cannot do this to a Russian.*

He agreed, knowing he had neither the resources nor the connections to make good. Killing the men was not the crucible. Drobyshev could mount their heads on spikes without a single haunting nightmare. The problem, for all his abilities, was that Drobyshev was a pale-skinned foreigner being asked to track down black teenagers in a ghetto of two hundred thousand black teenagers. Such a task demanded nuance, well-placed intelligence, and a lifetime of connections. Drobyshev knew of only one man who might possess these resources while also comprehending the unreasonable expectations of fellow countrymen.

To discuss the girl, Bielakowski met Drobyshev in his shop, where the running saw blades and mixers could camouflage their conversation. The Russian explained his predicament and the burden he bore. The sausage maker let him carry the conversation, nodding along as he kept his guest's mug full of hot coffee and rich cream. When the Russian finished, Bielakowski condemned the tragedy and agreed the young men should be held accountable. He loathed senseless violence and could think of no greater example than the plundering of a fresh-faced college woman.

Although willing to assist, Bielakowski explained he'd have no more success entering the ghettos than the Russians. Unleashing a hundred men wouldn't matter. The only option was shadowing the police and their investigation. When the Russian conceded he had no such connections, Bielakowski said he had many friends in Philadelphia and, if he spent some time on the matter, could probably think of one or two who worked in the investigating police district. *Keep a team and your phone ready,* he instructed Drobyshev; *you'll have little time when I call.* The price of the favor was never mentioned, though both men understood such services were not free.

Two weeks later, the front page of the *Daily News* carried pictures of three dead black teenagers slumped over one another on the basement floor of an abandoned North Philadelphia row home. No mention was made of the Russian girl's necklace in one of the men's pockets or of her repainted car parked out front.

It was this history that Bielakowski now relied upon as he reached out to Drobyshev. The debt of the Russian girl was still unpaid, and Bielakowski wondered what that bought him in today's dollars. Since that time, the Russian had added to his power and, while respectful of his Polish neighbors, wasn't shy about flexing his muscle whenever their business interests overlapped.

The two leaders met at a downtown Russian bathhouse that was once a private athletic club for Main Line Protestants with *Mayflower* lineage. New ownership limited access to a handful of Russian men bearing the tattoos of their homeland's prison system. The facility was an anonymous doorway midway down an alley off Walnut Street. The moment

Bielakowski rang the buzzer, the door electronically opened. A dozen feet inside stood a middle-aged man of average size in a black suit and white shirt. He waved for Bielakowski to approach and searched him without a word. Satisfied, he escorted Bielakowski to the locker room, presenting him with plush towels, a white robe, and shower shoes. Before returning to his station, the man said that Mr. Drobyshev could be found in the steam room at the end of the hall.

Stripped naked, Bielakowski chuckled at what it took to protect Port Richmond. He wrapped one towel around his waist, draped another over his neck, and left the sandals alone.

With a quick tap of his wedding band on the glass door, Bielakowski entered the designated steam room. The heat was intense though not unbearable, and the smell of mint was profound. On the top tiled shelf, in the corner, sat a single man. For the first time, Bielakowski saw the blackened knees he'd heard about. He remained motionless, waiting to be invited forward. A long moment passed before he spoke out. "Don't be rude, Kolya. I'm an old man. Invite me to sit."

"Yes, of course," said Drobyshev, snapping forward as if he'd been asleep. Perhaps it was his prison stay that accounted for his thinness. His cheekbones were high and wide; his nose marked by several skin piercing breaks. His blond hair, coarse like an animal's, had not yet begun to recede. "The steam has that effect on me. I get lost in my thoughts. I saw you, but my brain was convinced we were in a dream. My apologies. Of course, please, come sit."

Bielakowski was not shy about asking the Russian for his hand. He explained that tall steps were his hell and without assistance he couldn't climb to the top shelf. When the Russian's arm and upper chest pierced the steam, Bielakowski saw they were also marked by tattoos, some beautifully done, others scribbled by an amateur or Drobyshev himself. Once seated, he pointed to a line of writing beneath the Russian's collarbone. "Let me translate. I know a bit of your language."

"Of course," said the Russian, wiping sweat off the markings.

"I believe it says *Life will teach me to laugh through tears.*"

"Excellent, Anton. I'm both impressed and sorry to say I don't know a word of Polish."

"Too young for the war?"

"I was a youth, so no, I never visited your countryside."

Bielakowski turned his head and leaned forward for a better look at the Russian's art. "No war?"

"No."

"You have Lenin and Stalin on your chest. Knees blackened to show your defiance and yet leaders painted on your chest."

"You'll like the story."

Bielakowski nodded, though not in agreement. The obvious disconnect confirmed everything he understood of Russian duality. From his experience, they were vicious and conniving poets.

Drobyshev wiped the sweat from his face. "I was seventeen the first time I entered the Central Prison. In those days, the Communists were running the show, and it was not uncommon for them to line up a row of prisoners and shoot them dead. No reason, just target practice or because they needed the room. One day, after they'd ordered another firing line, they forced the prisoners to strip naked so their clothes could be reused. One of those men had Stalin tattooed on his heart. Why? Why, of all the things in this world, would he have that on his body? We never knew, just fate, or dumb luck. Well, this caused the soldiers all sorts of headache. Who wanted to shoot a likeness of the Great Leader? The soldiers just stood there, shaking their heads, looking for someone to tell them what to do. After a few moments, three fought for the right to pull the prisoner from the line. We couldn't believe our eyes, the only man in the Soviet Union ever saved by Stalin. But the other prisoners? The ones with birds or knives or baby Jesus on their bodies? All dead, shot a couple extra times because the guards were so cross. For the next week, we were lined up asshole to elbow getting that marking. I impressed everyone by including Lenin's portrait."

The men shared a laugh before the Russian walked through a few more of his tattoos. He said his life story was marked on his skin and any

Russian prisoner could read him like a book. They'd know his crimes, how many terms he'd served, and where.

"Which one for the White Swan?"

It was the Russian's turn to look sideways. "People talk too much. There are no secrets anymore."

"There's no shame in surviving."

"That's not what I'd call my experience. I died and was reborn. They had a cell they could flood, like a bathtub or swimming pool. A prisoner would go in and they'd fill the cell to his neck. Couldn't sit, couldn't sleep, couldn't eat. Most men drowned in forty-eight hours. Three times I lasted twice that amount of time. I think they just decided I couldn't be killed. Or if I was killed, no one would have me."

Bielakowski pointed to an angel on the Russian's right forearm. "That is the one, the one you took for making it out."

Drobyshev flexed the forearm before rolling his left arm across his chest. It was marked with the Grim Reaper and his sickle. "Yes, the angel is for me. This," he said, tapping his left forearm, "is for the prison guards who tortured me. Their dumb luck that Communism fell and money started to matter. They all died for less than it cost to buy a truck of chickens."

Both men fell silent. The steam valve had closed, and the air was thinning. Bielakowski noticed an ice chest by the door and wondered if it contained water. The heat had not yet overwhelmed him, but he wanted to proceed with care. Just as he was about to inquire, the Russian rose without speaking and retrieved two bottles.

"I recently saw a tattoo," said Bielakowski, thinking of the federal agent in the warehouse. "It was black, like yours. But something I've noticed with the Russians is another color no one else can match."

"In my day, tattoos were forbidden, so we had to improvise. For ink, we used our boot heels. We'd sand them down into a fine dust, strain it through a cloth, and mix with urine. That's where the blue comes from."

"Piss?"

Drobyshev shrugged. "I never knew why. We had water and tea, but I guess those didn't provide the right chemistry. The artist mixed the dust and piss and then used a sharpened guitar string for a needle. It's prehistoric, but you can see how some of the men mastered the art. Others, not so much."

"You Russians are willing to endure more than most."

Drobyshev took a long drink from his water. "Let's talk business," he said, capping the bottle. "I prefer my conversations here in the steam where no one else can listen. My fear is you won't last much longer."

Bielakowski drank half his water and poured the rest over his bald head. "You've heard of my issues with the Italians?"

"Of course. Nasty business."

"Even with the bikers, Rea has overreached. My men are ready."

"It's an interesting puzzle," said Drobyshev, as though he were participating in a theoretical debate. "Rea and the bikers are a formidable attacking party. Assuming they don't know much Russian history, I doubt they understand how difficult that can be. Rea sees retreat as surrender. You and I both know pulling back and letting the enemy come can be quite successful."

Bielakowski said, "Two reasons for me calling you. The first is financial, which we'll get to. The second is your role in the current dispute. I can see Rea courting your assistance. Him from the south, you from the north—that could pose problems for me."

The Russian shrugged. "I hardly know the man."

Bielakowski remained silent. He'd said everything he wanted. Now it was Drobyshev's turn to play a hand.

"The Italians did call on me," said Drobyshev, his head back against the tiled wall, "but of course you already suspected this. The offer was as you imagined—we join forces and split the treasure. I declined."

Bielakowski asked if the good turn was due, in part, to the Russian girl.

"If only I was so noble. What is gained by my participation? What's achieved now that can't wait until you two soften each other up? And if it goes fifteen rounds, I'll be able to push over the winner with a feather."

"You or him, Port Richmond stays the same. We'll fight."

Drobyshev paired a raised hand with a long blink. "No need. Like with a cornered badger, I know what Port Richmond offers. Between friends, I'd much rather expend my energies acquiring certain parts of the Italian's operations. The exact ones we needn't discuss."

Bielakowski leaned forward and pulled the towel over his head. He didn't know where Rea was, or what he might be doing, but the Italian leader surely wasn't achieving such a victory. Keeping the Russians on the sidelines was significant, the type of move that transformed battles into winning campaigns. Reemerging from his private thoughts, the sausage maker said, "I am ready to talk about my financial proposals."

"Before you do, there's one more thing."

Bielakowski waved him on, wanting to finish before the steam returned.

"The biker alliance may not be as strong as believed," said the Russian. "While they are from the same neighborhood and share some overlap, the tie that binds is meth. They have no allegiance outside the drugs. As you know, the Italians are pushing what the bikers are producing. That's a good deal for the War Boys and about thirty bucks an hour for the poor shits on the street. My people tell me Rea isn't happy and is looking to go end to end."

"What does he need?"

"Pseudoephedrine. It's an ingredient in cold-medicine pills. They have ways of extracting it to make meth. If Rea gets enough, he won't need his partners anymore."

Bielakowski paused. "If it's on the shelves, what's the problem? Go buy all the medicine, no?"

"You need a lot of those little pills. The War Boys have a connection. Rea is looking for his own. Not easy, though. He needs to do it without the bikers catching wind. They find out, he's tied to a tiger."

"Distract the bikers and undercut their business. Not new, but effective."

With so little respect for his Mediterranean rivals, Drobyshev scoffed at the compliment. "Rea makes moves like a child. He partners with idiots so they can't foresee the betrayal. If you and I can't outmaneuver him, we don't deserve our positions." Taking a moment to settle himself, he said, "Enough. Let's move on."

Since his meeting with Sonny Bonhardt, Bielakowski had been struggling with the telecom scam. The mixed martial arts proposal was a go, but siphoning from the Universal Service Fund was a heavier lift. While Bielakowski wasn't sure he wanted to drive such a far-reaching venture, he now had an alternative with a competent partner he needed to keep happy.

Weighing the benefits against his aversion to alliances, Bielakowski didn't see a real choice. He paused to organize his thoughts, then provided Drobyshev with a high-level sketch of the USF hustle. Once finished, he said, "I have a file that provides all the details including which phone companies to target, rate of return, the lobbyists in the respective states, the flow of payments from the Universal Service Fund to those companies, and the legal protocol for buying the targets. My plan, your people. We split down the middle. Should be between three and six million a year for two or three years. Then we roll down the blinds and count our take. My one condition is that only you know my name. I will extend the same courtesy. Unless your men bumble, blame won't find its way around the patsy management."

"Of course I'm interested," said the Russian. Opportunities in America never ceased to amaze him. Who'd ever heard of a government paying millions of dollars to tiny companies anyone could buy? For a man who had survived years on watery soup and maggoty bread, such a notion was decadent and absurd and deserving of abuse. "I agree to your conditions. I'd also like to buy an option on your idea man. Understand, Anton, I'd never wish you ill health, but you're not going to live forever. If your idea man is willing to work for another organization, I'd like the opportunity."

Bielakowski often wondered what Sonny would do upon his passing, whether he'd align with one primary partner or go the free-agent route. While he hoped his old friend would continue with his son, it was difficult predicting either man's priorities. "He goes his own way, same as ever. When I die, if he sells to you, that's his call."

Drobyshev blinked and shrugged his shoulders, as if the answer didn't matter because he'd handle the situation his own way.

For Bielakowski, the Russian's reaction confirmed why he'd sent Marcek to Florida. Sonny and his son would be targeted before his fingers grew cold and stiff. The stronger their relationship, the safer they'd be. "There's something else, not for today, but it could happen fast. As you know, drugs hold no interest for me."

"Yes, I have neither forgotten nor come around to your way of thinking."

Why others held so fast to the necessity of drugs was a mystery to Bielakowski. Without them, he'd avoided prison and run a successful, profitable family for forty years. Those who trafficked in narcotics either died or were traded in for plea deals. "The opportunity is not a street drug. It's called Viagra."

Before the Pole could finish his pronunciation, the Russian interrupted. "I'll take them all. Ten bucks a pill. When will you know?"

The steam started again, filling the room with a cloud. Without a word, Drobyshev rose, stepped down, and turned to assist his guest. As they shuffled together across the slick tile floor, Bielakowski had to raise his voice above the steam. "Fifteen. You'll be the only buyer, and I don't know the count, so you'll need a piggy bank. We deliver, you pay."

Stepping through the doorway, Bielakowski received the one-word answer he'd been seeking and turned for his locker. Drobyshev waved a hand, grunted a good-bye in Russian, and moved in the opposite direction with a subtle limp from a long-ago broken leg that had never been properly set.

21.

A Few Weeks Later

WATCHING THE WOMAN FLOAT in his rooftop pool, her French-manicured nails dapping the water, Sonny was feeling unimpressed with the inaugural meeting. What if she didn't have an extra bikini in the car, or had been unwilling to sunbathe? Then what? Would she be listening to Sonny's Day One lecture and offering her two cents? Bielakowski would have a stroke if he heard that Marcek started his internship with a girl in tow. Back in the day, the sausage maker didn't *talk* to women, let alone pal around with one during business hours. Sonny wasn't a torch-bearer for the old ways, but even he struggled with the curvy broad's presence. *Jesus Christ*, he thought, *what's with these young guys getting led around by their peckers?*

"Nice girl. Pretty," said Sonny, seated at a poolside table beneath an umbrella. After he'd opened his condo's front door and realized the party size had doubled, he suggested they head for the rooftop. If the couple had scoffed or Marcek countered, Sonny would have rescheduled or called Port Richmond to quash the whole deal. "Her name's Angie? Always liked that name. She's a real sweetheart."

Catching the sarcasm, Marcek knew there was work to be done. "Her old man's been in and out of prison since she was born, so the life is second nature." He smiled in Angie's direction. "And she's already proven herself with me." Marcek didn't need his mentor's indifference to tell him he'd tripped up. Bringing a stranger wasn't part of the protocol, which was why he'd brought the gift. Clearing his duffel from beneath the table, he opened the zipper, retrieved an envelope, and pushed it in Sonny's direction. "This will make everything smell better."

"What have you got there?"

"Check it out."

Sonny peeled back the fold and spread the sides with a puff of air. Inside was a decent collection of hundreds.

"I remember you having a gift for numbers," said Marcek, removing his sunglasses. "What's your guess?"

"You don't have to be Amarillo Slim to eyeball twenty grand." Sonny slapped the envelope back onto the table and did a quick check on the girl. Satisfied her raft wasn't too close, he said, "The question is for what?"

"My character defect is that I'm a romantic. I should have known better than to come as a pair."

Sonny noticed the genetic influence of Marcek's mother in his facial features and credited her for his impulsiveness. Marcek's parents were that oddball coupling that made everyone believe in the attraction of opposites. If Anton Bielakowski was the branch, she was the butterfly. Sonny imagined all the aggravation this mother/son synchronization must have caused his friend over the years. "For the future, keep these business sessions to you and me. At my age, I don't need the headache."

"Fair enough. Won't happen again."

"Now tell me the story behind this envelope, because I know it's not out of pocket. And make it entertaining. Florida has enough mouth breathers reciting their daily routines."

"The envelope comes from a job we pulled. Your taste is Dad's share plus something for me bringing Angie along."

"How's he doing?"

Marcek struggled reconciling his current role and responsibilities within the context of an accurate answer. His father was at war, men had died, and here he was in the Sunshine State with a beautiful girl learning how to think big. He'd initially refused to go south, but his father wouldn't hear of it. "Unresolved," Marcek offered, wiping sweat off his brow. "The Italians press and we strike back. They didn't like losing the bookie, which stung pretty good. We didn't like losing any of ours either."

"How many so far?"

"Three Italians. No War Boys. Three Poles."

"That's not like your father. He likes playing with a lead."

Marcek paused before answering. The issue wasn't trust, more Sonny's own safety. "The Russians are staying out. Dad won't say, but I think that was his doing. A week or two goes by with nothing. Guys relax, go out for a drink, maybe hit a club and it's on again. Seems like we're pacing ourselves. The men are ready, Dad just hasn't unleashed them yet."

"You think you have the numbers?"

"Same as always. Man on man, we're light. Neighborhood-wise, still plenty to protect our streets. Some of our guys—the ones you know— are getting gray, but they've been tested. Plenty of the Italians haven't done much more than talk tough."

Sonny leaned back and took a deep breath. He was glad those days of territorial warfare were behind him. While neither Polish nor a resident of Port Richmond, he'd still participated and suffered plenty protecting Bielakowski's operations. "Down here, your job is to forget all that. Don't be distracted, or what's the point? Concentrate on what I teach you. Here's the way your dad is seeing this—he doesn't need another soldier. You think one more gun makes a difference? What he needs is you ready down the line to lead Port Richmond."

The two debated the scenario—Marcek struggling with his desertion, Sonny countering he needed to trust his father. When they'd exhausted all their points and rebuttals, Marcek asked about Michael and whether Sonny would do the same with him.

"Impossible to answer. I'm not Anton, and you know Michael—there are special rules for him."

"Can I see him while I'm down?"

Sonny hadn't spoken to his son since he'd given him the two hundred grand. The morning of the exchange, they'd met for breakfast at Denny's, and Michael surprised his father with a set of house keys. *Keep an eye on things, Dad. I'm taking the cat, so just make sure nothing blows up.* Eating breakfast, Michael laid out his schedule for the next couple of months. *Go see Cassir, give him the money, and drive to Sarasota for ninety days at an inpatient treatment center.* Tears or smiles weren't served with the eggs, bacon, and coffee. That was for three months down the line. In the parking lot, father and son hugged, exchanged the money, wished each other good luck, and agreed to speak once Michael was in sober living.

"Michael's taking a break in California," said Sonny, figuring the lie would save him a sympathetic look. "He's got wife problems and needs distance. Let's get back to the envelope. Twenty grand seems generous, but that's your call. Must have been a pretty good racket with that kind of carve-out."

When he divvied up the haul, Marcek gave Sonny more than he was entitled to. He knew from his father how much the Depression generation appreciated long pours and generous cuts. "It's all thanks to Angie."

"You're just dealing heat. Don't try and make me like her. Make me like you and she'll be the beneficiary."

Marcek pulled his chair beneath the shade of the umbrella. Smoothing his slacks, he was glad he'd skipped the black-on-black outfit for linen and loafers. Acclimating to Florida heat was going to take some time. "Walking around Jewelry Row, I spied her working a counter. Few weeks later, when I started courting her as a connection, she was two steps ahead. I told her I needed help, and she asked what took me so long."

"Okay, I'm hooked. Reel me in."

"You know a lawyer named Billy O'Bannon?"

When Sonny acted committed to remembering the name, Marcek said it didn't matter and pressed on. "Angie's working the front counter at Roth's when her boss tells her to schedule a pickup appointment for O'Bannon. Apparently he'd ordered eighteen grand in custom jewelry and was paying in cash."

"You gave me twenty," said Sonny, eyeing the envelope. "Either you shorted yourself or she got confused with the numbers."

Marcek opened his hands as though there were no secrets left to hide. "Little of both, but let's not get hung up on the details. O'Bannon was supposed to be at the jewelry store around 1:00 P.M., so I took a position across from his office at 10:30 A.M."

"Where's his building?"

"123 South Broad. The Duke and Duke Building from that Eddie Murphy movie."

"Across from the Union League?"

Marcek didn't mind the interruptions. Meant Sonny was vested. "You got it. So I'm playing it casual, working my way up and down the block, keeping my eyes open for O'Bannon. I figured he'd have a couple morning cases at the Criminal Justice Center. Ten minutes to noon I look over and there's Raymond Rea. He's getting dropped in front of O'Bannon's building and heads in alone."

"No kidding?"

Marcek shook his head. "Rea's attorney is still Daniel Moss, and anybody watching his press conferences knows his office is on Rittenhouse Square. So now I'm wondering if Rea is there to see O'Bannon."

Sonny lifted his index finger off the table. "That's a stretch. You hear anything about him getting pinched?"

"Nothing on Rea, but you know those guys. They always have a family goon in trouble."

"Maybe it's unrelated," said Sonny. "Big building, lots of lawyers. Hell, there's a bank on the first floor. Rea was probably checking on his safety deposit box."

"That building has two towers and two sets of doors. He walked past the bank entrance."

"That narrows it to thirty other floors."

Marcek shifted in his chair, wondering how people managed such heat. Every part of him felt moist. "Fast-forward a couple minutes. I'm still across Broad Street, and here comes Billy O'Bannon skipping down the sidewalk, moving like he doesn't have a care in the world. He goes in the building, and twenty minutes later out comes Rea. He gets back in his car, but they don't drive away. Another guy, not the driver, gets out and goes into the building carrying a leather satchel. Five minutes later, he's back and they're gone."

"But you're still across the street, waiting for O'Bannon to shove off for his appointment."

"Right," said Marcek. "Nothing about Rea's appearance changed my plans. O'Bannon's office is eight blocks from the jewelry store, which means he could walk, drive his own car, or grab a cab. I scouted him the day before and had a plan for each contingency."

Instead of a quick response, Sonny took a second look toward the pool. Just because the kid bought into Angie didn't mean he was a blind believer. The only truth Sonny knew was that she'd worked her way from a Philadelphia jewelry counter all the way to his rooftop pool. There were a thousand off-ramps between Roth's Fine Diamonds and Boca Raton, and she hadn't taken a one. Either the stars were holding the young lovers together or the woman had an agenda. Tilting his head in the pool's direction, he asked, "Was she assisting or were you solo?"

"She couldn't do much because O'Bannon knows her face. I put her in a ball cap and mirrored sunglasses and had her close enough to catch a hand signal. When O'Bannon came out, he turned south and crossed over Broad Street, which meant he was headed for his parking spot at the Bellevue Hotel. All she had to do was shout *Watch out for pickpockets*."

"What did O'Bannon do?"

"Flexed his grip around the briefcase handle."

"So now you know where the money is and that he's driving himself to the jewelry store."

"And, at this point, I've already done the dirty work."

"Slashed his tires?"

"One front, one rear."

Sonny had a pretty good idea how the story finished. Marcek, dressed in a suit to allay suspicions, trailed O'Bannon into the parking garage, where he played the Good Samaritan once the lawyer discovered the vandalism. What he couldn't figure was how Marcek managed such a well-matched briefcase to pull the switcheroo.

Marcek said, "I thought I got a good look the day before but realized trailing him mine wasn't even close. I don't know—maybe he had two— but a convincing switch wasn't going to work."

"So it's on to Plan B."

Marcek nodded.

"That would have been your dad's choice from the beginning."

"Yeah, well, he's got knockout power. I'm not in that category. My blows have to be perfect to avoid a drag-out. And even when I have a clean angle, dropping the hammer is not my preference."

Sonny liked what he was hearing. Not necessarily the details, more so Marcek's realistic take on his weaknesses. Sons of talented fathers overestimated the transitive property of admired characteristics. Sonny had seen dozens trip on those false expectations. They weren't bad guys, just awful at self-analysis and thus liabilities on the job.

"When I bent down and acted interested in his tires," continued Marcek, "he didn't seem all that anxious to get close. I said, 'You should take a look because there's a knife jammed in this one.'. That's when he squatted down and I popped him. Out cold, one punch."

Sonny couldn't resist a smile.

Marcek didn't take offense. He had his mother's self-deprecating streak, which steered him clear of hot-blooded responses. "In case I'd guessed wrong, I checked his suit pockets for any envelopes, tried to roll his fat ass under the car, grabbed the briefcase, and beat a path back to Broad Street. Angie met me on Chestnut Street and off we went."

"I read *The Philadelphia Inquirer*. There haven't been any stories about O'Bannon or a robbery at the Bellevue."

They discussed the discrepancy and decided O'Bannon probably didn't make a report. A prideful criminal defense attorney wouldn't want the public knowing he was vulnerable and something less than the rock upon which all waves broke.

Marcek's turn to smile. "There's another fact explaining why there's no report."

Sonny thought back to the twenty thousand dollars in the envelope. "Rea's little visit."

"Right," said Marcek. "O'Bannon wouldn't want the head of the Philadelphia mob thinking his new attorney just lost the money he'd given him."

"Now we're coming full circle," Sonny said, eager to walk through the analysis. "The girl told you eighteen and had no reason to lie. The variable is Rea and his man coming in and out. Once you roll O'Bannon and pop the locks on his briefcase, he's carrying much more. Knowing you, my cut is generous and not necessarily indicative of the total. The girl was expecting a piece, probably half, so when you gave her ten, she was giddy. You kept ten and the rest is me. I'm thinking that puts forty in the briefcase, which you're figuring came from Rea."

Marcek gave Sonny a soft salute.

"Could just as well be nothing," said Sonny.

"I don't believe in coincidences like that."

"Okay, so what do they have cooking to explain that much money?"

Marcek shrugged. "No idea."

"You tell your father?"

"Of course. He didn't make much of it or wasn't in the mood to discuss. He stewed on it for a couple days and then got sore you were getting his share."

While Sonny figured the entire episode was probably a big nothing, he was glad the kid tried connecting the dots and shared the details. Out of respect for Anton, he'd give the sequence a second review later in the day. Time often provided a fresh perspective.

Sonny said, "Best lesson your old man taught me? Be quick to forgive. Grudges are too expensive to lug around. The envelope and your story make up for Angie Sugarpants."

Being the youngest of the Bielakowski children, Marcek grew up with a vague sense of Sonny Bonhardt. He had half-memories of cruising around Port Richmond in Sonny's convertible Cadillac and once or twice seeing a ball game with him and Michael. But by the time he was a teenager and ready for shaping, Sonny had split for Florida. Without him, Marcek's professional training was reduced to piecing together his father's mumbles and his own hard-fought, firsthand experience. Now, observing how Sonny tracked and dissected the O'Bannon scam, Marcek was grateful for a second opportunity. "Like I said, won't happen again."

Sonny sat forward, resting his hand atop a foot-high stack of newspapers he'd asked Marcek to bring up from the condo. "Let's get started. I'm supposed to teach you how to come up with good business ideas."

"I'm ready."

"One problem. I don't have a clue how I do it. Most ideas come in eureka moments. Best I can offer is explaining what I do in preparation of those times." Sonny paused as though there might be a question. When none was asked, he said, "This first part is like making chili. You know how to make good chili?"

Marcek didn't know where Sonny was headed, so he shook his head. Confessed ignorance at least guaranteed nothing could be assumed.

"Chili," said Sonny, "is pretty decent on Day One. By Day Two, it's coming into form. And by Day Three, the flavors have combined into a perfect blend. That's sort of me with these newspapers. I may read an article and have no reaction. Hell, I may read a week of articles and come up with eggs on the scoreboard. But then, out of nowhere, few days later and boom, an idea strikes. And it always comes back to something I read in a newspaper or magazine."

"I hate reading," said Marcek, only half joking. He'd spent two grand paying off an assistant high school principal to let him graduate.

"Don't say garbage like that. It annoys me when I hear young people reveling in dullness. There are plenty of uncharming, hands-on tasks in your dad's shop, so be grateful you're not boiling livers for the blood sausage."

A decent debater, Marcek saw it wasn't going to be much use going toe-to-toe with Sonny Bonhardt. Thumbing through the newspapers as if they were a pile of T-shirts on sale, he said, "Sports count?"

"I've gotten ideas in every part of the paper, but you must read the newspaper as it's packaged. Front to back, no skipping to the comics or box scores."

The newspapers were current editions from eight major metropolitan markets plus *The Wall Street Journal* and *USA Today*. Marcek settled on the New Orleans *Times-Picayune* for no other reason than that it seemed the least academic and most entertaining. "You ever see something right away and know it's good?"

"Sure," said Sonny, separating the sections of *The Atlanta Journal-Constitution*. "We don't need to make this a thousand-mile march. A beautiful woman falls in your lap, give her a kiss. If you read an article and get an idea, make a note or shout it out."

Paper in front of his face, Marcek wondered what Angie was thinking on her raft. A quick peek at Sonny's progress indicated he was already trailing, so he sped through some nonsense about the president's travels to Europe and offshore drilling regulations. Once he reached the local news section, the content got more interesting, particularly an investigative piece on the flow of narcotics into Louisiana. A map showed all the highways and interstates in the region and an arrest count for each of the corridors. Leading the way by almost double was I-10, which connected Florida to the Gulf Coast. Mentioned in the article was the recent arrest of a man who'd been pulled over twelve miles outside of New Orleans. With the assistance of a drug dog named Randy, four members of the Louisiana State Police discovered thirty pounds of uncut cocaine hidden in the car's rear panels.

"Sonny?"

"Yeah," he answered without looking up.

"Seems like maybe there's some easy money running drugs from Florida into Louisiana if you've got a process."

Sonny snapped down his paper and gave Marcek a hard look over the top of his reading glasses. "First, Anton gave me one rule with you—no drugs. That's the most dangerous money you'll ever make. Second, we're not reading the newspaper for dumb crimes to do better. And third, why you asking?"

Marcek wished he hadn't said a word. He was anxious to make a good impression and had pressed. Here on out, he'd be more discerning, wait for Sonny to offer up an idea or two so he'd have a better sense what they were targeting. "No big deal. I'm reading an article in the New Orleans newspaper about a Florida guy arrested for running dope."

Sonny filled his lungs with warm ocean air, wishing he could find permanent solace in that fleeting moment. "It give a name?"

"The guy? Yeah, he's called 'unidentified male.' The article is using him as an example of a bigger problem. Says he drove up from the Miami area. That's what gave me the idea, like maybe there's a better delivery system than driving past state troopers with drug dogs."

Sonny folded his paper, excused himself from the table, and stepped to the waist-high stucco wall wrapping the rooftop deck. He wondered about the time. How much did he have? Maybe a week, as little as a day. Tough to tell with desperate men.

He was reminded of the Iwo Jima photo, the famous one of the soldiers planting the American flag. One soldier's face was obscured, his head turned down so only his backside was visible. Even without a face or name associated with the photo, the soldier's mother saw the hazy black-and-white reproduction and knew it was her boy. After the man was identified as someone else, she wouldn't hear of it. Hundreds of thousands of men had stormed Iwo Jima, but that picture was her son, she could just tell. Turns out, after a bit more investigation, her mother's intuition was right. The man hoisting the flagpole with the hidden face was her son Harlan, a fine young Texan who died shortly after the photo was taken on that godforsaken piece of coral.

That was Sonny with the article. Could have been anybody busted with that cocaine—one of a hundred thousand drug mules working for maintenance money or paying off a debt. But deep in his heart, in that spot where truth cannot be denied, Sonny knew it was Michael. His son never went to rehab. He wasn't sharing personal demons in group therapy sessions. He wasn't graduating with a shiny coin. He wasn't moving into a sober living house. And he wasn't rebuilding any of his poisoned relationships. No, Michael wasn't doing any of that because he was in a Louisiana jail cell, feeling sorry for himself, trading food for cigarettes, and pondering life in Angola. Michael took the goddamn two hundred grand, bought cocaine, made a couple bets, bought some more cocaine, had another go with the odds, busted out, and went into hiding. Out of options and probably with Cassir's shotgun in his ear, he decided to drive a car from Miami to New Orleans. Tweaked, stressed, and impatient on I-10, Michael was suspicious enough to give the police probable cause to hit their blues and start the roadside dance.

At the wall, running the sequence a second time, Sonny realized none of it really mattered. Thinking about who did what and why was a waste of time. Stripped and boiled to the bone, Sonny was down a son and on the hook for another two hundred grand. That was the agreement he cosigned. Yes, he had the money, but it was all that he had. Paying it out, on top of what he'd paid for his own gambling obligations, tapped him for the year. He wouldn't have gas money.

He called Marcek to join him. Looking out on the Atlantic Ocean, hands in his pockets, Sonny said, "We're done with the newspapers."

Reading the sentence as more open than closed, Marcek held his tongue.

"I've got another project," said Sonny, still looking east. "High stakes. It goes right and it's the score of a lifetime."

Like a kid sprung from detention, Marcek wanted to ask a dozen questions, but the mood wasn't compatible. Whatever Sonny had gleaned from the article carried a somber vibe that favored silence.

"There's a new medicine on the market called Viagra."

"I've seen the commercials."

"You and me, we're going to steal some of it."

After internalizing the consequences of the last five minutes, Sonny decided a radical change was in order. Upfront fees were no longer meeting his needs. His ideas made millions while he'd settled for percentages and decimal points. For what? So he could feel full in January and margined by Thanksgiving? After working for most of his life, Sonny should have been able to handle Michael's double-down setback over drinks and dinner, not let it wash him down the drain like an old hair.

Watching the sailboats harness and hold their slivers of wind from his rooftop perch, Sonny knew the cure wasn't another year of newspapers and press releases from the U.S. Attorney's Office. To get well, to get truly independent, he needed to get balls deep into a score, one last big motherfucking score to send him on a never-ending sailboat ride. "I've discussed stealing a trailer of Viagra with your dad. Our usual arrangement is for me to sell him the idea after handling initial research and planning."

"But you've changed your mind."

"I'm keeping the heist. Whatever it produces, he'll broker."

Marcek nodded.

"Since you're down here, I want you as my partner. Full share."

"What's he going to think?" asked Marcek. The answer didn't dictate his decision. He was in. He was only asking because that's what was expected.

"Nonissue," said Sonny. "We kicked everything down the road except him lining up a bulk buyer. He'd need that regardless of the arrangement. In good faith, we'll cut him in for a partner's share. The standalone idea is worth a hundred grand. But the street value of a loaded truck is probably thirty times that. Instead of your dad's crew, you and me will handle the operation and delivery to Philadelphia."

Marcek had heisted six trucks in his career, two in the last year. Though not his specialty, they weren't far off. The problem in Philly or anywhere on the East Coast was the competition. Pick the wrong outfit or the wrong driver and half the take went to smoothing ruffled feathers. He figured Florida had to be a cleaner landscape. "Not to brag, but I'm pretty good with this type of thing."

"Hearing your O'Bannon story, you've got the ability." Sonny checked on Angie again, who looked as though she'd fallen asleep on the raft. "She's going to fry in this sun. Where are you two staying?"

"We have an apartment in Delray Beach." Marcek wondered what Sonny was considering for Angie. If he vetoed her participation, Marcek would struggle holding back his opinion. He wanted Angie close and could see plenty of ways she'd be useful.

Sonny leaned forward. "A truck of pharmaceuticals isn't like clipping a load of dresses or jacking a truck you've tracked off the loading docks. This is very specific. Pfizer manufactures Viagra, and much of the logistics is covert to protect themselves from people like us. Might be dangerous. Chance of getting pinched is above single digits."

Marcek said he understood the differences and wouldn't underestimate the details or risk. Wanting to push beyond the caution-and-warning stage, he said, "You got access to a second truck and warehouse? If we're hauling up to Philly, we'll need a stash house and transportation."

"I've got a secure warehouse. The other pieces will be on-site in a day. Clean truck. Clean trailer. Clean logbooks. I'll give you the address and a set of warehouse keys when we go downstairs. Can you drive an eighteen-wheeler, or do I need a wheelman?"

"I can handle us up to Philly. What do you need me to do right now?"

"The raw materials come in on an ocean freighter and are delivered to various manufacturing facilities for processing and packaging. I don't know the location or exact identity, and nobody else does either. All very hush-hush. What I do know is eventually those pills end up in a Walgreens or CVS or Publix. Start backtracking the shipments up through the supply chain. At some point, you'll unravel enough string to find our source."

"Find a trailer of Viagra and make a plan."

"Yes."

"How long do I have?"

"One week."

Sonny appreciated Marcek's approach. He was straightforward, concise, and—most importantly—trusted. If he had balked or insisted on his father's involvement, Sonny didn't have the resources to handle the job himself. Marcek in Florida was a good sign, like a swallow at sea.

In the elevator ride off the roof, Sonny stood by the control panel, his shoulders toward the center of the car. For twenty floors, the only movement was Angie reaching for Marcek's hand. When the elevator doors opened, Sonny took a half step out. Looking back in, he said, "Angie?"

"Yes, Mr. Bonhardt?"

"When you leave here today, Marcek will begin working on a new project."

Unsure what was expected, Angie removed her sunglasses. "Okay."

"If you aren't interested, I'll buy you an airplane ticket. You can fly home or anywhere in the world. That's an open offer. Call me anytime and I'll meet you at the airport."

She could feel the gaze of both men. She steadied her knees and made sure not to overgrip Marcek's hand. "I understand."

"The project is dangerous. Marcek assures me you're not naive, that you can handle yourself. Fair enough, I'll take him at his word. But if anything I've said is unappealing—or the risks unacceptable—I'll give you a plane ticket plus five grand. We'll all go our separate ways. No hard feelings."

Angie took note of the increased tender. She'd spent her life catering to a selfish bum of a father who didn't believe in options or outs. If he sneezed, she was expected to catch a cold. Well, those days were gone. "I get what you're laying out, I really do, but I'm not running. If Marcek is done with me, that's one thing. Otherwise I'm in."

Sonny nodded twice and turned down the hallway. He knew his thoughts were petty and misdirected. Still, he couldn't help himself. The problem wasn't Marcek or Angie as people or participants in the heist—he was solid, and she was growing on him. They'd be fine. His issue was resentment. They were hand in hand on a primrose path while Michael was rotting away, his best days a decade gone. Sonny was left sharing his experience, time, and wisdom with another man's son. For any father, that was a bittersweet equation.

22.

NEVER ANXIOUS TO PAY the same bill twice, Sonny had no choice with Michael's legacy. He'd already tasted Cassir's style once, could forecast his progression, and didn't need the bad energy.

Two miles from the marina, he stopped at a liquor store for booze, ice, and pretzels. If Cassir wasn't already in the parking lot or on the boat, Sonny would kill time with his old friend bourbon. It wouldn't be long. Like any halfway decent investigator, Cassir would begin with what he knew, the marina, pressing lower echelon employees until he made the right connection. Might as well save everyone the hassle.

Sonny parked his Cadillac opposite the security shack and hauled his groceries and brown bag of money to the dock. It was a quiet day at the club, all clear except for a wet footprint near his sailboat's portside winch. He unlocked the cabin, turned on the stereo, dropped in a Cannonball Adderley disc, and headed outside.

Two highball glasses into the bottle, Sonny found his groove. It'd been a long time since he was alone on the boat drinking to get drunk. The selfishness felt good, damn good, and he started thinking the solitary moments would be what he'd miss most. Just the thought got him chasing a refill. As an orphan kid, his fantasies were never outsized, like owning a Gatsby mansion or being a movie star. His mind was occupied by smaller milestones—food and shelter—so when he did fall asleep at night, he was too tired to dream. It wasn't until the sixties he had enough resources to start eyeballing luxury. Sailing imprinted on his brain after he saw pictures of the Kennedy clan outfitted in wool sweaters working the wind off of Martha's Vineyard. That's when he knew what he wanted.

Inside the cabin, dropping a few cubes into his glass, Sonny felt a subtle roll. Keeping his pour even, he spoke out of the side of his mouth. "You still a beer man or should I bring the whisky?"

Cassir stuck his head inside the cabin, hands on either side of the entryway. "My man, Sonny. Had a feeling you wouldn't fight the current."

"No sense playing grab-ass all over South Florida. It's only money."

"You could have sailed off."

"I considered it. Not like I'm too honorable. Just wasn't the right time." Truth was, without the FDA's recent Viagra approval and Marcek pressing forward, Sonny would have skirted for an extended stay in St. John.

Cassir said, "There's no testimony without a test."

"I've had my fill of both. One more isn't changing the gauge."

"Where do you want to do this?" Unlike at their first meeting, Cassir's hair was loose and hanging to his shoulders, making him look a few years older. Behind Cassir was a second man, another Cuban-looking tough guy who was all sunglasses and sideburns. His shoulders were too thin not to bring a gun to a fight.

Sonny grabbed a beer from the fridge and handed it up. "What's your pal's pleasure?"

"He doesn't drink. Makes him poor company."

Sonny shrugged as if he didn't see the point and took a sip. "I'm going to have some words for you. And I'm guessing you've got one or two for me. But the money is here, and since I think nobody's getting killed, we can sit wherever you like."

Clutching the cold beer, Cassir didn't want to go into the cabin. He had Sonny figured pretty well, but that didn't mean something nasty wasn't waiting for him. All things considered, he'd just as soon stay topside now that the sun had dipped and temperatures cooled enough to make a fine evening. "Come out of there," he said, unsure what else to add.

The men sat face to face on the port and starboard ends of the companionway, Team Cassir settling in side by side. "First thing I want to know," said Sonny, "is how much of my money Michael had left when he showed."

As Cassir took a sip, his elbow brushed his close-sitting partner. Grazing man skin pissed him off and he responded by whispering for some goddamn room. Back to the question, he said, "You saying you gave him the two hundred?"

At least Michael was consistent, thought Sonny. "We met that third morning for breakfast. Driving off the lot, he was paying you and heading north for rehab."

"He didn't post for a week or so," said Cassir. "I was getting ready to come see you when Michael came up for air. His net worth was four thousand dollars and clothes he hadn't changed in days. That boy smelled homeless."

"Jesus Christ."

Cassir took a long pull. "Said you bailed on him. *Dad screwed me.* Spun a tail how he was supposed to meet you here and when he arrived, you'd pushed off for a couple days. Mentioned Bermuda."

Sonny emptied his glass, rattled the ice, and took a final sip in case any extra booze had broken loose and filtered down. "So you put him to work."

"He call you?"

"New Orleans newspaper had a big spread about dope running. Michael was the anecdotal evidence."

"Antidote?"

"Anecdote—a story to prove a larger point. The reporter's take was Florida mules were fueling New Orleans's drug problem. He used Michael's arrest as proof."

Cassir paused, filing the lingual tidbit for future use. *Yeah, boss, my theory is the Puerto Ricans are stealing our action. Now let me continue with anecdotal evidence.*

"Was that legitimate or did you put him to the wolves?"

Cassir shook him off. "You said something like that before. We don't ship for loss."

"If he wasn't sacrificed, he was running lead. Otherwise, thirty pounds doesn't make sense."

"You're wasted talent, Sonny," said Cassir. "A silver fox still figuring the angles. As for your boy, yeah, he was out front, but he had as much chance as the second car. Nothing said he had to get pulled over."

"How much was in the second?"

"Four hundred pounds. Needed special suspension for all that weight. No guarantee that gets through either, even though hopefully the lead car draws the flies. Those Louisiana boys are getting smarter, starting to profile, so first car makes the run and thirty minutes later second car follows. If both make it to New Orleans, that's cool. Nobody wanted Michael to get arrested. And if they were profiling, we were covered."

Sonny looked off into the canal. All this could have been avoided if he'd just assumed the worst of Michael. If he'd conceded his son's rank and absolute depravity, he could have delivered the money himself and postponed the come-to-Jesus moment.

"Look, man, that was the deal," said Cassir. "He borrowed the money. He didn't pay it back. He got another chance with you and screwed it up. What was salvation supposed to look like? His choices were getting killed or driving. That's why he put his hand out for the keys. Michael did more than a few runs before getting careless. Believe it or not, he was pretty dependable once we got him into the program. I was sorry to see him go."

After watching two seagulls buzz the mast, Sonny said, "You guys aren't worried he'll trade you in?"

Cassir scoffed. "Shit, what does he really know? He picks up and drops off, and the second car was none of his business. Those end points don't mean a thing, and it's not like he has anybody's real name. Michael's best move is keeping his mouth shut. Make time go easy. Not like we don't have people in Louisiana. You tell him that, you get the chance."

"I'm in no hurry." For Sonny, his son dealing with the consequences was one thing. Assisting Cassir in spelling them out was another. If they wanted to threaten Michael, they'd have to write their own postcards.

"Well, he'll reach out to you soon enough. All the addicts get a little freaked when the court-appointed lawyer starts using words like *decades* instead of *months* or *years*."

"You should have tracked me down before putting him in that car. I've got money. Now he's going to waste in prison and I'm still paying."

"Fuck that," said Cassir, brushing hair off his face. "I like you, Sonny, but I didn't owe you any free courtesy. You know how much hassle rained on my head because of your boy?" He held his thumb and forefinger a quarter inch apart. "I was this close to getting my nuts busted. This close because I'd tippy-toed so far out on that Michael branch. Must have been crazy allowing that mess, like letting a cat pee all over the house and looking the other way. Insane."

"Yeah," said Sonny, with a slow nod. "I know the feeling."

That drew a dark chuckle from both Cubans. Sonny could see that the nameless one was missing an incisor and his gums were diseased.

"While I could chat all night, let's deal with the matter at hand. I've waited long enough." Cassir handed his empty beer bottle to his partner, who tossed it into the water.

Sonny called him a rude son of a bitch, and Cassir agreed, ordering him to fish it out. Leaning over the side, the man lost his sunglasses and almost fell in before he could swipe the bottle from the current.

Sonny didn't know what to make of Cassir's number two, figuring he was probably a slow-witted brother-in-law or cousin needing work. "The money is in the kitchen. A brown bag next to the pretzels. You can drop that bottle in the trash on your way down. Careful you don't hurt yourself."

Cassir's head nod looked like a dad telling his kid it was okay to hit the dessert bar. The silent partner disappeared into the cabin and returned with a fresh beer for Cassir, the bag of money, and Sonny's pretzels.

"Man, you've got no class," said Cassir, his mood rising. He looked left and right before opening the money bag. "Not that counting is all that polite, but you'll understand my distrust."

Sonny said the package was no longer his concern; he wanted them to leave as soon as Cassir finished his beer. Time to drink alone.

After a few minutes of peeling, Cassir pulled out a brick of hundreds. "You overpaid. Michael gets credit for his runs, ten grand each. He made four. So you know, last one doesn't count."

The first thought popping into Sonny's head confirmed how unsettled he was over Michael's situation. Forty grand was enough to hire his boy the best damn criminal defense attorney in Louisiana. Sure, the stack could finance the truck heist and keep *Eastern State* in good standing, but that was all too self-dealing. No matter how much Michael deserved it, Sonny wasn't the abandoning kind.

He scooped up the brick, peeled off two stacks of three grand each, and handed the money to Cassir and his wingman. "That's for the inconvenience. I'm also hoping it buys Michael some goodwill. If Michael ever gets out, just leave him alone. Treat him like a leper and run the other way."

Cassir slapped the bills against his assistant's distended belly. "You see that, Frank? Old doesn't mean old school except when you're dealing with this *gato*. Today's been one of a kind. We're going home with a bag of money, some sugar for the wife and kids, and a lesson in cool. Not bad considering the alternative."

23.

DRIVING HOME FROM SONNY'S CONDO, Marcek filled Angie in on the details. Her two cents was that even though their initial responsibility sounded simple enough—find a Viagra shipment and sketch a plan for stealing it—the end points felt a thousand miles apart. She especially didn't like the tight time frame. What was wrong with another month or two if the extension meant a better strategy?

Marcek explained how other factors were driving the compressed schedule. "A score like this, we aren't the only ones sniffing the fence line. Viagra is already on the street. How long did it take for that black market to develop? Ten, eleven days? And that's just from people selling off their prescriptions. Won't take much for other professionals to see what we're seeing. Right now, and maybe for the next week or two, a truck of Viagra is undervalued and underguarded. First shipment stolen will be the easiest. After that, impossible."

"If that's true, why didn't we start earlier? Like, you know, before it was being sold?"

Marcek was now wondering the same. His initial enthusiasm had him downplaying negative points Angie wasn't so willing to ignore. Unsure what to say, he answered her with a trust-me shrug and silent prayer that the delay wouldn't come back to bite them.

Inside the apartment, they time blocked forty-five minutes for preparations. The pair managed to shower, have quickie sex to release the adrenaline spike, pack simple accessories to alter appearances on short notice, and make a sack of peanut-butter-and-jelly sandwiches.

Mindful of organization, Angie suggested breaking the week into three parts, each one more refined than the last. Days one and two would be an all-out effort to accumulate information on the pharmacies. When did they get their drug shipments? Did certain pharmacies receive more than others? Were guards or store assistants monitoring the off-loads? She warned Marcek this stage would feel random and haphazard because they were starting at zero and tossing a wide net. These two days were also the most critical because mistakes begat mistakes, especially when stealing from corporations adept at preventing theft.

Once the raw data requirements were satisfied, she explained how the next forty-eight to seventy-two hours would be dedicated to trucks and routes. Where were the trucks coming from and going to? Any soft spots in their schedule? What was the typical driver like? That'd leave two or three days for synthesizing a plan, running scenarios, and doing a handful of test runs before presenting to Sonny. They'd be pressed to finish and have almost no chance at unwinding any missteps.

In agreement on the seven-day calendar, Marcek suggested starting with the all-night pharmacies. Ease in, play casual, and make small talk with cash register attendees or pharmacists working third shift. Both understood they'd need a breezier style, nothing too heavy or penetrating. Soft little probes by a couple of late-night wanderers. Even then it'd be like painting with mittens. Three stores in, they settled on finding open spaces on the shelves. *Hey, you guys are out of that antifungus cream— when's your truck getting here?* Or, to the pharmacist, *Hey, man, you need a prescription for that Viagra? Oh, damn, you do? How many trucks a week you got hauling that stuff in here? Must be like two or three, hahahah.*

By 6:30 A.M., they'd visited twenty pharmacies. The yield of that effort could be written with large letters on the back of a gum wrapper. Twelve hours of role-playing in exchange for fatigue, failure, and bad breath was a demoralizing start, one that had them questioning the entire proposal. And that's, of course, when they got their first break.

Wiped out and getting testy, Marcek and Angie agreed on hitting one more pharmacy in Boynton Beach before grabbing breakfast and a few hours' sleep. They walked into store twenty-one with long-shot hopes and exited with zero-point-zero help. Stepping outside the pharmacy's doors, as doubt leveraged exhaustion, both were quick to notice a tractor-trailer in the loading dock. Their reaction was to look at each other and shrug. *Well, now what do we do?* Marcek whispered something about sneaking into the pharmacy's back room and observing the unloading process. Angie was hung up on how, in six days, this truck would translate into a payoff.

Between them and the loading dock was a rough-cut picnic table for pharmacy employees on break. Perched atop the table was a bony, underweight white woman with a dozen piercings. Despite the warm temperatures, she wore a faded yellow sweatshirt with the sleeves stretched over her hands. Layered atop the sweatshirt was an employee smock and a name tag reading KALYNN. Unafraid of making eye contact, Kalynn stared straight at Marcek and Angie as she took a slow drag from her cigarette. "Hey there."

"Hi," answered Marcek, reaching for Angie's hand to lead her away. With the truck on-site, they didn't need any employees making mental notes of their visit.

Angie wouldn't budge. Something in the woman's eyes told her to stick around. "What's going on?" she answered, head to the side, a half-smile in the same direction.

Wiping her nose on the back of her sleeve, Kalynn rolled her eyes to the parking lot and back to Angie. "You guys like to party?"

"Come on, Ang—"

Angie shushed him as if she had an itch that needed scratching. Releasing his hand and stepping to the picnic table, she said, "He's working this afternoon, so it'd be for me. What'd you have in mind?"

"Pills. That's what you're doing, right, shopping for pills?"

"Yeah," said Angie, wondering just how bad she must have looked.

"Found the right place. The doctor is in. I'll have you high before you're two miles down the road."

Angie put a foot on the bench. "It's got to be good or I'm not interested," she said, doing her best imitation. She'd never bought drugs before. "No crap or sugar pills."

"Painkillers. For real. The sweet stuff. I've got a system for stealing one at a time. How many you need, baby?"

With the negotiation hanging between them, Angie acted wary of the loading dock, as if eyes were coming from that direction. "What's the story over there?" she asked, rubbing the back of her neck and working her jaw. "That truck is making me nervous. Too many people."

As the woman peeked over her shoulder, a neck tattoo reading PROPERTY OF SNEAKY PETE stretched above her shirt collar. "What do you mean? That truck is just our delivery."

"Aren't there cameras watching? Or security guards?"

The woman laughed, fished a pack of cigarettes from her sweatshirt pocket, and winked. "That truck is just for diapers and toothpaste and shit—all the crap we sell on the shelves. The pharmacy shit comes later."

"Oh."

"Yeah, one time they let me look inside the drug truck. Oh, damn, it has every taste under the sun. Like a river of chocolate."

Angie glanced again at the loading dock. "So two trucks—the regular truck and another for the pharmacy?"

"Yeah, relax. I just sold to that driver. He's cool. He's not going to bother us. The drug truck comes this evening, and you're right, I don't do nothing while it's around." She tickled the packet of cigarettes with her left index finger. "Sit next to me and have a smoke. They're menthol. High-end fancy smokes like that are twenty bucks apiece." She winked again in case Angie missed the import of the first one. "Half a cigarette—if that's your speed—is twelve."

All the necessary information acquired, Angie turned and walked away. Marcek was sitting in the car, his head pressed into the seat. Opening the door, she said, "You're never going to believe what I just learned."

Marcek raised his eyebrows.

"Three things, really. First, somewhere there's a Sneaky Pete with control issues. Second, that's not the right truck—it delivers everything except drugs. And third, the truck we need comes later today."

24.

MARCEK AND ANGIE had a few hours but no time to waste.

Figuring they wouldn't get another chance, they dashed from the pharmacy to a nearby Burger King for coffee, breakfast sandwiches, and a restroom. Next up was the Miami International Airport. Marcek dropped Angie at the busiest terminal to rent a car. Striving for shallow footprints, she drove her pregnancy-test-blue sedan straight to a low-rent apartment complex they'd scouted a few miles away.

Before rendezvousing, Marcek had his own list of to-do's.

He dropped their car in short-term parking and grabbed a shuttle to the long-term lot. He needed two sets of Florida license plates—no vanity slogans, and tags had to be current. Stashing the plates in his backpack, he returned to the terminal for a second high-mileage rental under a fake identity.

At the apartment complex they installed the stolen plates and discussed how to work the Boynton Beach pharmacy. The agreed plan was alternating thirty-minute shifts—staying close enough to observe the pharmacy's loading dock without drawing undue suspicion. Keeping one on-site, the other was parked two blocks away, ready to join when the truck departed for its next destination.

They leapfrogged for two hours until the truck arrived and completed its off-load. Given the early evening time frame, both agreed it was unlikely the truck had many more stops, and it was probably returning straight to its warehouse. When the truck merged south on I-95, each took a turn staying close for two or three miles before relinquishing the lead position.

Navigating medium traffic, they tracked the truck fifteen miles through Fort Lauderdale to west on 595 and then north on the Sawgrass Parkway. The truck took the third exit, made a half-dozen turns, and ended inside a soulless industrial park with a dozen warehouse facilities. Watching it enter the security gates of Allegiance Corporation, Angie and Marcek backtracked a mile to a semiempty warehouse parking lot.

Angie rolled her window down. "I'm tired."

"Me, too."

"What do you think?"

Marcek studied the surrounding warehouses and truck bays. "We're halfway there. The warehouse he went into—that has to be a distributor for all the manufactured drugs. The bulk drug shipments come here, and Allegiance creates individual delivery pallets for each pharmacy. You know, a little bit of this, a little bit of that. I'm feeling pretty good the bulk shipments of Viagra come here and get parsed up."

"And we have no idea where they manufacture Viagra?"

"No. That's why we had to start wide. Sonny says no one really knows."

She exhaled, catching herself short of a headshake. "If the goal is to find a tractor-trailer full of Viagra, you know how hard backtracking from here is going to be? How are we supposed to know which truck is from where? It's like looking at a bunch of geese and guessing where in Canada each one is from. Different trucks from different pharmaceutical companies, all with different loads. It's impossible."

Marcek tried sounding more optimistic. "It's good work for the first day. Time to sleep, and maybe we'll come up with something by morning. You hungry, or should we just head home? I think there's cold pizza in the fridge."

Angie was too tired to make a decision. She told Marcek to follow her out and she'd probably just make another peanut-butter-and-jelly sandwich at home. "There is some bread left, right?"

Feeling punchy, Marcek laughed at *left, right*, sending Angie off in a huff. He called to apologize.

25.

SIX HOURS OF SLEEP and long, steamy showers brought renewed hope. Angie was into her second piece of toast before Marcek brushed the night from his mouth and joined her in the kitchen.

Stirring two spoonfuls of sugar into his coffee, he felt her stare. Taking a sip, he nodded in appreciation and took another before looking at her sideways. "You going to keep me waiting or share the breakthrough?"

Her hair was damp, and she wore a wrinkled button-down oxford shirt above bare legs. Morning light suited her fine. "It came to me about an hour ago. I was lying in bed, thinking about home, and the answer popped into my brain. Just like that. The answer's the Italian Market."

Marcek responded with two blinks.

"Last night," she said, "we got discouraged because it seemed like the whole delivery thing was a closed loop. Trucks from some mysterious Pfizer manufacturing facility arrive at the distribution warehouse, and there's no way to identify the right one or catch it in between."

"But you've figured something out?"

"Delivery drivers are like anyone else when the boss isn't looking. They steal time. All those drivers rolling into the Italian Market? They have off-the-book stops before and after. Everyone knows because the trucks are double-parked as the drivers scurry to their favorite spots for booze, gambling, a woman—whatever vice they can squeeze in. Why? Because they're men and no one is watching. You think a driver hauling Viagra is any different? On the road, away from the wife and kids, in sunny Florida?"

Marcek found himself nodding. She was on the right path, although he was apprehensive about the final answer.

"Truck stops," she said, volleying his nod. "They're the break in the chain. They're the one place we have any chance of finding the right load."

"Damn. I thought that's what you were going to say. I hate truck stops."

Angie's eyes widened. "Think about it. We've got a natural corridor coming into South Florida. With the warehouse on the back side of Fort Lauderdale, there's a ninety percent chance all the tractor-trailers, at some point, are coming down I-95."

"Okay," said Marcek, jumping in when she took a breath, "but you're talking about a thousand miles of road."

"Let me finish. I put a lot of thought into this."

Marcek apologized with half a smile. "It's brilliant, you know. Really damn good."

Angie ran into the living room and returned with an oversized map book. Peeling through the pages, she said, "Since we have less than a week, we have to make choices. Educated choices to maximize our odds. While there's a chance we're wrong, I think I've got it figured pretty good."

"Am I still keeping my mouth shut?"

"That should have started with the coffee."

Marcek raised both hands. "The floor is yours."

"So two things. One, you said Pfizer imports the chemicals for making Viagra from overseas. That's got to mean Europe. Can't mean China, right? So unless they freight it west—which seems really extreme— Viagra is manufactured somewhere on or near the East Coast. Okay, assuming that's right, the general starting point is the northern section of I-95 with one of the end-point destinations being the distribution facility off the Sawgrass Parkway. I bet that warehouse handles all the Viagra for South Florida. And with it just hitting the market, that's got to mean a lot of supply trucks."

Marcek couldn't help himself. "Like I said, that's a long road. Eight or ten states' worth. Lots of truck stops along the way."

She stared him down. "Now my second point. This is the educated guess part, because you're right, there are too many truck stops to stake out. What we know is that these drivers are coming south after a long winter. They're in Florida, looking at the map, trying to pick a spot to spend the night. They peruse names like St. Augustine, Brunswick, and St. Marys before their eyes fall on . . ."

"Daytona Beach."

She hit him in the head with the map book. "You're such an asshole."

Marcek stumbled back into his chair. "This works, I need some basis to claim credit."

Angie leaned against the counter, her hip flared out in a smooth silhouette. "Kids dream about Disney, truck drivers do the same with Daytona Beach. The racetrack, bike week, the women. It's like catnip. They can't resist."

"No argument from me," said Marcek. "If Daytona Beach craps out, we're screwed, but what else do we have? Let's get dressed and pack a bag. We need to drop off the rentals, and I want to check out Sonny's warehouse before heading north. He's supposed to have the second tractor-trailer ready."

Before he could stand, Angie closed the distance and straddled him on the chair. Pressing her weight down, she could feel his spirited response between her legs. Kissing him hard on the lips, she whispered, "We have another stop to make."

"The bedroom?"

"Well, yes, there's that. But I need to go to Wal-Mart for my costume."

Marcek pulled his head back. "What?"

"My costume. You're cute, but no matter how horny those truckers are, none of them are going to mistake you for a lot lizard."

"Oh, Angie, come on. I don't know about you doing that."

She bit his neck. "Shut up, Marcek. We don't have time to argue."

26.

MARCEK HATED ALL TRUCK STOPS since he'd been beaten six ways to Sunday outside one near Scranton, Pennsylvania.

January a few years back—when the Pocono Highway slicked over—he and two hundred truckers ceded the road to the salt crews. Sitting in a diner, minding his own pie, he overheard four truckers in the next booth getting a game together. Nothing better to occupy his mind, he worked an invitation, even offering to supply the cards. Fast-forward a couple of hours, Marcek was bleeding in the parking lot, his pockets picked clean by eight hands. The truckers felt entitled to their original stakes plus an extra six hundred dollars because why not. Short of being gang raped, Marcek's night couldn't have ended worse. In his car, too embarrassed to seek help, he assessed the damage at two chipped teeth, no money, no wallet, and a punch line with fifty years of legs. Oh, and an icy road to Saratoga Springs still to be traveled.

Now, parked with Angie at the truck lot's farthest edge, Marcek had no reason to believe the Flying J Truck Stop south of Daytona Beach wasn't the same hellish variety. A hundred lined-up eighteen-wheelers spewed diesel fumes while their denim-clad drivers slept or wandered inside the glorified minimart for soda and showers. The setting's lone redeeming qualities were a cloudless sky and a stiff breeze clearing away the exhaust.

"If we're right," he said, "it's either this stop or the next one up the road."

"I've got a good feeling. Woman's intuition maybe. This one's closer to the beach and the racetrack."

Marcek scanned the testament to highway convenience as he ran a nervous hand through his hair. "What other options do we have? Can't jack a delivery outside the distribution warehouse, so we've got to walk back up the line."

"I guess."

"You having second thoughts?"

"No. Just want to be right."

"It's how these truck deals go."

Angie nodded, unable to take her eyes off all the eighteen-wheelers entering the lot. Judging from their pace, the count could double in an hour.

"Say the word and we're out of here."

"And waste this outfit?" Angie was wearing acid-washed jeans and a T-shirt with soaring red, white, and blue eagles knotted tight around her waist. When she'd mentioned a costume, Marcek thought she meant high heels and fishnet stockings. Angie explained how she'd learned from a Lifetime Channel movie that truck-stop hookers were more trailer park than streetwalker.

Rubbing her knees to soften the denim, Angie felt her first butterfly. A few more followed, though not enough to make a to-do with Marcek. She'd convinced herself that the parked truck rows were a giant flea market where she'd wander in search of the right product. "I'm not doing anything but shopping. We've got to start somewhere, and switching places isn't going to work."

Marcek had no counterargument. From his Scranton experience, he'd learned truck stops were their own ecosystem, a unique collection of subtle communications that outsiders couldn't quite hear or duplicate. Port Richmond was no different. Or a locker room or the VFW on a Friday night. In those circumstances, an unknown man asking questions could expect something between stone silence and a stiletto shoved in his kidney. Only a woman stood a chance.

"Keep it simple," he said, a protective hand massaging her left thigh. "You're looking for anything that suggests Pfizer. The ideal scenario is Pfizer owns the truck or trailer and the driver is their employee. That would give us some kind of insignia or marking. Pfizer outsourcing the entire operation to a third-party hauler would be bad news. The driver might not even know what's in the truck. All he has is an address and a schedule. If that's the story, we're dead. Thing is, we won't know until you make a run."

"Relax." The way his fingers moved, Angie could feel his tension. In the months since meeting, they'd become close. Not just the physical stuff, although that was sweet frosting each time. The two mattered to each other, perhaps more than anyone else at that moment in their lives. They didn't talk long-range plans, but they had momentum. That was enough for now. Pointing to the football-field-sized parking lot, she said, "I'm just dipping a toe. No commitment. Anything I learn, I'll either call or hustle back."

"I'm worried about you."

"Marcek, you think those truckers are any harder to handle than neighborhood boys? I've got game they've never seen before."

Her joking relaxed him enough to discuss next steps. "I've been thinking—we may end up stealing the trailer tonight."

"Why?"

"Think about it. If we find the right truck, all we know is that it's here now. We have no idea when another is due. Tomorrow? Later this week? While we know they've got to be ramping up the Viagra supply, who knows if that's one truck a week or ten. If we find one, we hit it. And if it's the wrong one, well, oh shit. At least we didn't let our opportunity flush south."

Angie knew all along that had to be the routine. She was just waiting for Marcek to catch up. For her, the wild card was Sonny. Her understanding was they'd been charged with the plan. No one said anything about turning nouns into verbs. "You think we should call Sonny for a green light?"

"No."

"Can I ask why, or is that on a need-to-know basis?"

Marcek took a deep breath, needing to convince himself as much as Angie. "Guys like Sonny—and my dad—what they want most are results. If I screw up, there are consequences. But if I freeze or hesitate, I'll never get a second chance. They won't tolerate indecision."

Hearing the rationale, Angie couldn't disagree. "It's almost five o'clock. Tell me where you'll be when I'm walking through there."

"Right here, holding my phone. If I don't hear from you every twenty minutes, I'm coming in. No debate."

"What about the keys?"

"What do you mean? The car keys?"

"Yeah," she answered. "The keys need to stay in the car. Like you said, at any moment we might be stealing the trailer. We can't have you tooling down I-95 with the car keys in your pocket."

Marcek wished he'd had this type of evidence when Sonny scoffed at Angie's involvement and potential. She was three levels better than any typical partner.

They discussed best hiding spots for the keys, both stalling the inevitable opening of the car door and her walking away. She said the priority was fast access and wanted them under the floor mat. Marcek was more concerned with the car getting stolen. After five minutes, Angie won the point because she was driving and unwilling to compromise.

Time to go, they hugged until the center console dug into their sides. Marcek repeated his warnings, and Angie answered she wasn't looking to be a superstar, exiting with a wink. He watched her walk toward the trucks in her lot-lizard attire, thinking she was the finest piece of white trash ass he'd ever seen. He also tabbed her chances of coming back with anything decent at ten percent.

Breeze in her face, Angie appreciated the parking lot's wide expanse. The walk to the trucks was an opportunity to get her mind right. Smelling the diesel, she imagined the desperation of selling one's body and the self-loathing of counting the day's receipts. The mental exercise dropped her mood, drew her elbows in, and curled her shoulders around a sinking chest.

A hundred feet away, she began feeling the physical presence of the engines. Vibrations up through her shoes pulled sweat from her belly and lower back. Closing in on the first row, she saw how the trucks were purposefully parked and staggered, each angled with just enough space to pull forward. She wanted to share the observation with Marcek but knew they were too far apart for hand signals. Touching the outline of her phone in her front pocket, she wondered how long it would take for him to respond if there was trouble.

Moving along the far back edge of the parked trucks—pavement to her right, taillights on her left—Angie passed six rows before encountering her first man. He emerged from the camouflaged truck side, hurried enough to make it feel like a game trail ambush, bumping shoulder-to-chest and almost knocking her over. As he stammered through an apology, she jab-stepped around his lean mountain-man build and hustled away, too terrified to even look back.

Double-timing along another dozen rows, Angie screamed inside her head at the insanity and inaccuracy of what she was doing. Nothing meshed with what she'd envisioned. Her mind's eye had pictured some kind of Florida bazaar with truckers hanging from their open windows, some staring, others making conversation. Dangerous but social. What she found peeking between the trucks was far more unsettling—empty, isolated cavernlike spaces where she'd be alone until she wasn't.

After two more chance encounters with men—resulting in all parties scuttling away—Angie decided to get real. She didn't have it in her to start a conversation. She knew that now. If a trucker initiated, maybe she could respond, but no way was she capable of going door to door, playing the whore role to acquire information. That reality narrowed her focus to the only option left—visually inspecting the outside of each truck for a link to Pfizer or the distributor's warehouse.

Finishing her walk around the perimeter took another five minutes. Making the lap and observing the indifferent truckers settled her nerves enough that she was willing to begin exploring the individual rows. With the falling sun, enough light still filtered between to give her a good look at all the tractor doors and trailers. Each of the sixty rows—crosscut by three paths—took half a minute to walk. Midway through, she leaned against a bumper and called Marcek. "It's all wrong," she said. "The whole stupid plan, just wrong." He asked how many rows she had left, and Angie said thirty with new trucks arriving every minute. He asked if she felt safe, and she said it was just like walking South Philly. Sun up, no problem. Come night, things might get weird.

Finishing her weave through the final thirty rows, Angie found more of the same—no useful information and shy men who dropped their eyes within fifteen feet. There was zero support for her hypothesis or encouragement to continue. Needing a break and some air-conditioning, she trailed a chubby trucker inside the minimart and duplicated his purchase. Back outside, she settled on a curb and gave herself five minutes to enjoy sixteen ounces of Mountain Dew and a bag of teriyaki-flavored beef jerky.

Two sips into her drink, Angie heard footsteps, felt a light tap on her shoulder, and scrambled to her feet faster than her role should have allowed.

"New girl, huh?" said a middle-aged woman with a rounded belly, gap-toothed grin, and chin pulled into her neck. As though they shopped off the same rack, the woman wore a cat T-shirt, dirty jeans, and white sneakers with the tongues pulled out high and wide. Her frizzy hair was overrun by Florida's humidity, and there were four freshly picked scabs on her face. Angie liked her immediately.

"I guess," said Angie, wondering how her accent would play in the Sunbelt. "First day."

"Any luck?"

"Never."

That got the woman laughing. "Can I have a sip of your Mountain Dew? It's hot, and I ain't got paid anything yet."

"Oh, sure," said Angie. "Take the rest and this jerky, too. I'm all through."

The wild-haired woman smiled into the bag of dried meat. "Nobody does nothing during the day, you know. Sunlight makes them all polite and chicken shitty. I saw you walking and wanted to tell you but figured that's just something you had to learn. Guys are napping, showering, or maybe touring the racetrack. Fun starts around ten or eleven o'clock. That's when the other girls arrive."

Angie reached her hand out. "My name's Penny with a y."

The woman fought the curls off her forehead before taking Angie's hand. "Stardust," she answered with a smile. "That's what I'm called around here. You stay a week, we'll come up with something special for you. Nicknames have to be earned, though."

"That is my nickname," said Angie. "You know, *Find a penny, pick her up*. How long you been working the lot?"

"Oh, on and off for ten years. Got married, so that was a two-year break. Back now five, so I guess it's twelve total. Never thought I'd be here so long."

Angie noticed how she quoted a decade plus two without a hint of regret. "Can I ask you a question?"

"Sure—those other girls, the ones coming later, they can be some nasty bitches. They won't help you. But not me. I'm just trying to get along. Stay away from my regulars and we'll be fine partners. You ever need a condom, just ask, and I'll do the same, okay?"

Angie tried remembering the line so she could share it with Marcek. He'd think it was as funny as she did. "You know most of the truckers that come in here?"

Finishing off the soda, her tongue darting inside for the last drops, Stardust said, "Yeah, I'm like the mayor of truck town. We actually have a Christmas card mailing list for the regulars. I start handing out copies in November. Next year I'm planning on e-mail."

Angie dropped her gaze to a pebble and worked it with the toe of her sneaker. "I'm not real experienced at this."

"They'll like that, the men, I mean."

"When the parties start, what do you usually charge?"

"As much as I can," said Stardust, glancing around to make sure potential customers weren't passing by. "Minimum is twenty for a blow job, but it depends how bad I need the money."

Angie pulled a pack of gum from her pocket and offered her new friend a stick. "Night like tonight, what can you expect to make? Ballpark figure—two hundred bucks?"

"Oh," said Stardust, her mouth grinding a beef strip into brown mash. "Baby, this ain't the big city. Two hundred dollars? These cheap-ass truckers aren't paying money like that."

"So what, then?"

"Eighty bucks is my target. I hit that, whether it's on my first or fourth trick, I'm done. Some nights, that's the hardest eighty bucks you'll ever earn. But I'm a good talker, fellows like me. Two or three think we're dating, so when they drive through I'm booked for the night."

Angie had met full-time prostitutes in Philadelphia. And a couple girls she knew from school dabbled in the craft, though she'd never met anyone like Stardust, a woman so resigned to the oldest occupation she discussed her day-to-day routine without irony or sadness. Angie decided her last act of the evening would be giving Stardust all her cash. Buying the redheaded prostitute the night off was the least she could offer.

"Mind if we sit?" asked Angie, pointing a finger at the curb. With the truck stop to their backs and the overnight lot on the other side of the gas pumps, she had a good angle to see all the arriving tractor-trailers.

Stardust dropped onto her haunches, leaning into Angie when a foot got lodged beneath her thigh. "You sure you're done with this?" she giggled, jamming the last piece of jerky into her mouth.

"Stardust?"

"Yeah?"

"You said you keep a list of all the drivers? For Christmas cards?"

Stardust nodded. Her mouth was too full of beef juice to speak without leaking.

On a hunch, Angie asked, "You ever heard of Viagra?"

Stardust swallowed and ran her tongue over both rows of teeth. "Is that a type of spaghetti?"

Angie hesitated with her last question, not anxious to hear the wrong answer. "How about Pfizer? That name ring any bells? Pfizer, starts with a *P*? Maybe you've seen it on a truck or one of your mailing lists?"

"Penny, you chasing an old boyfriend? Because I know everybody on this lot and I've never heard of a Pfizer. I once had a man I loved so much I tried hunting him down. His name was Gowen, and I went all the way to Virginia for his hairy red ass."

Angie leaned back on her palms, closed her eyes, and lifted her chin. Late day orange and lemon sunlight leaked through her lids, unexpected reminders of summer breaks at South Jersey beaches—classic rock on every radio, high school boys tossing a football, little brothers and sisters riding waves, her girlfriends bitching how they couldn't get tan without using oil, and Angie not wanting the time to end because of home's reality.

"Oh, shit," said Stardust.

Angie opened an eye.

"Here comes Gary the Preacher. Coming to shower before tonight's service."

A dozen men moving in every direction, Angie asked which one.

"See him in the white shirt, all clean? With the ironed jeans? Yeah, by the trailer right there. That's him. Fresher than a baby, the man still showers before he eats and preaches. You ain't Baptist or anything like that, are you?"

"I'm Catholic."

"Oh," said Stardust. With hips so wide she couldn't cross her ankles without splaying her knees, her crotch was on full display to approaching traffic. "Well, Gary the Preacher is Baptist. I mean, like, really, really, Baptist. Set your mind to saying no to anything he asks. He's tricked me before. Start answering his questions and the next thing you know, you're at his Bible study group on the other side of this building and you've missed three hours of work. Oh hell, here he comes. Just know his favorite thing is saving whores."

Angie considered walking away but didn't want to abandon her new friend. The man Stardust identified was indeed making a straight—though not uninterrupted—line in their direction. To each passing trucker he offered a hearty hello and a business card, which Stardust explained was his verse of the day plus the time and location of tonight's prayer meeting.

Before he was close enough to hear, Angie asked, "How many go to his services?"

"Depends," answered Stardust. "I have no bias against preaching, though he tends to run long when taken by the spirit. He tries grabbing every new trucker, has six or seven regulars, and a few will drift through. Says he likes stopping over in Daytona for all the sinners."

Gary the Preacher made eye contact with Angie a dozen steps away. He was the type of well-built, joyous man who looked younger than his true age. His belt was buckled a notch too tight, and he carried a leather gym bag, which Angie assumed contained shower supplies and a change of clothes. The only marking on the bag was a white patch with a single blue word. Unable at first, she could read it as he got closer—PFIZER.

Holy shit, she thought. *Jackpot.*

Stopping a yard off the curb, Gary said, "Hi, Stardust."

"Hi, honey." True to her nature, Stardust accepted his approach with the same easy aplomb she brought to every other facet of her bumpy life. Blow jobs for twenty bucks received the same emotional investment as Baptist truckers spreading the Good Word.

"Have you read the verse I mentioned?"

"Yes. I mean, I looked at it, but I haven't had a chance to really think about it."

Gary nodded at Stardust's answer while looking at Angie. "I'm Gary," he said, handing her a card. "I haven't seen you before. What's your name?"

When Angie inhaled, Stardust tapped her with an elbow, like, *Careful, this is how he got me.* Angie couldn't help smiling. "Penny with a *y*."

"Well, Penny with a *y*, have you accepted Christ as your Lord and Savior?"

Angie read the card before rolling it over in her hand. "I'm Catholic."

Gary winked. "You don't think Catholics can be saved?"

"My priest thinks I'm okay already. What's up with the card?" she asked, holding it up between her first two fingers. She'd never flirted with such a religious man, figuring it couldn't be too different.

"It's my prayer meeting. Love for you to attend. Since being dipped in the holy waters, I've personally saved twenty-six sinners."

"How long?" she said, extending the last syllable with her glossed lips.

"Excuse me?"

"How long are the meetings? Me and you, how long would we meet?"

Stardust's snicker made Gary blush. "Oh, I see," he said, his mood dimming as he tightened his grip on the bag. "You're having a little fun at my expense. Well, it's not too late for you, Penny. There's still time. Listen to your heart and join me tonight. From seven to ten o'clock we'll be near the tree line. Stardust, you're of course welcome."

Angie pointed to his bag. "Hey, on the patch, that the name of your church?"

Mouth falling open, Gary locked eyes with Angie as he experienced what he would later describe in sermons, testimonials, and self-published materials as The Epiphany. *Yes, of course,* he thought, the message was so clear. *My church, indeed, if they had their way. How could I have been so blind? This is my moment of deliverance.* Shifting his focus upward, he shouted, "How you do work, sending me this courier of truth. Yes, I've been weak, allowing myself to be led by a false prophet. I'm shamed and sorry."

Smile restored, Gary knew God had spoken to him through this beautiful prostitute. He'd wandered. The bag—that prideful leather bag adorned with corporate patches—was Pfizer's gift to him for ten years of service. He now understood it as a lure, the devil's work to ensure he'd haul their unholy intoxicant. Sex was a spiritual gift, and if taken away, who'd be so brazen as to defy this mandate with a pill? The devil, he thought, that's who.

Pulling his shoulders back, resolute in his newfound peace, Gary the Preacher said, "No, Penny, despite their intentions, that's not my church. Pfizer is the company I drive for, my employer, but not much longer. Truth be told, I now believe they're peddling false idols."

"Never heard of them. What do they make?"

"Fool's medicine."

"Is that what you're delivering?" asked Angie. "Are you the Medicine Man?"

"I'm sorry," he said, stepping around the two women. Knowing he had the beginnings of his most powerful personal statement, there was much to consider before the night's prayer meeting. "I need to shower. Seven o'clock, Penny. Don't forget."

Angie closed her eyes and leaned her head back. She'd celebrate the victory for five or ten seconds, call Marcek with the news, and wait for Gary the Preacher to reemerge. Finding his truck was her final task. Marcek could handle picking the keys off the preacher and driving his truck off the lot.

"Hey," said Stardust, shaking her new friend's shoulder. "You see that? Your boyfriend's name is printed on the preacher's bag. You did it, you found him, Penny. You found the man of your dreams."

27.

THE PLAN WAS SIMPLE. Avoid using cell phones while traveling from Daytona to their own warehouse. Stay close, drive a few miles under the limit, and hug the right lane regardless of slow drivers. If there was an issue, neither was allowed to flash headlights or honk, because both were police attractors. Just wave a hand or run the windshield wipers, which meant take the next exit.

With almost no traffic and perfect spring conditions, they pulled into Sonny's warehouse just as Gary the Preacher finished his closing prayer and blessed the flock.

Inside the warehouse, with the stolen truck parked alongside the new one, Marcek and Angie allowed themselves a moment of celebration. They jumped up and down, hugging and high-fiving their success. Even if Stardust remembered the new prostitute and Gary could describe the fellow who bumped him hard enough to knock heads, how did that information help the cops recover the truck? As long as they got the product unloaded and onto a new truck heading north within the next twelve hours, they'd be tough to pin down.

Walking through their future timeline, they realized the immediate issue was whether they should open and unload the truck before calling Sonny. He knew nothing of their progress. He didn't know they'd found the distribution warehouse in Fort Lauderdale or traveled to Daytona Beach.

Marcek said, "What if this thing is full of packing peanuts or aspirin? How does it make sense bringing Sonny down to embarrass ourselves? If it's a bust, we still have time to steal another truck or come up with a second plan."

Angie acknowledged his point before countering with the winning argument. "Sure, this truck could be bogus. But what if we open it up and find Viagra? Sonny might already be sore because we kept him out of the loop, like we're going a little too rogue. Then he sees we opened the truck and rooted around?"

"So?"

"Come on. In his position, you and I'd be thinking the same thing— *I wonder how much Viagra was in the trailer before I arrived.*"

That was all the convincing Marcek needed. She was right. Again. It was Sonny's project, and he needed to share in the joy or disappointment of opening the doors. For the moment, Angie and Marcek would have to define success as hooking the truck within forty-eight hours. Whatever they found inside was the purview of Lady Fortune.

Sonny arrived within an hour of receiving the call. They picked him up at a fast-food parking lot to minimize traffic coming in and out of the warehouse. On the five-minute drive, Sonny asked two questions—*How did the truck handle on the road,* and *why was Angie dressed like a truck-stop hooker?* Heavy enough it wasn't empty, Marcek answered to the first. And for the second, he explained their plan required her to dress down. Those were the last words until they reached the warehouse.

Once they popped the back doors and unloaded the pallets to the warehouse floor, it took a few moments to appreciate what they'd stolen. Best-case scenario was a trailer full of Viagra. They didn't get that. Worst case was all niche pharmaceuticals for treating gout or swimmer's ear— obscure products with zero street value. They didn't get that either.

In total, the truck held twenty-six pallets. Twelve pallets were a mystery—a hodgepodge of scientific-sounding, unrecognizable names.

Eight pallets were Viagra. For all involved to walk with six hundred grand, Sonny said, each pallet needed twenty thousand pills. By a rough count—given the rows and columns—they were playing math in the right neighborhood.

The final six pallets were dismissed until later that night at Sonny's condo. Standing around his dining table, thinking of next steps, they agreed to call Bielakowski. Sonny had already cleared the air about roles, so no issues were expected. As Marcek had predicted, his old man was fine with the arrangement. He was getting a half-million or more without assembling a team or running the operation. His sole responsibility was middle-manning a northeastern buyer with the resources and willingness to appreciate the hottest pharmaceutical drug in the world. What complaint could he have?

Sonny assumed the lead on their end of the call. Once his partner answered, Sonny explained the truck contained twenty-six pallets and eight were worth hauling north for sale. The buyer needed three million with a half-million reserve in case their preliminary count was low.

"What's getting left behind?" Bielakowski asked.

"Twelve are a grab bag of medicines we can't pronounce."

"And the others?"

"Six pallets of Sudafed. Can we make money off them? Sure, meth cooks need the pills and would pay a price, but—given your position on drugs—we're leaving the pallets in the warehouse."

"Walking away?"

Sonny didn't want to get pinned with a committed position. "To be determined."

A thinking man's pause from Anton. "Those are the pills with the pseudoephedrine?"

"Yeah," said Sonny, his face playing out the surprise. "Six pallets of cold pills with pseudoephedrine. While it's probably one-fifth of the Viagra's value, there's still something there."

Anton paused again, this time twice as long. "Give me those cold pills and you and Marcek get my cut of the Viagra."

"You certain?" Sonny didn't understand the angle. Part of him wanted an explanation. The other part said *Shut up and take the deal.*

"Yes, Sudafed for the Viagra. It's what I want. Tell Marcek to start driving."

"Hit the road tonight?" asked Sonny, protective of his young partner. "He's looking a little beat-up."

"He there?"

"Yes."

"Put him on." In Bielakowski's world, if a job required one hundred hours of straight work, then one hundred hours of straight work happened. No debate.

Sonny handed over the phone and tried making sense of Anton Bielakowski's shift. Not once in sixty years had he known the man to get involved in street drugs. And here he was giving up six hundred grand for the privilege. Didn't add up.

Turning his back, Marcek said, "It's me, Dad. We did good."

Bielakowski agreed, giving his son well-deserved credit. Never one to need the pat on the back himself, he sometimes forgot his boy liked the approval. "Sonny says you're sleepy."

Marcek looked over his shoulder to give Angie the winning-team smile. "Long days. No worries, though. I'll sleep a few hours tonight, load the second truck in the morning, and be on my way. Probably a two-day haul with an overnight in North Carolina. I've got clean books, so there shouldn't be any problems as long as I take it nice and easy."

"Start driving tonight," said Bielakowski, his tone no longer the complimentary father. "When your eyelids get heavy, light a cigarette. If the nicotine isn't enough, use the hot end to blister the back of your hand."

Marcek didn't want to alarm Sonny and Angie with a wordy question so he stuck with "Why?"

Bielakowski stoked his son's fire. "There's a million dollars waiting. And if that isn't enough, the sooner you get here, the better chance you have at blasting an Italian with one of Big Bern's shotguns."

"I'll be there." Marcek had figured the heist was just a money grab.

Now his old man was making clear the truck was a chess piece in the war with Rea. He couldn't get to Port Richmond fast enough. "Tell Mom I'm bringing home a guest. Her name's Angie."

Marcek set the phone down, grabbed his woman by the hand, and told Sonny he'd be back in a week with his share of the sale.

28.

ANTON BIELAKOWSKI WENT ALONE to meet the Russian.

Time was short, too short to waste an hour traveling back and forth downtown for more towels, flip-flops, and Russian courtesies. They agreed on a strip-mall tavern ten miles north of Bielakowski's neighborhood, a shot-and-beer joint wedged between a barbershop and a check-cashing store. The Russian had started his gambling operation in the tavern and, on occasion, still took calls there. Bielakowski parked in a handicapped spot, popped an antacid, and waited. His custom before any meeting was spending a few moments studying the scene. Up, down, left, right. Who's hanging around and where's the exit? More than once he'd rolled off, spooked by a suspicious van or odd-looking pedestrian. The antacid was his timer. When it was gone, he was ready.

Entering through double glass doors, Bielakowski paused to let his eyes adjust. The tavern's blinds were drawn, leaving the room in a state of smoke-tinged twilight. Three old men sat at the bar, getting drunk staring at a noiseless television. A bartender—cleaning glasses at the far end—turned his back when Anton entered. Kolya Drobyshev was in the corner booth, seated with a second man who shared the same wide face and broad features. The *vor* wore a tailored blue suit without a tie. The second man, dressed in a smooth black leather jacket, was two decades younger, which meant his value depended upon certain physical qualities and the willingness to use them.

Crossing the room, careful not to trip in the dim light, Bielakowski stood before the Russian with his arms relaxed at his sides. He wasn't interested in sitting or sharing a drink and refused both when offered. "The shipment is arriving," he said. "You'll need three plus in cash."

"Congratulations," said Drobyshev, raising his glass to the success. A bottle of unchilled vodka rested in the middle of the table. "I'm ready when you are. This man will represent my interests in the exchange. His name is Alex. I knew his father from prison and promised to look out for the boy if anything should happen."

Bielakowski waited for a sign of respect from the younger man and returned the nod in kind. He wondered if the introduction was Drobyshev's way of hinting Alex was his son. Given the physical similarities, he would not have been surprised.

"I have other business I want to discuss," said Anton.

Since the Russian was hosting, it was his choice who listened in. Anton Bielakowski's obligation was providing the opportunity to clear the decks, nothing more. When Drobyshev waved off the concern, Bielakowski said, "You told me the Italians want to expand their role in the meth market."

The Russian frowned and nodded. "Yes, this is true. It's a delicate dance, but they have feelers out. No success yet from what I understand."

"I want to accelerate the process."

Drobyshev didn't flinch. "How so?"

"I have what the Italians are looking for."

The Russian paused, then chuckled and backhanded his assistant in the chest. "They should have never started with you, Anton. I warned that Rea. I told him, *Provoking that Polack will not end well.* You know what he said? He called you *old.* See how backwards he is? Isn't that the point? Does he think you've lasted this long because you are dumb?"

Bielakowski disapproved of the crowing. He preferred better done over better said. "Before I make my request, let me explain the payoff. Once I defeat the Italians, you may have what you want from their operations.

Pick the bones. I don't care and will not object as long as Port Richmond is left alone. All I ask is that if the War Boys survive and are capable of continuing, you leave their meth market alone."

Drobyshev's face was now flat and cold. "How long does this grant for the bikers last?"

Bielakowski let a few seconds pass before answering. "One year. Nothing is guaranteed after that."

"Fine." The Russian understood Bielakowski's sensitivity for maintaining Philadelphia's balance of power. Too much, too fast was never part of the man's history. "What is it you ask of me?"

With his hip hurting from the spring moisture, Bielakowski was careful not to reach for a chair or the table's edge. No sense clouding the discussion with his frailty. "I have six pallets stacked head-high with Sudafed. I need you to do a blind sale with the Italians."

Thinking back to their meeting in the steam room, Drobyshev was pleased with his maneuvering. He'd planted the seed and it had grown accordingly. He wasn't foolish enough to imagine Bielakowski was unaware of the guidance. That level of stupidity was reserved for Rea. And who steered, for the moment, was irrelevant. General direction was enough. "Your Viagra trailer was perhaps a bit more crowded than planned, eh?"

Bielakowski's easy shrug answered for the Sudafed's origins. "Anything you're able to negotiate for the cold medicine, half is yours. But you must keep the price low enough that they don't balk. Offer to finance if you must, and I'll make up any difference."

"I understand the value here is not the sale."

The old man nodded. "If you don't want your fingerprints on the play, you're free to outsource. Perhaps our Armenian friends would be willing to assist, but that's to your discretion."

Drobyshev raised a finger to his assistant. "Alex, pay attention to what you are hearing. The sausage maker is setting fires in South Philly."

"No violence is required of you," said Bielakowski. "Set the meeting, pick up the trailer, deliver it to the Italians. You get half plus whatever you obtain when the Italians and War Boys start shooting each other."

Downing his second drink, the Russian reached for the bottle. His assistant had no glass on the table. "With that much trouble inside their own neighborhood, the Italians will have to settle with you. What will you demand?"

Watching Drobyshev enjoy the alcohol, Bielakowski decided to have a drink when he got home. He'd ask his wife to sit and they'd reminisce about when the children were young and Philadelphia was a different place. "We want to be left alone. I have no ambitions beyond protecting my neighborhood. This squabbling over city blocks has lost its appeal."

"I'll call right now," said Drobyshev, pulling his cell phone from inside his suit jacket. "Would you care to listen?"

Anton Bielakowski raised a hand, shook his head, and turned to leave. The crumbs had been sprinkled. It was time Rea learned why his predecessors left the Poles of Port Richmond alone for so long.

29.

WINTER HAD BEEN HARSH to the ball fields, and spring temperatures still hovered in the low fifties. Neither was enough to stop Raymond Rea from organizing the year's first softball practice. Two o'clock at the FDR fields, no excuses. Cleats, sliding pants, and gloves were encouraged. No-showing was not.

The old guys thought Rea was nuts for having a team of wiseguys in a public softball league. Other than attention, what was the purpose? He reminded the grumblers it was his call and if they disagreed, they could complain to Monte or Anticcio. *Oh, I forgot—one's in jail and I killed the other. Guess we're playing ball.* Rea's humor was a reason why the twenty-somethings idolized him and the fifty-somethings prayed he'd catch cancer.

Coin Operated Partners, a corporate front for Rea's video game and poker machine business, sponsored the Italian's softball team. Despite the two guys in charge of uniforms not knowing acronyms from embryos, they thought blue jerseys with COP in black lettering were nice middle fingers for any spying law enforcement. Team COP finished fourth its in-augural season and hoped for better production in year two. Rea pitched and batted third, both justified since he was the only team member who'd played high school ball.

Once practice started on the muddy FDR fields, players took turns in the batter's box, catching fly balls, and fielding grounders. It was still a month from the opener, so coolers of beer were on the field and cigarettes dangled from every other lip. Rea was manager and court jester, throwing softballs behind the batters, cracking wise about the differences between catching and pitching, and enjoying being the center of attention.

After practice, as the men gathered in the parking lot, Rea made a point of pulling Nick Martin to the beer cooler and keeping him supplied. The undercover agent wasn't half finished with one when Rea was pushing another into his hand, opened and ready to go. On top of the booze, the boss was patting Martin on the back, even wrapping an arm around his shoulder after an okay joke that hardly broke through the noise.

One by one, as the coolers emptied and the spring sun lowered, men gave excuses for heading home or to their girlfriends. The three oldest were grabbing dinner and groused about who was supposed to have made reservations at the new joint on Spruce Street.

Not giving it much thought at the time, Martin realized he'd accepted a ride to practice from an outfielder who had since disappeared. As numbers dwindled, Rea made clear he'd drive him home. "Get in," he said, waving him toward his Lincoln. "Been meaning to catch up with you on a few things."

For the first few miles, the two men talked ball. Rea hoped they had sufficient power in cleanup. Martin said he didn't know enough to give an opinion because their four-hitter drank a six-pack before taking his swings. They joked how fat some of the men looked in their baseball pants, and each made excuses for the pitches he'd missed.

Heading north on Broad Street with City Hall in the distance, Rea said, "Anyway, glad you're on the team. Last year's lineup was a hot mess. No balance, you know? Don't get me wrong, we had good players. But Bill, rest his soul, even Bill knew he sucked. With you in center, our defense got upgraded."

Martin nodded, knowing the dialogue was subtext. He wasn't riding with the boss so they could bullshit over South Philly softball. This kind of attention meant he was moving up, down, or out.

"Since we've got the time, some things I've been meaning to get straight."

"Okay." Martin was glad Rea was sticking to Broad Street instead of I-95. With lights every block and a speed limit of thirty miles an hour, he could bail with a decent chance of surviving. He started considering how to position his feet so he wouldn't hook his heels or get run over by the rear tire.

Rea looked sideways at his passenger. "All that beer is making you antsy. You got to piss?"

"No."

"Settle down, okay? You think I'd give you lead-off, then drive you to the swamp after our first practice?"

Martin tried acting cool, but his shrug came up short. "I'm a paranoid guy. Too many movies."

"Nick, man, I'm wearing baseball pants. Use your head. What, I'm going to choke you with my bare hands or use a baseball bat? Fuck's wrong with you?"

Martin swore under his breath, acting a little put out without crossing into anger. It wasn't time to prove he was a tough guy. This sequence was all about him getting his balls busted without losing his cool.

"You live in a dark world. Chill, man. You're making me too much money to be thinking like that."

Martin tapped his finger near the door handle and nodded. *Keep earning* was the message.

Rea checked his mirrors before sipping the beer he'd brought along. "There is some stuff, though. That's why we're doing this in my car. I flip rides every month through my cousin's lot. That way, I know they're clean. This Lincoln hasn't been too bad."

"That's smart. I never heard of anyone else doing that."

"It's because everyone else is lazy. They'd rather do twenty years than two minutes in front of a notary signing over the title."

"I might copy that routine."

"Good by me. I need all you guys taking precautions, too. I'll give you my cousin's address. He'll set you up. You ready for the other stuff?"

"Yeah."

When Nick Martin started with Jimmy Zoots's South Philly crew, he moved from Jersey across the bridge to a townhome in Queen Village. There wasn't a perfect route from the FDR ball fields to Martin's place, but Rea was taking the long way. Martin figured the extended route meant heavy business.

Rea stopped talking at a red light and didn't start again until it turned. "How's your operation in Jersey? Okay despite the move?"

"Good. Could always be better. After ten years I've got it dialed in pretty good. Eagles killed me this year, know what I mean?"

"Wiseguys in Jersey are funny to me," said Rea. "It's like they all have this inferiority complex."

"Yeah, maybe."

"Not quite Philly, not quite New York. They're like that story of the wandering Jews—you know that one? Monte was telling me about them once. There are some crazy Jews that have been wandering all over Africa looking for a home for a thousand years. That's those Jersey guys. They should make a show about that."

"Yeah, that's a funny idea."

Rea's voice dropped an octave. "Anyway, and this is what we need to discuss, after last year's tug-of-war with Anticcio, relations got a little strained with our northern cousins. New York wasn't *formally* backing either of us, but they weren't exactly neutral. Anticcio was their guy."

Martin looked for a read and drew a busted flush. "I heard it's been getting better, like we're not so much the kid brother. Least that's what Costa's been saying."

"Costa? The thing with Costa is he shouldn't be talking out of school."

"I was just saying . . ."

"No, it's okay. This time he's actually right."

"Yeah? That's a good thing."

Rea opened his right hand to help explain. "For New York, yeah, I think the perception is we're getting it together—first with the tax and now our expansion. And they seem to like us pushing on Bielakowski and the Poles. That's where you come in."

The mention of the Poles made Martin's skin tingle with memories of the binding rope. Even though he'd given Bielakowski his word, time had whittled away at the commitment. Truth was, between the Italians and Poles, Martin needed Rea to win or what was the point of the last ten years? All down the toilet because the Pole had gotten lucky snatching an undercover FBI agent in Kensington? Hell with that.

Rea tapped Martin's arm. "Listen up. On this New York thing, I've been handling the communication myself, but that can't work forever. One, it's too damn much exposure. And two, it's bad for business, like a ballplayer handling his own contract negotiations. Impossible to keep personal feelings out."

Martin turned his hands up, unsure what to say and wanting to keep his options open.

Rea didn't speak again for another three blocks. At Third Street, instead of going straight, he turned left into Northern Liberties. He drove half a dozen blocks, eyes tracking the cars parked curbside until he stopped in front of a metered parking space cordoned off by orange City of Philadelphia cones. With cars stacking up behind him on the one-way, he told Martin to hustle out and clear the space.

"What are you talking about? You serious?" Rea's look was enough to get Martin out and tossing the cones onto the sidewalk.

Once Rea swung into the space and Martin was back inside, the boss made a point of twisting in his seat to make eye contact. "Here's the deal. You're getting bumped up. I want you as my guy with New York. It's working and needs to stay on the rails. Any business involving New York and North Jersey is your responsibility. I'll have final say and will attend most negotiations, but you're my day-to-day point person. Their guy is Dom Bidanno."

Martin had been wrong. The drive had nothing to do with the Poles. It was one hundred times bigger than the Italians' ongoing friction with Anton Bielakowski. Rea was opening him up to the most significant undercover accomplishment in FBI history. Ten years infiltrating the Philadelphia mob and now he was being invited north. New York City.

"Yo, Martin, I'm asking about Bidanno. You know him or what?"

"Yeah, sorry," he said, with an exaggerated nod. "Sure, I know Bidanno from card games in Atlantic City. Smart. Not as smooth with the ladies as he thinks. Probably eight years I've known him. No bad blood. No good either."

"I figured you could handle him. What do you think? I send Costa up and he'd come home wearing a New York Giants jersey from Chinatown. But if you're in, this can't be no half-ass thing."

"Of course. I'll do good."

Rea broke off eye contact and turned forward. A light rain was falling, and headlights were splitting drops on the windshield. Pointing a finger toward the next parked car, he said, "Look there, what do you think that car is worth? Give a guess."

When he was moving the cones, Martin hadn't paid any attention to the run-down four-door Ford Taurus parked off their front bumper. Nothing stood out except two Marine Corps stickers and a Harley-Davidson emblem in the window. "Maybe a couple grand. Three tops."

"Wrong. Way more. Couple million, probably."

With the number, Martin knew, Rea was giving him another puzzle piece. Each movement and line was by design—being asked onto the team, the practice, the arranged pickup, the drive home, the parking space, the promotion, and now this car. To what end, Martin had no idea.

"Tommy Paschol."

"What?"

"Tommy Paschol. I'm asking if Tommy Paschol means anything to you."

A name wasn't what Martin had predicted. His mind raced to make the connection. "Never heard of the guy. He saying he knows me? That I did something?"

"No, nothing like that."

"What's up with him?"

"Paschol is a War Boy," said Rea. "Turns out, he's more involved with our side of the business than I ever knew. I can't say he's the brains of the operation because that's too much credit, but he knows to the ounce how much meth is sent our way."

"What, like a bookkeeper?"

"Yeah, that's probably a way of explaining it. No formal ledgers or anything, but yeah, he's their bookkeeper." What irked Rea was that other than him and Chuck Trella Jr. nobody on either side was supposed to have Paschol's knowledge. They'd agreed on dealing directly so no intermediaries could cause too much harm or sabotage the relationship.

His voice low, Rea said, "Paschol got arrested about two months ago. I found out on my own, nobody from the War Boys clued me in. Typical of those assholes. When I reached out to Trella, all I got were assurances. No action."

"You thought Paschol was going to talk?"

"Basically," said Rea, pulling a pack of cigarettes from the armrest. "He hired an attorney known for dealing. When I tried a soft sell to get him to change, that crapped out, too. Smoke?"

"Sure."

Thinking of the money he'd wasted on Billy O'Bannon, Rea lit his cigarette and pressed his head against the seat. "My hands were tied. Me and Trella have an arrangement. War Boys don't mess with my men and vice versa. Difference is, none of you have been arrested on anything serious. And if you were, you wouldn't know much about the bikers' side of the business. That was supposed to be the deal. Experts call it operational deniability, but those fucking motorcyclists run their business like a monkey house."

Martin paused, wanting to remember every detail. Looking up the sidewalk for anything he could use to slow the conversation, he saw a meter maid heading their way. Martin tapped Rea's elbow, rolled his eyes toward the cones on the sidewalk, and mentioned maybe he should drop a quarter if they were sticking around.

"Yeah," said Rea, pulling some change from a cup in the console, "and see if that Ford needs love. Hate to see a veteran get a fifteen-dollar ticket for nothing."

Martin didn't bother asking what he should say if questioned about the cones. Shit honored gravity, which meant it was his job to handle the situation. He took the change, opened his door, and exited into the drizzle.

Watching the meter maid ticket a red Honda, Martin dropped two quarters for the Ford and two more for Rea's Lincoln. She caught the move, snapped the windshield wiper down on the ticket, and skipped the dividing cars. A half-sized women with a plus-sized backside, she closed the distance with fast little steps. Winded, she placed her right hand on the Ford's trunk and looked ready to dip the hip for additional support. "You know I can still write him, don't you? And give you one, too?"

If Martin had read those words on a page, he'd have figured she was boom-ready, but her body language defied the stereotype and suggested a milder interpretation. She looked tired and in no mood to fight.

"Just being a good neighbor," he said, a little slower than his usual pace. "I wasn't messing with you. Figured the owner of that car could use a break. No need to pile on. All about the karma."

She looked him up and down in his baseball pants before turning her attention to the nearby cones. "Where'd those come from?"

Martin shrugged.

"Last lap I swear those were in the street. You moving them for a spot?"

Hands up and smiling, he said, "What do I look like? A car pulled out and we pulled in. Road crew probably left them after filling potholes. No wonder our taxes are so high."

"Don't look at me, baby." Her head bobbled side to side, making her hoop earrings dance. "I'm a revenue generator. Look down your nose if you want, but I'm saving the city money. Can't tell people nothing, though. All they have is hate."

Eyes open wide, Martin agreed on each of her points, saying they couldn't pay him enough to do her job. "Toughest shift in the city. Total respect. Me? I'd rather patrol for stray dogs or guard a judge."

She rechecked both meters and made a point of mentioning another meter maid wouldn't be back for a couple of hours. If Martin wanted to skip a quarter, no sweat off her ass because her shift was almost over. Time to head home.

"Power to the people," said Martin.

She answered with a peace sign over her shoulder and disappeared around the nearest street corner.

Back inside the car, Rea told Martin he should have called the meter maid a bitch, because who cared whose money fed the meters? "Put her in our line of work," he said. "She'll drop those distinctions real quick. Money doesn't care who earns it or owns it."

"She's all right," said Martin, noting Rea was halfway through another cigarette. "End of her shift and it's starting to rain, so I think she just wanted a reason to hopscotch to the end of the block."

Checking his side mirror, Rea said, "We're good with the New York thing?"

"What, I'm going to change my mind in five minutes? It's perfect."

"Big bump, you know. Historic. People will know your name."

Martin got the feeling Rea was unsatisfied with his gratitude, like a grandparent gifting a savings bond. Time to show some love. "I want New York," he said. "I want it, okay? And I appreciate the opportunity. Whatever it takes, Ray, because nobody will do a better job. And I promise, Philly is done drawing short straws with those boys. I'll handle the duty, no problem, man."

Rea took a drag and flicked the butt out his window, bouncing it off the quarter-panel of a passing car. "We've got some housekeeping, too."

Martin wished for another beer so he could steal a second to think. Rea had the benefit of a script. He was read-and-reacting. "It doesn't matter," he said, deciding to say as little as possible as the conversation rolled forward.

Using his chin like a pointer, Rea said, "Back to that Ford. I mentioned it was worth something."

"I remember."

A double-length pause. "Its value is its cargo."

Martin looked back and forth, waiting for the punch line.

Rea said, "Tommy Paschol is in the trunk."

"Dead?"

"Shot six times."

"Jesus" was all Martin could manage. If Rea was telling the truth, Philly's mob boss had just identified the location and identity of a murder victim. "In that car? You're telling me a War Boy is stuffed in that frickin' trunk? Ray, what the fuck, man?"

The question marked Rea's face with shaded black lines. "Don't get all dramatic. Two minutes ago you'd never heard of the guy. All that matters is Mr. Tommy Paschol is out of the singing business."

The picture had come into focus. While Rea was a street-savvy player, Martin never took him for fifteen moves of clairvoyance. At best, he was two moves out or—like with the New York offer—just one. *Hey, Nick, you get one of the highest-profile spots in the family, the one you've been busting my stones about. Oh, by the way, see that car? Let's talk about what's doing with the dead body in its trunk.* Typical meatball, right down to the parking job on Third Street.

"So what's the assignment?" Martin said, his voice matching the boss's intensity. "That's why we're here, right? 'Cause you've got something for me to do?" The task was more than just disposing of a body. There were ten guys on payroll better suited for burn-and-bury work. Whatever the job, it was important enough to have New York as its prologue.

"There are changes coming," said Rea, going for his third cigarette.

"How so?"

"Until tonight, our enemy has been the Poles and our ally the War Boys."

Second mention of the Poles struck a nerve for Martin; he figured he was being introduced to the ending. If Rea had a gun, it was probably under his seat. Martin's was beneath a towel in his backpack. Either one getting the draw would be a tall order. "You going for peace with the Poles?"

"Screw that," said Rea. "That's a long day from being done, especially after what they did to Louis and Bill."

"Then I'm not following."

"We're redefining the relationship."

Martin didn't know what to say. Without more clues, he was flailing at the possibilities.

Rea tossed his hands up at the silence. He'd been hoping Martin was smart enough to grasp the big picture and run with the details. "Christ sake, Nick, I gotta connect every dot? Take Paschol's body and pin it on the Poles."

"Set up Bielakowski?"

"Yeah, now you're getting it."

More silence from Martin, a strategy he'd stick with until it stopped working.

Rea tapped the steering wheel. Staring out the windshield at nothing in particular, he said, "This isn't some regular everyday thing. We're making a move. That's why you're involved. I trust you'll keep your mouth shut."

"I'm down for whatever. Just point me in the right direction."

Rea looked at his passenger with thin eyes. "Trella has to think the Poles killed Paschol. He's a frickin' hothead about protecting his people. We can use that."

Martin nodded, mentally summarizing the move for later recollection. Rea was manipulating the War Boys into joining his fight against the Poles. Okay, so far, he wasn't overwhelmed with the material.

"Give Trella our blessing for revenge. In fact, tell him I want the Poles wiped off the map. Bielakowski, his son, the whole lot of them."

Martin turned toward the passenger-side window, disgusted at how self-impressed Rea was with his clever little plot. All this drama and a dead body just to jazz up some bikers into making a charge through Port Richmond? *Fucking amateur hour*, he thought.

Rea lit his fourth cigarette and turned up the radio. He waited through an entire Bon Jovi song before turning it back down and leaning across the armrest. "And then let the Poles know the War Boys are coming."

Martin flinched. Couldn't help himself.

Rea leaned back into the driver's seat, hands atop the steering wheel, cigarette ash dangling over the column. He was so damn close. If Martin could convince Trella to mount up—and the Poles did their part killing the bikers—he'd control the city's meth market from A to Z. No more partners, no more testifying assholes like Tommy Paschol. He just needed a little luck, because once word was out about him buying cold medicine—and word always got out—the War Boys would rebel. That's why Paschol had to die. He was the starter's pistol.

"There's an important sequence," said Rea, his index finger up. "Do the thing with Trella, that's got to be number one. So far, the Poles haven't targeted the bikers." He pointed to the Ford. "Paschol's corpse will change that perception. My guess when Trella hears? Out of his head—almost wish I could be there to see it. Stand back, let him freak a bit, and then tell him to target Bielakowski. Here's the thing, though—focus him on the old man's shop. Last headache I need is the bikers terrorizing Port Richmond and drawing in the news crews. The point is getting Trella at a specific time and place trying to kill Bielakowski. Follow so far?"

Martin nodded and said yeah, he followed.

"Then call the Pole's shop and tell anybody who answers the War Boys are coming. Bielakowski can handle it from there."

Martin decided to change the conversation's rhythm. He needed Rea explaining the why behind his maneuvers. Bold, yes. Smart? To be determined. "If Trella gets hammered, doesn't that leave us scrambling to replace their capabilities? The cook has always been their deal."

"One step ahead of you, brother."

As an undercover agent, Martin loved Rea's arrogance. Like the sausage maker said, it left him vulnerable. "I'm not following, Ray."

The rain slowed enough for Rea to lower the driver's-side window. A passing car stopped, and a mom with two wide-eyed screamers asked if they were leaving and could they have the spot? Rea gave a big wave like just another happy tourist looking to help a fellow traveler. He pulled out and again headed north. "If all goes right tomorrow with the bikers in Port Richmond, I'll need you tomorrow night."

"Where?"

Rea acted like he didn't hear the question, instead tossing a set of keys into Martin's lap. He was enjoying his role as director. "Entirely up to you how Trella gets launched into action, although I'm figuring these might be handy—they're for Paschol's Ford. When you're done, make sure you dump them in a sewer or the river. Under no circumstance do you keep them as a souvenir. Scalps like that get us all convicted."

"No shit."

"Watch your mouth. That is important enough for me to repeat ten times if I want. Don't be a wiseass thinking you know everything."

Martin studied the set. There were four keys—one ignition, one for the trunk, and two generic cuts probably for Paschol's house. While he wasn't sure how he'd manage the biker's body or finish the night's ruse, he sure as hell wasn't losing the keys down any hole. As evidence, maybe the four keys were tainted and inadmissible in court, but they were also a crucial component of his narrative and proof of his access.

They traveled another two blocks north before Martin realized Rea hadn't answered his question. "After the bikers are handled, where do you want me to be?"

Finally swinging south toward Martin's place in Queen Village, Rea said, "Can you drive a truck?"

"Sure."

"Good. I bought some cold medicine. It's being delivered tomorrow."

Martin's tumblers fell into order. "Holy hell, how much?"

"Enough to make me okay putting Tommy Paschol in that trunk and walking the War Boys into a shooting gallery."

At last, Martin had acquired enough tile pieces and perspective to understand the mosaic. Raymond Rea's ambition equaled his own. Under different circumstances, he didn't doubt each could have worn the other's clothes. "Who's selling that much pseudoephedrine?"

"The Armenians. That's why I need you. They're clowns."

30.

FEELING LIKE ONE of those casualty notification officers visiting a fallen soldier's parents, Martin arrived at the War Boys' clubhouse bearing the same variety of bad news. He only hoped his version of Tommy Paschol's death contained enough shavings of truth to conceal the lies. If he flinched, or the story failed to hold up, the audience's notorious lack of impulse control meant his certain death.

Allowed inside, Martin didn't waste time on small talk or formalities. He explained to Trella and the surrounding bikers how patrolmen found Paschol's Ford in Pennypack Park. Following procedure, the cops checked its registration, opened the trunk, and discovered the dead War Boy's body. The news circulated in the department until a badge on the payroll caught wind and called Rea.

All Chuck Trella Jr. needed to hear was Tommy Paschol was dead.

He grabbed a pry bar and attacked a waist-high toolbox, gouging its gauged steel and splashing wrenches across the oil-stained floor. Martin stood to the side, one eye on Trella, the other on the dozen bikers watching this unleashed force of nature. No one moved or said boo. While Trella's intelligence was credited for the club's rise, he didn't lead the East Coast's most violent motorcycle gang because he had an academic demeanor. His willingness to both lead and fight—with guns, knives, or fists—was the only technique he needed for absolute control.

Exhausted and palms bloodied, Trella dropped the pry bar, spit on the floor, and turned for his office. Halfway across the garage he shouted for Martin to follow. Behind a metal desk—bikini and motorcycle calendars decorating the walls—Trella leaned forward on his knuckles like a silverback in the jungle. "Who did this fucking thing to Tommy? I want to know."

No hesitation. "The Poles."

An emotion other than rage crossed the gorilla's face. "How do you figure? We've got no beef with them."

"It's not in the papers yet, but the cops told us Tommy's mouth was stuffed with blood sausage. That's their move. Plus, finding him in Pennypack, it's a dumping ground for Northeast Philly."

Trella slammed both fists onto his desktop, wrapped his fingers beneath the front lip, and pitched it forward. "Fuck Rea if he thinks I'm waiting. Those Poles are bleeding for this."

Martin stood in the doorway, like an observer of a bomb detonation crew ready to take cover. The hope for the outburst was Trella becoming too clouded to decipher the setup. The risk was the breadth and depth of any collateral damage. "That's why he sent me, so there'd be no misunderstanding. When we heard about Paschol, Ray was devastated. His words to me, honest to Christ, were *Unleash the War Boys*. No restrictions. Hit Bielakowski full force. Burn him out of his shop if you have to."

The wheezing of Trella's inhalations was almost asthmatic. "Goddamn it, he ain't going to be at the shop. He'll be hiding, scared of popping his head up."

Martin had grown weary of criminals projecting fear upon an opponent. He hadn't met many—friend or foe—that shied from aggressive attack. Their propensity for matching or exceeding an opponents' intensity was why they were in the life to begin with. The only man who didn't attribute fright as an adversarial motivator was Bielakowski. Perhaps because he didn't care.

"We're setting a meeting," said Martin. "Rea wants this over, too. This afternoon, Bielakowski thinks we're coming to his shop to propose peace based on his men dying and what happened to Paschol."

Head down, too emotional for eye contact, Trella said, "Tommy Paschol, man."

"Four o'clock. He thinks it's just Rea and me. He'll probably be in the back of the shop, finishing his shift."

The biker turned his back and stared at a corkboard covered with party fliers and bumper stickers. With his arms crossed, his flanks flared like jousting armor. "I'm going to skin that damn Polack with his own knife."

Nick Martin had one more call. If all the moves fell into line—and Rea didn't have a heart attack or catch a stray bullet—the Federal Bureau of Investigation and the U.S. Attorney's Office would have the case of a lifetime.

Walking from the bikers' clubhouse to his car, he heard the word *hero* repeating in his ear. He wished his old man had lived long enough for the press clippings. The first week would be a media storm, like for a Medal of Honor winner coming home for Christmas. He figured it'd take another year to wrap up the Philly crew, the War Boys, New York, and now the Armenians, plus eighteen months preparing for trial and testifying. Then he'd be liberated. A lifetime pension, a book deal, and a sweet consulting gig in Manhattan. His head swirled with the possibilities.

With the air-conditioning on high and the radio off, he decided to remain parked until he finished with Bielakowski. Movement might distract him from making the perfect call. He dialed the Port Richmond shop and waited three rings.

"Hello, Bielakowski's," answered a woman young enough for enthusiasm at work. "What do you need?"

"I'm a friend of Anton's. He in?"

"He's with a customer. Can you wait a sec, or is there something I can help with?"

"No. Tell him the Irishman from the warehouse is on the phone. He'll know."

Martin heard a metallic clink and the background chatter of a busy shop, as if she'd set the phone down on a steel counter. The temptation was to go with a light warning, less specific than what Rea demanded. Instead of giving a date and time, more along the lines of *Hey, I don't know the details, but the War Boys think you were involved with Paschol.* If the bikers killed Bielakowski, Martin was free. The warehouse incident would be twenty-four hours that had never happened. Gone, erased, ciao baby. At the same time, if the War Boys survived and discovered the meth play, they'd go for Rea, an unacceptable possibility. A dead Rea was ten years flushed down the toilet like last night's dinner.

"Hello," said Bielakowski. "I thought you lost my number. Back in the warehouse we'd agreed to be friends. But you never call. You never write. I began thinking I'd done something to insult you."

Because of the man's age and accent, Martin struggled reading his tone, but the words were pretty clear. "I have a warning."

"Of course, why else would you call?"

"The War Boys are coming to Port Richmond. Four o'clock at your shop. There're coming heavy."

If Martin had been sitting alongside Bielakowski, he'd have thought it was the old man's birthday. A wider smile could not have been had. "I guess Rea can't handle us anymore. Time for the poodles and professional wrestlers."

"I've got to go. That's all I know."

"Please send my condolences to the Paschol family," said Bielakowski. "A very unfortunate accident. And in Pennypack Park, too, so close to Port Richmond. Such heartbreak."

Martin's answer was silence.

Bielakowski said, "Rea isn't the only one who knows friendly police."

"The reasons why don't change this afternoon. Trella is on his way."

It was the Pole's turn to pause. Using the Russian for the blind sale was making it too easy. The irony, of course, was that it was going to cost the FBI agent his life. Sure, Bielakowski could save him. Only a few words were needed. The problem was Martin himself. Once warned, he'd turn around and protect Rea. And if the Italian ended up living, what was the point?

Anton Bielakowski hung up the phone.

31.

AT 3:45 P.M., a scout positioned in South Philly reported eight motorcycles riding out of the War Boys' clubhouse. Chuck Trella Jr. held point,
no car or van accompanied the herd, and the bikers were decked in their
official colors. The scout had little trouble tracking them through the
neighborhood—they took the shortest, straightest route to northbound
I-95. Once their direction was called in, the scout returned to the clubhouse to watch for another wave.

Twelve minutes later, a second scout at Allegheny Avenue reported all
eight bikers exiting I-95 and turning right at Byrne's Tavern. Bielakowski
liked the bikers taking the lazy route into Port Richmond—they were
underestimating him. He also noted the travel time. Twelve minutes
meant no stops for additional weapons. And if the first scout's report was
accurate, they weren't traveling with shotguns or AK-47's. Pistols and
smaller automatics were still possibilities, but Bielakowski was more interested in what firepower they didn't possess.

In the sausage shop's back room, Bielakowski updated his men—*Eight
have arrived*—and ordered them into position. Man One—dressed in a
hard hat, worn jeans, and dirt-stained shirt—headed out the shop's front
door to lead the East Ontario Street roadblock.

Man Two had the easier task. He just needed to make sure his team was clear on rules of engagement. Since shots hadn't been fired for some time in Port Richmond, his job was reminding the men that killing was okay—and expected—as long as protocol was followed. The only true mistake was any on their side dying. Errors were to be at the opposition's expense. Mercy wasn't a consideration.

Out the shop's back door and down the rear alley, Man Two zigzagged to Salmon Street. His destination was a block-long, two-story warehouse with no signage. Three hard knocks on a steel door gained him entrance. Moments after receiving Bielakowski's orders, Man Two was on the warehouse rooftop, confirming his men's positions.

Four blocks away on Richmond Street, Trella and the bikers were caught in slow-moving traffic. They tried passing, shouting profanities, and slapping fenders to speed up the line—all to no avail. The locals just didn't share their impatience. After a few minutes of stop-and-go momentum, the bikers' first turn was left onto East Ontario Street. That's where their route troubles started. With the necessary Tilton Street intersection in sight, two flagmen—backdropped by a seemingly engaged pothole crew—detoured all traffic off East Ontario onto Salmon Street.

The tight Salmon Street one-way started with row homes but quickly dropped the neighborhood feel in favor of automobile shops, tire sheds, and deserted lots. At the East Schiller Street intersection, two flagmen motioned the bikers onward toward the Tioga Street intersection, where another flagman awaited their approach. If Trella had suspected the noose, Tioga was his moment to break free. Short of the flagmen, nothing was stopping the bikers from pulling off Salmon Street and circling back. They did not. And as they say in Port Richmond, it was all over except the screaming.

To one side of the Salmon/Tioga intersection was a corner lot with a half-dozen semi-trucks and long-haul trailers. As the bikers followed the flagmen's directions up Salmon, traffic behind them slowed enough to allow one of the trucks to ease off the lot and fall in to their rear. The tail blockade was in place.

Past the Tioga Street intersection, the Salmon Street landscape transitioned again, this time to the back walls and loading docks of parallel-running warehouses. On the right side of Salmon Street was a single, cinder-block facility stretching the entire block. It was a two-story building marked by little more than a dozen metal doors. The street's left side was a collection of one-, two-, and three-story buildings of mismatched shapes, materials, and sizes squeezed in over the last one hundred years.

Ten seconds after cruising into the open-air chute, the bikers looked between the walls and each other. Trella was out front, his head swiveling left, right, and up. *Shooting gallery* was the thought repeating in his head, confirmed when the cars they'd been following accelerated past a loading dock and a U-Haul truck backed into the street. The U-Haul's driver pressed his rear tires into the opposing curb, leaving no room between the bumper and warehouse wall.

The bikers stopped, steadied their bikes, and turned back to the Tioga intersection. Instead of the line of trailing traffic they expected, the only vehicle was the semi-truck creeping down the street with two feet of clearance on either side. The bikers looked to their leader for answers. Trella stayed stone-faced; his only concession to the moment was cutting his engine. "This ain't good," he said, dismounting. Surveying the immediate area for an emergency exit, all he saw was knobless metal doors and bricked-in windows.

Sixty seconds passed before a man appeared on the rooftop of the two-story warehouse, forty feet up and on the bikers' right side. They could see he was older and smaller with a sagging peasant cap atop his head.

Trella waited for him to speak. Nothing was uttered until the biker could no longer help himself. "What the fuck is all this?" he shouted, the echo reverberating down the cordoned-off street.

In unison, as though answering the question, forty-nine more men stepped to the rooftop's edge. They were of all ages, shapes, and sizes— only similar in the shotguns they clutched. No pistols, rifles, or machine guns. All 12-gauge, pump-action shotguns aimed on the street below.

Neither group spoke. The bikers staring up felt like time was frozen. The men staring down didn't care. Their sole concern was listening for word from their leader to pull the trigger, pump, and repeat until the eight bikers had fallen and stopped breathing.

The break in tension came when a street-level warehouse door opened from the inside. The bikers backpedaled three steps before catching themselves, worried the shooters would mistake the movement for panicked flight. Out the door walked Anton Bielakowski. He was alone and dressed in the same trousers and button-down shirt he'd worn to work that morning.

Bielakowski studied the rooftop before swinging his gaze to Trella. "Welcome to Port Richmond."

Fifty shotguns in his direction, Trella still looked ready and willing to charge. No one could accuse him of weakening when the attention got personal. "You expecting us to piss and moan, you got the wrong guys. This ain't the first time we've had guns aimed at our heads."

Bielakowski had no physical reaction. "Now that I'm in the street, if you or any of your men move a finger those fellows above will fire. And the line between life and death is even thinner than that equation suggests. There may only be ten or twelve professionals on the roof—men who've killed before with the weapon in their hands. They are skilled and ruthless and all that is needed to handle eight of you. But how could I have known all the War Boys wouldn't come? That's why I've called the others to join. Among the men looking down are the sons, brothers, and uncles of Port Richmond. Of course, the problem with these volunteers is they aren't only protecting me. These men are also protecting their wives, children, and parents. Think how much quicker a man pulls the trigger when he's fighting for family. And think how much harder he fights."

Trella rolled his eyes to the roofline and back to Bielakowski. "You're telling me I can listen or I can talk. Anything more and the negotiation gets messy."

"Let me be direct," said Bielakowski, dropping his voice so as not to share with the men above. "You've been played for a sucker."

"Me? You killed Tommy Paschol and I'm the sucker?"

"My condolences," said Anton, his eyes closing a brief moment. "I don't know Mr. Paschol. Never had a problem with him or you. My issue is with Rea."

Trella's breathing was on the rise, his face reddening. "Then you should have stuffed the blood sausage down the Italian's throat and shot him six times."

"Oh," said the Pole, feigning surprise. "Is that what you've been told? That your friend had a mouth full of blood sausage? How tidy. Perfect and neat, everything but my driver's license shoved up his nose. Look at me, Trella. I'm an old man. Did I get this age because I leave provocative, unintended calling cards?"

The biker shook his head an inch in either direction.

"I'll bet a man called Martin told you this story."

Trella paused. "Yeah, he's the one."

"He also told you to come get me. And here you are with fifty shotguns aimed from the rooftops."

The biker squinted, then lowered his chin as though eye contact blocked his thoughts. "Fuck me."

Bielakowski stepped up the street toward the blocking U-Haul. "Inside that truck are six pallets of Sudafed."

Trella raised his chin back up. "Yeah."

"Rea is buying them tonight. I doubt he's told you of that deal. It's why Tommy Paschol was murdered and stuffed into a trunk and why you're supposed to be dying in Port Richmond. Consolidation. That truck means Rea no longer needs the War Boys."

"That motherless bastard."

"Here's my offer. You are invited to attend the sale. It's scheduled to go down in an hour in South Philly. By that time, you were supposed to have been dead forty-five minutes. Rea is accepting delivery. I don't believe anyone else is attending other than Martin."

Trella looked at his men and back to the Pole.

Bielakowski wondered if the biker understood there was one answer to his offer. "We are not friends, but I also do not wish for any more enemies. You can refuse and die here on this street. Or I'll give each of you a shotgun and you can ride in the back of the truck. Maybe you still have doubts. So be it. If Rea is the one opening the doors and shining a flashlight in your eyes, you'll have the answer."

"I've already got my answer."

"Yes, I suppose you do."

"What do you want in return?"

"Kill Rea and leave me alone. You get the cold medicine in the truck. I don't want anything to do with that. The money Rea brings with him, that's for the men driving the truck."

Trella felt comfortable enough with the negotiation to reposition his feet. It was the first War Boy movement in five minutes. "Who's that going to be? Couple of your guys?"

"No, we don't deal drugs. They'll be Armenians."

Trella shook his head. "Shit."

"Don't worry," said Bielakowski. "You'll have shotguns to protect yourselves. And it'll be eight on two."

32.

"YOU HEARD ANYTHING YET?" said Rea.

Martin shook his head. "Too soon. I can tell you Trella was fired up. Bought the whole story. And Bielakowski had plenty of warning. I think he knows about the Paschol thing, though."

"Why do you say that?"

"He was a smart-ass about Pennypack Park and that you weren't the only one with cop friends."

Rea paused. "Doesn't matter what he thinks. It matters what Trella thinks."

Martin nodded. Both were talking low and slow, confident of their moves. "Might not hear anything for a while anyway. If the Poles slaughter those bikers, not like they're leaving a crime scene and calling the news crews. Those bodies will be floating down the Delaware before rush hour."

Rea chuckled and joked about watching the river for one of the bikers bobbing by. *Oh, I think I just saw Trella, hahaha.* "Like I said, would have been fun to be a bird on a wire."

Martin leaned forward, his hands pressing the dash. "How do you want to play this?" They were in Rea's Lincoln, parked on an overgrown lot on the banks of the Delaware River, a quarter mile from the nearest boat launch. River grass blocked views in all directions except for the waterfront and entrance road.

"Straight-up exchange. Armenians heisted a truck, heard I was in the market, and reached out. Knowing them, I insisted we do the buy in our territory. Rules are simple. They arrive in a truck and are allowed a single trailing car to drive home. One guy in each vehicle, no more. Otherwise, the deal is off and we drive out."

"Why can't we go heavier?" asked Martin. He'd heard enough about the Armenians to appreciate their tendencies.

"Nobody can know about this yet. Can't afford word leaking. Besides, they get two, we get two. When they pull in, you stay in the car. I'll take a peek inside their delivery truck, and if it looks good, I'll give you a wave. You come up with the money and they give you the truck keys."

"You know the two Armenians who are coming?"

"Nope," said Rea, none too concerned with the question. "Could be the boss, could be anybody. Don't worry, we'll be out of here in ten minutes. Once you're driving the truck, keep a low profile until we confirm Trella isn't coming back. Drive to where we store the poker machines. Park in back and I'll pick you up."

Waiting for the sellers, the men pissed in the river, smoked cigarettes, and watched a coal barge motoring north toward the Ben Franklin Bridge. Both used the quiet to daydream about their respective legacies and what the future held. Neither had any reason to doubt a healthy stream of back slaps, bank accounts, and the spoils of success.

Five minutes passed before the top of a U-Haul truck appeared above the river grass, followed by a trailing dust plume. Entering the gravel lot faster than expected, the truck jerked to an angled stop thirty feet from Rea and Martin's front bumper. A dented sedan missing hubcaps and gas-cap cover stopped alongside. Both drivers cut their engines and exited without hesitation or pause. Looking like wild-eyed cousins, the men wore their hair without a part and their jacket sleeves pushed to their elbows.

"So far, so good," said Rea. "Two guys, like they said. Those bastards do look half crazy, no?"

"Yeah, was thinking the same thing. You packing?"

"One on my ankle, another in the glove box if they start blinking too fast. But don't go looking for trouble. Money for cold medicine is as simple as they come—pretty tough to screw this up."

Martin nodded while making sure the keys were still in the ignition.

"Again, I'll check inside their truck. If everything looks good with the pallets, I'll wave." Rea stepped out of the car, paused, and looked back with a prankster's grin. "Some day, hey pal? Un-fucking-believable what we've done. Let's remember the details, okay? Going to make a good story."

One eye on the Armenians, Martin slid into the driver's seat. Through the open door, he said, "When it's time for the money, come back or send one of them. No sense giving these guys an opportunity to have us both on open ground."

"Relax. This is the easy part. We have to remember, things are different. Not like with Anticcio and Monte. We can't just trade with our own kind. These days, business is international. We've got to learn new ways of earning, be a little open-minded." Nodding to close his soliloquy, Rea climbed the steep flood plain in ten long strides.

Rea stuck his hand out between the two men, a favorite move for determining who was in charge. As the first Armenian shook, he looked in Martin's direction, mouthing a few words. Rea shrugged but didn't wave his partner forward. Seemingly satisfied, the lead Armenian tossed a thumb in the truck's direction, and all three men nodded in agreement. The larger of the two escorted Rea to the U-Haul's rear door. The other sat on the front bumper, staring at Martin and cleaning his teeth with a toothpick.

Martin had heard the phrase *in the blink of an eye* his whole life but didn't understand until that moment. As a kid, he wondered what could happen in a tenth of a second, even experimenting with the television, blinking to see what he missed. Not a thing, was the conclusion. But now, on the banks of the Delaware River, he got to see a much more convincing experiment. Rea was standing at the truck's back corner. His hands were on his hips and his chin up as the Armenian opened the door.

Martin blinked and Rea was gone, replaced by a cloud of red mist. *In the blink of an eye.* Now he knew what could happen in a millisecond. Death.

The first man jumping down was Chuck Trella. Holding a smoking shotgun across his chest, he took half a dozen steps toward the grass line, aimed at the patch compressed by Rea's fall, and fired two more shells. He followed the fireworks with four hard kicks and a mouth full of spit. Done mourning, he turned in Martin's direction as the seven other bikers jumped down to join him. A quick shout from Trella and the bikers were marching across the gravel patch toward Rea's Lincoln, shotguns belly high, all aimed at their mark.

Martin let go of the moneybag, tossing it into the passenger seat so he could reach for his wallet. He didn't have much time and wanted to see his little boy's picture. Thoughts of his son had saved him before, like with Bielakowski in the warehouse. That situation hadn't looked too rosy either, and he'd survived. Maybe, with a peek at the picture, he could figure out a crease, talk his way out. Then he blinked and it was all gone.

33.

THE BIKERS DIDN'T EXPECT another car. With their line of sight blocked by the overgrown grass, they tracked its approach by listening to the grinding gravel and watching the rising dust cloud.

Trella made a list of three possibilities. The bikers were included in the setup, a patrol car was investigating, or the unluckiest bastard in the world was driving down for a scenic look at the Delaware River. Racking his shotgun, he checked on the Armenians. Arms crossed, they gave nothing away. Just two blank faces looking back at him, still as statues, not talking but also not drawing down. Like the bikers, they were in a wait-and-see mode. Trella told his men to spread out, find cover around the truck and Martin's car. After what they'd used on the two dead bodies, they still had enough ammunition for thirty seconds of hell.

Slow and steady, a late-model sedan emerged from the river grass, stopping short to block the entrance. No one in, no one out. A single man was in the front seat. Through the windshield, Trella had a hard time getting a positive identification other than the man was larger than any of the bikers. "Back up and drive off," he muttered. "Your clock is ticking."

The driver wasn't listening. After pointing at each of the bikers—as if tallying numbers—he stepped from the vehicle and walked a straight line to Chuck Trella.

Hands to his sides, the man said in a voice loud enough for everyone to hear, "I'm Big Bern Jaracz of Port Richmond, and I've come for my guns."

His calmness and confidence rattled the bikers. One asked Trella if he should kill him; another took two steps forward for a better angle. Trella held his hand up and shouted for his men to calm down.

"Bielakowski send you?" asked Trella, shotgun in his right hand, barrel pointing at the ground.

"He doesn't need to send me," answered Big Bern. "My job is guns, giving them and getting them back. I was on the warehouse rooftop when Bielakowski allowed you the ones you're holding." Looking around, first at Rea's feet poking out from the grass and then at the pockmarked Lincoln with the shattered windshield, the one-eyed Pole asked, "Is your business done here?"

"I was promised the truck," said Trella, tapping the metal side with his knuckle. "And the cargo."

"I'm not here about the truck. I'm here for the guns." Big Bern extended his hand. "You have eight of them. Give them back and I leave. I have no other business. Shotguns, that's it."

Trella took a quick assessment of his men. He knew some were thinking they should blast away and go home. Take the truck, its pallets, and the bag of money brought by the Italians. Fuck everyone. But there was a reason he was the chief and they were the Indians. He tossed his shotgun in the air, catching the barrel on its decent. Handing the wooden stock to Big Bern, he said, "You can take them one by one, but probably easier opening your trunk and we'll put them in."

Keys in hand, Big Bern walked back to his Cadillac, followed by the footsteps of seven bikers. Collecting the eight shotguns balanced his sheet. Fifty shotguns ordered, fifty shotguns delivered, fifty shotguns returned. All that remained was picking Little Bernie up at McDonald's and driving to the storage facility. A few miles before reaching the river, he'd dropped off his grandson and told him he'd be back in thirty minutes. *Eat some burgers, don't leave, and don't talk to anybody. Grandpa will be back, don't worry.* Maybe, while picking up the boy, he'd have some fries and a Coke. Big Bern Jaracz was feeling like he deserved a special treat.

34.

THE MONEY WENT FAST. A million bucks is a fortune except when you spend dough like Sonny Bonhardt. After receiving the Viagra payout, he evened up with the casinos, got current on the boat and marina slip, sent a check to his building manager, funded a college account for his grandson, and bought Tatiana a big-bodied BMW with gold wheels and a twenty-grand stereo system. His unshared logic was that if the relationship didn't pan out—or anything happened to him—she'd at least have something of value to remember him by.

Taking care of Michael's legal woes cost Sonny less than he'd figured. For thirty-five grand he retained a decent bayou mouthpiece that negotiated a drug treatment plan and plea deal. Jail time was unavoidable, but at least Michael wouldn't die an old man behind steel bars. The attorney got him ten years, which could have been cut in half if Michael shared information on Cassir and his employer. He didn't and wouldn't. All things considered, Sonny considered the punishment a square outcome and even started sending his boy postcards and care packages. It was a start. Deep wounds, slow healers.

Sonny's last decision was the mausoleum. What'd started off as a must-do had faded to a may-do. Four hundred grand was a lot of scratch for an after-dinner party he'd be too tired to attend. Sipping bourbon on his balcony, he reread the investigator's report, paying special attention to the part about his brother's grave. He could tell his feelings had softened, getting philosophical as he watched seagulls flying low over the horizon. Nobody buried birds when they died—did that make their lives any less significant? Birds flew until they couldn't and then disappeared. Wasn't that enough?

A couple of drinks into the one-man debate and he still didn't have an answer.

Needing a second opinion, Sonny reached for his phone, set it down, picked it up, and dialed the number he'd memorized. Same as every time, a woman's voice answered.

"Bielakowski's," she said, rushed as though she'd just put another call on hold.

"Anton in?"

The awkward pause spoke more than her words. "Is this a friend?"

Sonny sat up in his chair. "Yes. We're friends."

"Mr. Bielakowski hasn't been feeling well. Perhaps you'd better call his home. Do you know the family?"

Sonny's mind raced. Anton didn't miss work. Shoot the old man in the leg and he'd be back running the bone saw in three days. Must be pretty damn sick, he figured, like the dying kind of sick. He called information for Bielakowski's home number and was told it was unlisted, sending him to find his little black book. Number in hand, he refilled his bourbon and took a seat. He hated getting old.

"Hello?" answered a frail voice, with more accent than word.

"Anton, it's Sonny."

A long quiet hung on the line. "I'm glad you called. Are you here in Philly?"

"No, I'm on my balcony in Florida. You don't sound so good."

"I've been better."

Sonny took a drink, his ice rattling into the phone. His friend must have recognized the sound, because he said to have one for him. Sonny answered he'd have two, followed by "Sick or dying?"

Anton's chuckle started fine and ended with a wheeze. When he was able to catch a breath, it was soft and shallow. "That's a question only an old friend like you can ask. But I'm sorry I don't have an answer. A little of both, I'm afraid."

"How's your wife holding up?"

"Smiles on this side of the wall. Cries on the other."

Sonny swore, unsure what else he could offer.

Anton spoke next, the energy in his voice suddenly rising. "He married that girl."

Sonny asked who, and Anton explained that Marcek had run off to Vegas with Angie—he called her *the South Philly girl*. "You think my wife is crying with me in this bed? You should have heard her handle that news. Her baby boy abducted to Vegas. Only thing that got her to stop was Marcek promising they'd been married Catholic. I think he was lying."

Sonny said they were a good match and meant it. She'd proven her smarts on the Viagra heist and made Marcek happy. What else was there? "I'll send the kids a card. Tell your wife they'll do fine. Remind her not everyone was convinced you two would last."

Anton grew quiet again, the banter giving way to heavier thoughts. "You must look out for him. My boy will need you."

"Yes," said Sonny. "Loyal to the end, whatever Marcek's path. Nothing held back."

"Like with us."

"Yes, like with us."

Sonny could hear Anton tiring. He thought of asking for the diagnosis but knew it didn't matter. Either Anton got well and lived or he didn't. Hashing out the details wasn't a factor.

"Sonny?"

"Yes, I'm here."

"Our lives—the way we've lived—I'm not sure we're guaranteed to see each other again."

Sonny understood they weren't talking about this world. "No one knows," he said. "Your wife has lit a lot of candles for us. Got to count for something. Let's promise each other, first one at the gates argues with Saint Peter for the other's admission."

Anton managed his second chuckle. "With you making the case, I'd stand a decent chance. Unfortunately, I believe we'll die out of order."

"You can be pretty convincing."

Anton coughed twice and wiped his lips clean. "One more thing, then I must go."

Sonny closed his eyes and dropped his face, preparing for what might be the last words shared with his longest-living friend. "Okay."

"Time comes, I want you buried in the Bielakowski family plot. Dad bought a spot for you along with the rest of us."

"I never knew that."

"It's not a conversation for young men."

"No," agreed Sonny. "I suppose not."

"Will you be buried with my family?"

Sonny wiped his nose. "Yes."

"That would make the old man happy. Me, too."

Before speaking again, Sonny made a point of spotting a seagull in flight. The bird soared alone toward open water. "Glad there is a place for me."